Amish Identity

Book 7 in the Covert Police Detective's Unit Series

Ashley Emma

Copyright © 2022 by Ashley Emma

All rights reserved.

No portion of this book may be reproduced in any form without written permission from the publisher or author, except as permitted by U.S. copyright law.

Contents

GET 4 OF ASHLEY EMMA'S AMISH EBOOKS FOR FREE

www.AshleyEmmaAuthor.com

Your free ebook novellas and printable coloring pages

Novels by Ashley Emma on Amazon
USA Today Bestselling Author
UNDERCOVER AMISH
AMISH UNDER FIRE
AMISH AMNESIA
AMISH ALIAS
AMISH ASSASSIN

ABRAHAM & SARAH'S
Amish Baby
HOSEA & GOMER'S
Amish Secret
BOAZ & RUTH'S
THE AMISH
Prodigal Son
ASHLEY EMMA
ESTHER'S AMISH
Bravery
ASHLEY EMMA

PART ONE

1

Alexis Fernandez looked up as the doors of the utility van opened and the traffickers shoved in another victim—a young Amish woman. The doors slammed closed before any of them could even try to escape, shutting out any sliver of sunlight or hope. The back of the van had no windows, concealing its secret cargo.

With her prayer *kapp* askew and terror glimmering in her eyes, the young Amish woman sat up from the floor of the van and looked around at the other captives.

Alexis watched the woman as she sat in the van among the other two terrified-looking teenage girls who had just been kidnapped a few hours ago.

Alexis had been taken months ago, but she had to act like she'd just been kidnapped that day.

All of their hands were tied, but Alexis was used to the sting of the rope binding her wrists. They only tied her up so she would blend in with the others. It wasn't like she was going to try to run—she'd tried that before over the past several months and had the scars to prove it.

Now they kept her with the others, forcing her to spy on them and report back any escape attempts or other useful information.

"What's going on? Where did you all come from?" the young Amish woman whispered. The teenage girls stared blankly at her with eyes devoid of hope.

Counting the other Amish women who were now being kept at the warehouse, this was the third young Amish woman the traffickers had kidnapped recently. Alexis didn't know much about their customs, but she supposed that the traffickers figured they were easy targets with their pacifist beliefs.

Another reason was that their customers were demanding more innocent, unique, and diverse victims, which made her sick to her stomach. Alexis squeezed her eyes shut, not even wanting to think about the atrocities these young women around her would endure—atrocities that Alexis was now growing used to, if that was even possible.

They had no idea what was coming. They would never see their families again. They'd be lucky if they ever saw the sun again.

One girl piped up, "I don't know about anyone else, but I was taken from the Maine Mall today. There was this guy I met who was really cute and nice to me, and we hung out all day. I thought we were friends. I thought he liked me. He offered to take me to a movie, but instead he drove me to the back of a building where this van was. He threatened me with a knife and made me get in." The young girl dropped her head and began to sob. "I can't believe I fell for it all. I'm so scared."

Alexis' heart broke for her.

The Amish woman asked, "Did you see any other young Amish women who were taken? They wear dresses and bonnets like me. There were two that were taken from my community." The girls shook their heads. She dropped her voice as low as possible. "I'm going to try to get us out of here. I have a son. I have to get back home to him!"

Alexis sat up straighter. No, no. This Amish woman had no idea what she was up against. If she tried to escape, she'd be caught—and they would make her wish she was dead before they were through with her.

Trying to dissuade her, Alexis spoke up, making her voice sound harsh. "There's no point, you naïve Amish girl. They'll catch you, and you'll wish you wouldn't have tried. You'll never see your son again." A lock of her black hair fell over her eyes like a mask, hiding the person she used to be. Alexis was once full of hope and life like this woman who had no idea what was about to happen to her. Alexis used to have a spark in her eyes, too—until the traffickers had beaten it out of her and stolen her innocence. "You might as well give up any hope you have of escaping now."

"Aren't the police looking for us?" the woman demanded. "Especially because of all the other kidnappings in the area?"

"Of course," Alexis said. "But haven't you ever heard that trafficked people aren't usually found? There's no use in hoping to be rescued. These guys are going to make us disappear. It's what they do."

Yes, it was what they did, and they were exceptionally good at it. How many girls and young women had Alexis seen disappear forever, never to be seen again?

Too many to count.

A few sniffles and whimpers sounded from the girls.

"Can't we try to escape then?" the Amish woman said. "Maybe we can if we all work together. We outnumber them. Isn't there anything we can do?"

"They have guns. As I said, if you do, you'll wish you wouldn't have tried. Trust me, I tried when they took me a few hours ago," Alexis lied. She had tried to escape once, but that was months ago. "Besides, they'll most likely start drugging us to make us dependent and compliant soon after we get to wherever we are going, probably with heroin or fentanyl." The traffickers didn't drug Alexis so that she could be alert and spy for them. She continued, "Whatever hope you have, Amish girl, you might as well give up on it. There's no way out, no way home."

Alexis normally wouldn't speak to anyone this way, but she had to get it through this woman's head that it was a terrible idea to try to escape.

She just might be saving her life.

"I'm not giving up hope," the Amish woman whispered.

Just stop talking, Alexis thought. *And stop hoping.*

"No talking!" a man's loud, deep voice boomed from the front seat of the van, as if on cue.

The youngest girl scooted over to the Amish woman and clutched her hand, looking up at her with big blue eyes. Alexis had to look away, guilt and shame causing her eyes to fill with tears.

More than anything, she wished there was something she could do to save them. She just wanted this never-ending nightmare to end. She'd considered taking her own life so many times.

The Amish woman got that determined look in her eye again and began looking around the van suspiciously.

What is she up to now? Alexis wondered. She better not try anything, or they would both pay.

When the van stopped, the van doors flung open, and two traffickers herded them into an old abandoned warehouse—a familiar sight to Alexis by now. But soon, they would move on before the police caught on to where they were. Alexis was the last one in line, knowing she'd be questioned.

"Alexis." The gruff voice slithered over her ear as a hand roughly grabbed her arm from behind. Though she was expecting to be stopped, she still jolted from his touch. She looked up to see Sebastian, the leader of the sex trafficking ring. "Did you hear anything useful, dear?" He spoke the last word mockingly, only rubbing it into her face further that he cared nothing for her and wouldn't think twice about having her beaten.

"The Amish woman wants to try to escape. I tried to discourage her, but she seemed like she might still try something," Alexis stammered.

"Those Amish women are so naïve," Sebastian spat out, chuckling mirthlessly as his stale cigarette breath washed over her. She bit back a gag, trying not to lift her bound hands to cover her nose. He'd only slap them away. "Fine. Get in there with the rest of them, but keep a very close eye on those Amish girls. They're up to no good." He got a sly look in his eyes that made her skin crawl. "They're much feistier than they look. I like that, and so will our customers."

Her stomach churned with disgust from his words as he ran a tattooed finger down her jawline.

"Remember where I found you, Alexis. You were half-starved in an alley, higher than a kite, and beaten beyond recognition. I took you under my wing and gave you food and shelter."

So, that's what he called it? Taking her under his wing? She wanted to scoff and roll her eyes.

Sebastian leaned forward, causing her to hold her breath so she wouldn't gag from his stench. "You owe me."

I owe you nothing, she thought, but wouldn't dare say that aloud. He thought he owned her, but she would never let him break her.

When he shoved her into the musty room, she was just relieved to get away from him. A faint ray of gray light shot in from the opened door only for a fleeting moment before it was shut out when the door slammed. The other captives were so busy crying and talking in low voices that they hadn't even noticed her slightly late arrival.

Alexis squinted as her eyes adjusted to the dim light, and she saw two other Amish women huddled on the other side of the room.

When they saw the new Amish woman who had just arrived, they both cried, "Maria!"

The three of them embraced, and Alexis sat down in the corner, hidden in the shadows as she observed their conversation closely.

"I'm so happy I found you. Are you hurt? What's happened, Anna?" Maria asked, looking at a bruise on the blonde woman's arm. Maria gestured to the cut on her friend's leg, whose strawberry blonde hair was mostly hidden underneath her dirt-smudged prayer *kapp*.

"We are okay so far, except that Liz cut her leg while trying to get away from the men when they took her," Anna, the blonde one, said. "I've been trying to take care of it, but as you can see, I have no supplies. We've been in this room since we were taken. We've heard them talking about who among us will be"—she hesitated, shuddering—"sold first."

Liz burst into tears. "I just want to go back to the farm. What's going to happen to us?"

Alexis' heart broke for them. Didn't they know they would never return to their homes again? Now that they'd been sucked into the dark, bottomless void of trafficking, they would never return home to their families. All they would know from now on was a life of bitter misery, only numbed by the drugs that would soon flood their veins. If they were lucky, the drugs might even prevent them from being aware of what was happening to them once they were indeed sold.

"You're a long way from the farm now," Alexis told them, making her voice callous as she crossed her arms. She looked at Maria. "I told you in the van. There's no way out of this."

"Don't listen to her," Maria quietly told her friends then whispered something to them. Alexis couldn't hear, but she knew she would have to find out what they were planning if she wanted all of them to survive this.

If she failed to discover their plan, the traffickers would hurt them terribly—or worse. It would be better for everyone if they kept their heads down and complied silently.

"Come on. Let's pray together," Maria said as she moved to a corner of the room, sat down, and leaned against the wall, bowing her head and folding her hands as if praying. Liz and Anna sat beside her and also bowed their heads.

Maria had something in her hand, then hid it behind her skirt. Alexis leaned forward from where she sat, trying to get a better look. What on earth were they doing? They were going to get themselves killed! Alexis had to stop this before one of the traffickers came in to check on them or ask her for updates.

Maria took her prayer *kapp* off and set it on the ground. Why would she do that? Didn't they always keep their hair covered? Alexis furrowed her brows in confusion.

Two of the kidnappers strode in. "You, there. You come with us," one of them said, pointing to Maria.

"No," Liz whispered in a panic, grasping at her friend's arm. When Maria hesitated, the man stomped over and dragged Maria away.

Liz grabbed Anna's hand, and Anna held on tightly. Maria's eyes locked onto theirs as long as possible before Maria was gone. The door slammed shut once more, causing Alexis to jump even though she knew it was going to happen.

Why had they dragged Maria away like that? Was it because of what Alexis had told them? Were they going to hurt her—or worse?

A moment later, one of the other men came in and grabbed Anna by the arm, also dragging her away. Liz fought and protested, trying desperately to pry the man's huge hands off her friend, but the trafficker shoved her away as though she were a pesky insect.

The door slammed shut again, causing a chilling silence to descend over the room of captives. Alexis' eyes filled with tears as she wondered what was happening to the women on the other side of that door—and how it was all her fault. It was only a matter of time before they would come for her too. But why had they left behind Liz, the last Amish woman?

They probably wanted Alexis to keep watching her and see if she could get any information from her now that she was separated from her friends.

Liz suddenly crawled over and placed her hand on the *kapp* in the corner. What on earth was she hiding under that head covering? The chatter in the room gradually returned as Alexis made her way over to Liz, wondering if she could find out what she was hiding.

"What are you doing?" Alexis asked.

"What? Nothing. Just sitting here." Liz's eyes darted left and right, a red flag that she was lying. When Alexis moved closer to see what was under the bonnet-like head covering, Liz quickly sat right on top of it.

"What are you hiding under that bonnet thing?" Alexis demanded, tugging on her arm. Her heart felt as though it was being torn in half as she yanked on the innocent woman, knowing that she'd receive much harsher treatment if the traffickers found out what she was hiding.

"Let go of me!" Liz cried. A few of the others looked over to see what was going on, but no one moved to help. Not knowing how else to get this stubborn woman to move aside and reveal what she was hiding, Alexis swung her fist, landing a blow on the side of Liz's face.

"I'm sorry," she whispered under her breath.

Liz held her face, wincing in pain. Alexis used the distraction to shove Liz aside and grab the prayer *kapp*.

"Wait!" Liz cried, scrambling to get up. She held her hands up. "Please, it's in the best interest of everyone here that you don't say anything."

There was something inside it—a cell phone.

Alexis' eyes widened in shock. She thought that the Amish didn't use cell phones. How on earth had they managed to smuggle that in here unnoticed when each woman was checked thoroughly before being put into the van?

Alexis looked up at Liz, feeling her eyes sting with tears. Now she had to report this, and Liz would pay dearly. But if Alexis didn't report this to the traffickers, they might kill Liz or hurt both of them much more severely than if she just reported it.

Her heart wrenched in her chest as she tried to make the impossible decision. But no—she had no choice. She had to do this.

“Is this yours?” Alexis whispered. She moved to the corner where they could talk more privately.

“No, it’s my friend’s. But that’s why I didn’t want anyone to see it. I don’t want them to find it.”

"I thought the Amish don’t use cell phones,” Alexis said.

“Some of us break the rules sometimes,” Liz said quietly. “It’s a good thing she did. This is our ticket out of here.”

“Really? You think so? Why?” Alexis couldn’t help but feel a small spark of hope igniting within her. What if she didn’t report this and they used the phone to call the police? This really could be their way out.

“Because the police will track it if she calls them. They’re going to use it to find and rescue us. I don’t know how, but they will,” Liz explained.

“How do you know that?” Alexis demanded. Maybe this really could work.

“My friend said so. That’s all I know. I don’t know very much about how cell phones work.” Liz shrugged.

Of course. Alexis wondered if Liz had ever used a cell phone in her life. “Has this been on the whole time?”

“I think my friend might have turned it on when she got here, but I’m not sure. It made some noises and lit up.” Liz shook her head slowly. “I think she called the police and turned down the volume. I can’t hear them.”

Alexis slowly nodded. “That’s good. It’s been on long enough to give them a signal.” So, maybe it was true. Maybe the police really were tracking them. “May I check to see if she called 911?”

Liz nodded and handed her the cell phone. Sure enough, the police had already been called and the call was still connected, but it the volume was down, so Alexis couldn’t hear anyone on the other line.

“Please tell them where we are. I don’t know the address,” Liz pleaded.

Alexis hesitated. Should she take a few seconds to tell the police where she was? What if one of the traffickers barged in here while she was on the phone? She would be as good as dead—or wishing she was dead.

“Don’t you want to go home again? Don’t you want all of these poor souls to be rescued?” Liz made a sweeping motion with her hands. “You could be the one to save them.”

Alexis hesitated. This could work. She felt it in her bones. When would she ever get a chance like this again? She’d never seen a woman successfully smuggle in a cell phone before.

She pictured her parents’ faces in her mind—she hadn’t seen them in so long. They hadn’t spoken in so long that they probably had no idea she’d been kidnapped. As far as they knew, she was still living on the streets, addicted to drugs.

They must be worried sick about her. What had she put them through?

And what about all these innocent young women? She had to do something to help them.

It was worth the risk. Before she could change her mind, Alexis turned the volume up a little and held it to her ear.

"Hello?" she whispered.

"What is your emergency?" the man on the other end asked.

Alexis quietly rattled off the address of where they were into the phone. She whispered, "There are several women and girls being held here by sex traffickers. Please hurry."

"CPDU has already been dispatched to your location and will arrive in a few minutes. Do you want me to wait on the phone with you?"

"I can't stay on the phone. I have to hang up."

"We have your location. They will be there soon."

Alexis hung up immediately, erased the call from the call history, then faced Liz. "The police are coming," she whispered.

"Oh, thank the Lord." Liz clasped her hands together, tears in her eyes. "Thank you."

Alexis still had to report the cell phone, but maybe she could buy some time until the police arrived. Did she dare hope that could happen?

Alexis stared into the young Amish woman's eyes apologetically, holding the cell phone she'd just taken from her. "I'm really sorry. I wish I didn't have to do this, but I have to or they'll kill one of you—maybe even all three of you."

Liz stared at Alexis with wide eyes as realization slowly set in. "Do what?" she stammered.

Everything within Alexis wanted to fight the orders from the kidnappers, but she knew there'd be deadly consequences if she disobeyed them again.

And she didn't want to see Liz end up dead.

"I'm sorry," Alexis choked out. "They're forcing me to spy on all of you."

Maybe, finally, they'd be rescued, and she'd be able to leave this place for good.

"Wait." Liz grabbed Alexis' arm, revealing the burn marks on her arms. "Did they do this to you?"

Alexis cringed, remembering the last time she'd refused to tell them about a woman's plan to escape. Her name was Caroline. Alexis had been pretending to be just another kidnapped girl, as usual, and Caroline had even asked her for help with her plan. It was a decent plan until one of the kidnappers found out about it. And when they realized Alexis had hidden it from them, they'd tortured her.

But worst of all, they'd killed Caroline.

"They'll do worse to you and your friends if I don't go tell them about this right now," Alexis warned Liz, jerking free from her grasp. "If they walk in here and see us with this phone, they might kill us."

"Wait," Liz whispered so no one else could hear. "You can erase the call after so they can't see it, can't you?"

"I already erased the call."

"What's your name?" Liz asked.

"Alexis," Alexis whispered. "My name is Alexis."

"I'm sorry they're doing this to you. Please, don't tell them, Alexis," Liz pleaded.

"I have to." Alexis ran to the door, pounding on it. "It's Alexis. Let me out."

One of the criminals swung the door open, and Alexis gave the Amish woman one last apologetic look before dashing out.

"No!" Alexis heard Liz scream before the door slammed.

2

Diego, the burly man who often guarded the room where the women were kept, shoved Alexis into the largest room in the warehouse. "What have you got there?" He snatched the cell phone out of her hands.

"One of the Amish girls had it."

"Oh, Sebastian will want to know about this. Come on." Diego grabbed her arm and marched toward the leader of the human trafficking ring.

"Leave her alone! Please believe me. I'm Amish. The Amish don't lie," someone cried.

"Everyone lies, missy. Ready to talk now, Maria?" Alexis heard Sebastian say, cocking his gun. "Three, two, one—"

Alexis ran toward the voices until they came into view. Sebastian had tied one Amish woman, Maria, to a chair while another one of the other kidnappers held a knife to the other Amish woman's throat.

He was going to kill her. When Sebastian threatened something, he did it. How could she distract him and buy time?

"Sebastian, wait! I heard them talking about escaping. I found this under her bonnet in the corner." Alexis held up Maria's cell phone. "By now, the police have probably already traced the phone. We don't have time for any more questions or to kill anyone. We've got to go, boss. Right now. They could be here any second."

At least, she hoped so. But it would take them a while to pack up all the women and erase any evidence that led to their next location.

And that might just buy them enough time for the police to get here unless they were already close by.

Sebastian lowered his gun and roared, punching Maria in the face. Alexis' stomach lurched as he struck the innocent woman.

And it was all Alexis' fault.

"Why didn't any of you search her, you idiots?" Sebastian demanded.

"But... We thought the Amish don't use cell phones. One of the guys did search her," one of the traffickers countered.

"Apparently not well enough! Amateurs," Sebastian snapped, throwing his hands in the air. "What other secrets do you have up your sleeve, missy? Or should I say, in your bonnet?" he asked Maria, then turned to Alexis, setting his icy eyes on her. "You're right, Alexis. We don't have time for this. Load up all the girls into the vans. We have to get out of here right now. I said now!"

All the doors to the building burst open, and dozens of CPDU officers and agents stormed the warehouse, shouting commands and aiming their weapons at the kidnappers. The man holding Anna whirled around in surprise, cutting her face.

"You're surrounded! Lay down your weapons, or we'll shoot!" one of the agents cried.

Most of the kidnappers complied, slowly putting down their assault rifles and other weapons—all except for the stubborn Sebastian, who would rather die than surrender.

"Sebastian, we have no choice! Drop your gun!" Alexis told him, holding her hands up.

Sebastian continued to aim his gun at Maria. Would he truly shoot her? Alexis felt as though she might be sick as she watched in horror.

An agent fired and hit Sebastian in the torso. From the floor, Sebastian dropped his gun and clutched his bleeding side as CPDU agents spread out across the building. Sebastian wouldn't go down without a fight, but he was immediately surrounded and handcuffed while shouting threats.

"And you, Amish lady, you better keep watching your back," he shouted at Maria, sending icy shivers down Alexis' spine.

The two Amish women embraced, sobbing as CPDU agents unlocked the door where the other kidnapped girls and women were held. The agents and officers led the survivors out of the warehouse toward freedom. They shielded their eyes from the light as if they had been in captivity for months like Alexis had. Soon they would be reunited with their families.

While Alexis was filled with gratitude that they had been rescued, she was also overwhelmed with grief and regret, knowing she had been a part of their suffering. She collapsed to the floor as the other traffickers around her were seized, handcuffed, and hauled outside to police cars.

She was next. She looked up through her tears, expecting one of the officers to grab her wrists, handcuff her, and drag her to prison.

As Sebastian was wheeled past her on a gurney toward the ambulance, his cold stare was trained on her.

"That girl is as guilty as the rest of us!" he shouted, his eyes never leaving hers. "She spied on the kidnapped girls and told us everything. She belongs in prison!"

A male police officer with kind eyes approached her where she sat crumpled on the floor.

"Yes, I was their spy, but they forced me to do it," she told the officer. "They would have killed that Amish girl and her friends if I hadn't told them about her cell phone." Alexis held out her hands and hung her head. "Arrest me. I understand."

He looked at her hands and clearly saw the burn marks on her arms. "Want to tell me how you got those?" He gestured to the burn marks on her arms.

"They did that the last time I didn't report an escape attempt to them."

"Let me help you up," the officer said, gently taking her hands and helping her stand. She flinched when he took her hand, then realized his touch was gentle, entirely different from the rough grabs and blows she had now become used to. She looked up into his face, gazing into his brown eyes as everything else around her faded.

"My name is Agent Ben Banks, and I'm going to take care of you. I'm going to bring you back to the station for questioning. Do you think you could help us by giving us information on these criminals and the sex ring? Do you know about any other locations they have or any other kidnappers involved?" he asked.

Alexis' eyebrows shot up. She knew everything about how the human trafficking ring worked, from how they kidnapped the girls and women, how many hideouts they had, and how many other men were involved. "Agent Banks, I've listened to countless conversations and meetings between these evil scum-sucking parasites. I know names, dates, locations—everything you need to know. They ruined my life and hurt me more times than I can count. I would be happy to give you every detail I know about them. And I'd be happy to see them rot in prison."

Agent Ben Banks held out his hand. "Follow me, then." He led her to the ambulances, where the three Amish women were huddled together in prayer, thanking God for their rescue. He said, "The Covert Police Detectives Unit thanks you for your help." He gave her a beautiful, heart-stopping smile. "What's your name?"

"My name is Alexis Fernandez," she said, standing a bit taller as her heart beat faster. She glanced at his left hand, noticing he wore no ring. He was one of the most handsome men she'd ever seen in her life, and his smile was so warm and kind.

For the past several months, all the men she had encountered were the worst kind in the world—men who wouldn't think twice before hurting women in the worst ways imaginable, which they did.

After seeing so many men like that, she knew in her heart that this man was a good, honest man. Somehow, Alexis knew. She felt something ignite in her heart that she didn't think she would ever feel.

"Miss Fernandez," Agent Ben Banks said in awe, wrapping a blanket around her shoulders and handing her a hot cup of coffee. "You are the bravest woman I have ever met."

As they locked gazes, she stared into his dark eyes as they studied her. She became suddenly curious, wishing she could get to know him and learn every detail about him. When she took the cup of coffee from his hand, she felt sparks of electricity shoot up her arm and straight to her heart.

But he was a police officer. After this was over, she'd probably never see him again, and she would just be another victim to him that he had helped.

Those eyes. For the rest of her life, she would never forget those incredible eyes.

Alexis' eyes shot open. She gasped in a lung full of air, then sat up in bed.

She looked around the room, seeing her familiar bed, nightstand, and dresser in the small house she rented near the Amish community in the town of Unity, Maine. Relief overwhelmed her as she sighed.

It had just been a dream. Well, it had been a memory in the form of a dream—one that she had over and over again. It haunted her like a phantom, never giving her one night of peaceful sleep.

She wiped her cheeks which had been wet with tears, and her sheets were damp with sweat. Alexis took a deep breath, trying to calm her racing heartbeat.

"Just a dream. Just a memory..." she told herself, arms crossed over her body as she rocked back and forth. "It's over."

Oh, God, please take these dreams away, she prayed.

While usually dreams feel so real, even after waking, these night terrors had mostly actually happened. They were extra hard to shake off upon waking. Memories and guilt kept haunting her.

The worst part was she would never be able to apologize to so many of the women she had betrayed who had been sold, never to be seen again. Where were they now? She didn't even want to think about what they endured every day—and how she'd been forced to play a role in their demise.

Glancing at the clock, she jumped out of bed.

Maria's wedding!

Alexis quickly brushed through her thick black hair, which flowed almost to her waist. Her eyes ran over her clothes that hung on wooden hangers. Time was a luxury she couldn't afford, and she had to try her very best to look presentable. She grabbed a long dark green dress, a sweater, and some gloves.

Tears sprang up in Alexis' eyes as remnants of her dream played in her mind. She moved to the bed; she sank into it, carefully dropping her dress next to her.

It was a miracle that Alexis and her new friends who had been kidnapped by Sebastian's sex trafficking ring—Maria Mast, Liz Kulp, and Anna Hershberger—had been rescued. It was an even bigger miracle that they had forgiven her for betraying them by spying on them.

Alexis had been shocked when Maria invited her to the wedding even though she hadn't even apologized to her in person yet. Alexis had already apologized to Anna and Liz and was taking it one step at a time. Her next step was to apologize to Maria. But with everything going on in Maria's life lately, Alexis hadn't found the right time to talk to her about it yet. Clearly, Maria had already forgiven her anyway. Maybe today she'd have the opportunity at the wedding, but she didn't want to cast a sad shadow on Maria's happy day.

A wave of guilt rushed over Alexis again, but she rebuked it. She'd no choice but to play the part of the traitor. Alexis wanted a taste of love and happiness. Sometimes she envied the bright smiles and glowing faces of her friends.

Someone pounded on the door, and Alexis opened it.

Her dear *Englisher* friend Freya Lapp, who was also close friends with the Amish, stood at the door. After their kidnapping, Maria, Anna, and Liz had introduced Freya to Alexis, and now they were all close.

"Alexis, hurry up and get dressed! The wedding starts at nine. We have to leave now or else we'll be late. I just need to stop by Maria's house before the wedding. What, did you sleep in too late by accident?"

"Yeah, you could say that." Alexis averted her eyes. "I'm really sorry. Come in. I'll just be a moment. I'm just so honored I got to know these wonderful people well enough that they invited me."

Freya stepped inside and closed the door, peering at Alexis with concern. "How are you doing? Like, how are you really doing?"

Alexis sighed. "I'm okay."

"You had another nightmare, didn't you?"

Alexis looked away from her friend's insistent eyes. She grabbed her dress and walked toward the bathroom to change, sighing. "They aren't going away."

"I still get nightmares too, you know. And when I drive on that road where Robert died, I still cry," Freya told her. "You don't have to hide it, Alexis."

"I am not trying to hide it," Alexis snapped, pulling the dress over her head. She grabbed her shoes and coat, then saw Freya's frown. Alexis reached for her hand. "I'm sorry. I didn't mean to be harsh."

"You know I'm here for you always. Right? I might not have been through the same things as you, but I still have flashbacks of when I accidentally killed Robert in that blizzard." Freya squeezed Alexis' hand. "So, I can kind of relate to what you're going through with the nightmares and the guilt. I'll always be here for you to talk to. You're like a sister to me now. I love you."

"You're going to make me cry." Alexis threw her arms around her friend. "I love you like a sister too."

Freya released her and dragged her to the door. "I know. Come on, let's go. Maria's getting married today!"

3

The Mast home was simply furnished, like every other Amish home. The interior was plain and uncluttered but lovely and clean. The walls were painted cheery shades of blue and yellow with a white border running along the lines near the ceiling. It had surprised Alexis at first, who had expected that all Amish homes lacked color altogether. There was no TV or radio, but the house was filled with the sounds of conversation and laughter.

The house overflowed with Maria's friends and family, and many of them bustled around the kitchen, finishing the food preparations.

Joshua Lapp stepped outside, needing to get some air. He smiled when he saw his cousin, Adam, getting out of his car in the driveway. Joshua jogged over to him.

"Adam!" Joshua called, then wrapped him in a big bear hug. "Where's your wife? How have you been?"

"Great! Freya is helping Maria's family with food preparations. Married life is incredible," Adam said with a grin.

"That's wonderful." Joshua smiled and pulled back. "I'm just so glad to see you around here again. I missed you after you left."

Adam had left the Amish to become a police officer at the Covert Police Detectives Unit. His brother Robert had been accidentally hit and killed by Freya's car while he'd been out on the road looking for his horse in a blizzard, but that was a whole other story.

"At least I wasn't shunned," Adam said. "Good thing I didn't get baptized before I left."

Joshua waved away his comment. "Bah. I hate that rule, to be honest. I never agreed with it. Actually, there are a lot of things I don't agree with here. I still would have talked to you even if you were shunned."

Adam's eyebrows shot up. "Are you thinking of leaving too? You could move in with us until you get back on your feet. You could go to college. You still want to be a veterinarian, right?"

"Whoa, slow down." Joshua lowered his voice, looking around to see if anyone was nearby. "I wouldn't want to impose on you and Freya like that. I'm not sure yet, but I won't lie. I have been seriously considering it."

"You always told me you wanted to be a veterinarian and work with animals. I think you'd be great at it."

"Thanks. And I still want to. But no one else knows that. Has it been worth it to leave all this behind for the outside world? Do you ever regret it?"

"Never. Not for a second. Leaving home and *Maam* and *Daed* to become a police officer was a high price I had to pay and the hardest choice I ever made, but I love Freya more than anything, and I love our life together. She's amazing. In fact, we're expecting our first baby. But don't tell anyone. We haven't announced it yet."

"Adam! That's wonderful news! I'm so happy for you." Joshua threw his hands up in the air and gave his cousin a friendly slap on the shoulder, hiding the fact that even though he was elated for his cousin, his heart ached as he longed for a wife and children of his own.

"Thank you. God brought her to me in a miraculous way. For the longest time I never thought anything good could come out of such a terrible tragedy. I still don't understand why my brother had to die, but somehow that must have been in God's plan too. I have learned to trust in Him and His plans, but it's not easy."

"She really is great. To be honest, sometimes I'm still in awe that you fell in love with the woman who accidentally killed your brother. But now that I know her, she really is one of the kindest people I've ever met." Joshua reached for Adam's arm. "The story you share is truly inspiring."

"Thanks, Josh. I know what happened was terrible, but with God's grace and each other, we got through it. She's the love of my life. In fact, every day I love her even more, if that's possible. And I love my job. I get to help people every day. I wouldn't change anything if I could go back in time. If you want to leave to pursue your dream, then I think you need to follow your heart, even if that sounds cliché. If it's meant to be, you won't regret it."

"You weren't shunned, but I would be. I don't want to break my parents' hearts." Joshua sighed. "But you're right. I'm so happy for you. You got everything you ever dreamed of. But in my case, it's different. I would devastate my parents, not only because they would never see or talk to me again, but also because they want me to take over the farm."

"Of course, they do. They adore you. But if you believe it is God's plan for you to leave and become a veterinarian, then you need to do it. Or else you'll spend your whole life wondering what could have been. You could always come home, repent, and become Amish again. But if you don't leave, you might always regret it."

Joshua sighed. "I know. You're right. I didn't think about repenting because I don't consider it as an option. Even if I become successful and love being a veterinarian, I would also miss my parents dearly. Still, once I decide to leave, I would never come back. I need to pray about it more."

"God will show you what to do. I have no doubt. But enough about that. Did you find a date for the wedding or what?" Adam playfully slapped his younger cousin on the shoulder.

Joshua laughed and shrugged. "I'm not interested in any of the girls here."

"Another perk to getting out of here. There are tons of women. Lovely Christian women, to be precise. In fact, I know a few I could set you up with at our church. Freya has a lot of friends in her women's Bible study."

Joshua chuckled and pushed him jokingly. "Okay, let's not get ahead of ourselves, Adam."

Joshua had a strong admiration for Adam. Joshua wanted to be free, liberated from the unseen chains that his society had on his dreams. He wanted to explore the world like Adam, but he couldn't let anyone in on that just yet. It was too risky.

"There is no dream more important than finding the right woman. Speaking of which, Freya is inside, helping with the food and other preparations. I need to go find her. It's starting soon," Adam said.

"I'll go inside with you," Joshua said.

He looked up to see a young woman with the most striking dark eyes piercing into him. Her eyes were so intriguing as if they held dark memories. She stood on the front steps of Maria's parents' house and looked out over the fields. Her long black hair fell in waves over one shoulder, and she wore a long green dress the color of pine trees. She looked at him, and he forgot how to breathe.

Who was that lovely, mysterious woman?

Alexis had noticed the handsome stranger at the entrance of Maria's house, but she'd quickly averted her eyes from him to be polite. The young man went inside the house, where several other men greeted him and began asking him to help with transporting food to the church in buggies. Adam went into the house to put trays and pots of food in the trunk of his car to take to the church.

"Look, Adam's here. Let's go," Freya said, and they walked the distance to his parked car.

"Hello, ladies. How are you, Alexis?" Adam asked, shaking her hand.

"I'm good, thank you. I'm glad to be here," Alexis said, and she meant it. "I'm glad you're here with me, so I'm not the only *Englisher*. I feel a bit out of place."

Freya waved her hand. "It's actually common for *Englishers* to be invited to Amish weddings around here. They live close by, so the Amish have many *Englisher* friends. There might be others there besides us."

"Let's go. It's starting soon," Adam said.

They drove the short distance and pulled into the church parking lot. The church was a two-story structure that the community had built together rather than hosting church services in homes as many other Amish communities did. People were already arriving and walking inside, carrying food. The three of them got out of the car, and a few men came over to help them carry the food inside. So many of the young men volunteered that Freya and Alexis didn't even need to carry anything.

Alexis swallowed the bitter lump that clogged her throat as they made their way toward the church. Weddings were always so romantic. Perhaps that was why she never really liked attending them.

They reminded her of what was lacking in her life.

Who could ever see beyond her past and learn to love her?

"I'm just curious, Alexis, when will we be coming to your wedding?" Freya grinned.

Alexis brushed off her question. "I don't know." She knew her friend was just making conversation. "Not for a while, probably."

"Oh, I'm sorry. I didn't mean to offend you."

"No, you didn't offend me, Freya. I'm just not sure I'll ever find love like you and Maria did," she admitted somberly.

"Oh, now that's ridiculous. You're beautiful, kind, and caring. Any man would be crazy not to fall in love with you. Don't worry, Alexis. God has someone special just for you. Come on," Freya replied sweetly. "I have a surprise for you."

Alexis fell in step behind Freya until they reached the edge of the woods behind church, out of sight from anyone passing by.

"What are we doing back here?" Alexis asked.

"Alexis!" Anna Hershberger rushed toward her, followed by their friend Liz Kulp, the strings of Liz's prayer *kapp* trailing behind her as they ran. Anna wore a conservative navy-blue dress and no head covering since she had decided to leave the Amish to become a nurse after being rescued from the traffickers. Because she'd been shunned for leaving, Liz could only speak to her secretly, so she wasn't shunned as well. That rule didn't apply to Freya and Alexis, who were *Englishers.*

Alexis had missed Liz and Anna along with Maria. They all shared a special bond since they had all been victims of the same heinous crime. But most of all, Liz and Anna's forgiveness showed Alexis God's love like nothing else ever had.

Anna bounded over to Alexis and practically jumped on her, shrieking. "I missed you! How are you?" Anna held Alexis at arm's length and hugged her again, lowering her voice. "You look gorgeous."

Liz laughed at Anna's typical enthusiastic behavior, hugging Alexis once Anna let her go. "It's so good to see you, Alexis. I'm sorry we have to meet out here in secret, but this is the only way I can talk to Anna."

"I understand. It's good to see all of you." Alexis flashed them a gracious smile. "I'm so glad to be here. How do you like your new *Englisher* life, Anna?"

"I love it," Anna gushed. "Every day is a new adventure. We've missed you," Anna added.

"I've missed you too," Alexis said. "All of you. I'm sorry I haven't been around lately." Alexis stared at the ground.

"What's wrong?" Freya asked.

"You have all been so kind and welcoming to me, but I feel so guilty. I guess it's been keeping me from visiting," Alexis admitted, kicking a pebble with her toe.

"We don't want you to feel guilty," Liz said, grabbing her hand.

"We want to see you much more often," Anna added. "None of what happened was your fault. Don't forget that."

"I feel like it was."

"No, no. We love you, Alexis. We want to see you. Don't be a stranger. We're going to keep inviting you to come to visit until you do." Liz grinned.

"Thank you," Alexis said, barely above a whisper, her heart swelling with gratitude. "You all are the best friends I've ever had."

Freya's eyes filled with tears. "So are you, Alexis."

"Anna has some exciting news," Liz told Alexis, squeezing her hands.

"I got into nursing school!" Anna clasped her hands together with excitement.

"Wow! I'm so happy for you," Alexis said, wrapping her arms around her.

"Congratulations!" Freya added.

"Thank you," Anna said.

"Have you applied yet, Alexis?" Freya asked.

Alexis looked at the ground. "Not yet. To be honest, I'm scared I won't get in. Also, I've been thinking... I'm not sure I want to be a nurse. I want to work with horses, but I don't know anything about them. Maybe that's a pipe dream."

"If that's what you want to do, you should go for it!" Anna said.

"When I was younger, I'd go to horseback camps, and it was so therapeutic for me. I did some research on how therapeutic working with horses and learning to ride can be for people who have survived trauma. I'd like to help people in that way somehow and become certified someday."

"That sounds incredible," Freya said. "I think you'd be good at it."

"I only know how to be a waitress." Alexis sighed.

Alexis dreamed of the day when she could quit and walk out of the diner where she worked, but in order to do that, she had to figure out what she wanted to do.

"Well, you won't know until you try other things," Anna said.

"Whatever you choose to do, you'll be great at it, Alexis," Liz said.

The group nodded in agreement, offering her words of encouragement. Alexis blushed, but her soul was filled with gratitude for such supporting friends.

Thank you, God, for blessing me with these friends, she prayed.

"Oh, look. Here comes Adam and his cousin," Freya said.

"Have you met Joshua Lapp?" Liz asked.

Alexis followed her friends' eyes. Her heart jolted the moment her eyes met with the handsome man she had first seen at Maria's house.

"No," Alexis murmured. "I haven't."

Unsettled by the depth of his brown eyes, she quickly broke eye contact and stared at the ground.

4

“Who is she?” Joshua whispered to Adam as they approached the group.

“Patience, man,” Adam replied with a mischievous smile.

Joshua chuckled. He trusted his cousin completely and would always abide by what Adam asked him to do. He couldn’t stop staring at the alluring beauty who stood in the midst of Freya, Liz, and Anna.

She was so unique and different from all the other women he had met, like a rose in the desert.

Please act normal, he cautioned himself, unable to take his eyes off her.

Never in his life had a woman had such a striking effect on him.

He was eager to speak with her. He was eager to know her more. This was his chance, and he wasn’t going to ruin it.

As he walked over with Adam, Alexis caught the young man's eye again and quickly looked away.

"Hey, everyone," Adam said. "It's so great to see you all."

Freya did the introductions. "Alexis, meet Adam's cousin, Joshua. Joshua, meet Alexis, one of my best friends."

Alexis felt a tingly sensation in her palms as Joshua extended his hand for a handshake. She stared at his strong, wide hands, wondering what his touch would feel like.

"Hi. I mean, hello," Alexis stammered, and her face heated in embarrassment. What was so hard about just saying hello?

"Nice to meet you, Alexis. Beautiful name you got there." Joshua grabbed her hand gently and gave it a light squeeze.

Alexis quickly pulled her hand away.

"So glad you get to meet my less handsome cousin." Adam chuckled and punched Joshua jokingly.

"I see the resemblance now." She blushed as she looked at each of them. "You definitely look like cousins." But she had to admit, Joshua was very handsome, though she'd never say so.

"Yep. There's something special about the men in our family. Maybe that is why the ladies can't get enough of us." Adam winked at Freya, and he got everyone laughing.

"Oh, stop it, Adam." Freya chuckled. "You think you're so funny."

"Well, the wedding is about to start. Let's go inside," Alexis said, turning to Anna with a frown, knowing her friend wouldn't be able to come inside.

"It's okay," Anna said. "I know I can't come inside. I'll be with you in spirit. Oh, look. Here come Olivia and Isaac. They're going to be outside with me too."

Olivia and Isaac had also left the Amish and were now police officers for CPDU. Unlike Adam, they were shunned because they had been baptized into the church before they left.

"I'm glad you won't be alone," Alexis said.

After briefly saying hello to Isaac and Olivia and exchanging pleasantries, Freya, Adam, Liz, and Alexis went inside the church to the top floor. Liz, Freya, and Alexis sat in the back of the room where there were chairs instead of backless benches. One of the elders came up to them and told them the translator would be sitting on the opposite end of the church, so he led them to different seats so they could hear better.

"The sermons will be in German and Pennsylvania Dutch," Liz explained. "So, this way, you'll be able to understand."

"Okay." Alexis had no idea there would even be a translator.

The church was made up of three rooms. Downstairs, in the basement, there was a hall where the after-church luncheons were served and where the reception would be. The floor was cement, and there was a wood stove and propane burner.

Liz explained, "One half of this floor is usually the school room we use during the weekdays, and the other half is the room where church is usually held. But there's a collapsible wall in the middle, and today we took it down to make more room."

Alexis nodded, looking around in awe. All the chairs faced the center, where the two rooms met.

"That's where the speakers will stand and where Derek and Maria will be married at the end of the service," Liz said, gesturing to the middle of the large room.

In the school side of the room where the walls and ceiling met, there was still a border of numbers and letters. Book shelves still stood, holding encyclopedias and textbooks. The chalkboard and dry erase board remained on the walls, but everything else that was school-related had been temporarily moved out. However, there were no decorations or finery.

The bride and groom wore clothes that looked just like clothes they usually wore, and they did not at all stand out from the guests. Alexis could hardly pick Maria and Derek out from the crowd.

The room was packed with Amish, Mennonite, and *Englisher* guests. Alexis turned to a group of young women sitting next to her.

"Hi, I'm Alexis," she said. "This is Freya and Liz."

"Hi, so nice to meet you all. I'm Loulie, and this is my sister Abigail," Loulie said. Alexis wasn't sure if they were Mennonite, Amish, or a different religion, and she was too shy to ask. They wore dresses similar to Amish attire, but they had beads and patterns on them. Instead of prayer *kapps*, they wore handkerchiefs on their heads.

Everyone got a pamphlet with songs from the *Ausbund*.

Loulie whispered to her friend, "This is all in German."

"The English part is written right below the German words," Liz pointed out. "I can sing the English part with you if you want. Do you know German?"

"No, we don't," Loulie said.

"Where are you from?" Freya asked.

"Tennessee. We are distant relatives of Maria. Oh, look, I think it's about to start," Loulie whispered.

Everyone stopped talking as the wedding began at five of nine, and they sang very slow hymns in German for the first fifty minutes. Alexis had to admit that it felt like hours because she didn't understand the words.

Then a man gave a message in German. Right before the man started to speak, another man came into the church and sat near them.

He then began speaking in a loud voice over the sermon, "Brothers and sisters, we are gathered here today to celebrate the marriage of this young man and woman..."

Why was he talking so loudly? Alexis looked over at him, puzzled.

He received several strange looks from other people.

"That must be the translator," Freya whispered, leaning closer to Alexis.

"Oh," Alexis whispered in realization.

The man spoke so loudly that Alexis guessed the whole church could hear him. It was confusing to hear both the translator and the preacher speaking at once.

Next, a different speaker gave a message in English about how a good marriage takes two good forgivers.

The third speaker was the bishop. As the third hour ticked by, Alexis felt very fortunate to have a chair with a back. Many people sat on not-so-comfortable benches for the three hours. The group of boys who sat on benches across from Alexis put their elbows on their knees and their chins on their knuckles, looking like they would much rather be doing something else. But everyone was patient throughout the long service. However, Alexis knew that Amish church services were often three hours, so maybe they were used to it.

The actual vows and marriage ceremony took about five minutes out of the entire service. The bishop called the bride and groom forward and asked them vows similar to those Alexis had heard before at other weddings, but they were worded a little differently. At the end, the bishop joined their hands together. He said that a three-cord strand is not easily broken. The three-cord strand represents the husband, the wife, and God. Instead of saying "I do" in response to the vows, they simply said, "Yes." Maria looked so calm, yet joyful.

Someone's phone went off loudly during the vows, and Alexis jumped. Several of the wedding guests looked toward the sound, and Alexis double-checked that her phone was on silent. She would have been so mortified if her phone had gone off during the wedding.

When the vows were complete, Derek and Maria did not kiss. Instead, the bishop announced that they were married, and then another speaker began closing the ceremony. Then, several girls left the room to get ready to serve lunch.

Alexis glanced at the clock, and it was exactly noon.

"What did you think? Was it different from the weddings you've been to?" Liz asked Freya and Alexis.

"It's very different. There are no flowers or big cake, no wedding party, no photographers, no dancing, and no white dress for the bride," Freya said.

"It is really different. I'm so glad I got to come to this. This has been an amazing experience," Alexis added.

"Well, it's not over yet. Come on, let's go downstairs and eat so you can experience some of the best Amish food you'll ever have," Liz said excitedly, and they headed downstairs.

"Alexis," Joshua said at the bottom of the stairs when he saw her. She turned to him, and someone in the crowd bumped into her. The church wasn't that big, and so many people were cramped inside. "What did you think of the wedding?" he asked.

"What?" she asked over the din, touching her ear to signal that she couldn't hear him well.

He grabbed her hand and led her out of the crowd and out the back door. The cold autumn air rushed to meet them, but it was a welcome change from the stuffy air inside of the church.

"Thanks. There are so many people in there," Alexis said. "I needed some air, even if it's freezing out here."

"*Ja*." A smile curved the corners of Joshua's lips.

She stared at the ground.

"Alexis? Are you okay?" He moved closer to her. It seemed she had not heard him.

Joshua placed his hand lightly on her shoulder. She flinched.

"Sorry, I didn't mean to startle you," he said.

"It's okay. I'm just jumpy."

"So, how do you know Maria? How long have you been friends?"

"I just... I got to know her and some of the other girls, just recently actually." Alexis wrapped her arms around herself and looked down at the ground.

When she didn't elaborate, he pressed, "How did you meet?"

"Why are you asking so many questions?" she snapped, her dark eyes blazing.

He took a step back, put his hands up, and couldn't help but laugh nervously. Why was she so upset? "Alexis, I'm sorry. I'm just trying to get to know you better."

She lowered her head. "I'm sorry. I just don't see why you'd want to get to know me, I guess."

"Are you kidding? It should be the other way around. I'm shocked a beautiful woman such as yourself is even talking to me."

She laughed, blushing. "Oh, come on, really?"

"*Ja*," he said. "Really. I'm just a boring farmer." He had sensed he was intruding, and usually, he would have walked away, but he didn't. This one was worth fighting for. "You can be yourself around me, Alexis."

"I am myself." She furrowed her brows.

"I just want to get to know you better and for you to feel comfortable around me. I'm a pretty good listener." She seemed tense, and he just wanted her to feel at ease.

She took a step away from him.

Had he made her feel uncomfortable? "I'm sorry if I overstepped. I was just hoping we could become friends. I really would like to spend more time with you." There was something about her that drew him to her.

"Look, I know you are just trying to make conversation when you ask about how I met Maria and the others, but I just can't answer those questions. Not now. Not to you."

Why not to him? Her words seared his heart. Joshua wanted to ask about her even more now that she'd raised his curiosities, but he decided to keep his questions within.

"I'm so sorry if I offended you. You're right; I was just making conversation. You don't have to answer anything you don't want to. I respect that. I respect you." He wished he knew her real reason for behaving this way, but he was a man of his word and would give her the space she desired. Maybe he'd been too forward.

Joshua drew a deep breath and walked to an area hidden from people's immediate view, near the edge of the woods.

5

Tears welled up in Alexis' eyes as she realized she had spoken rudely to him.

All Joshua wanted was to be friends with her, and she had overreacted when he'd just been trying to make conversation with her. She was so wracked with guilt by just being here that she'd let her emotions get the best of her.

She was unsettled by his willingness to walk away. Some men would have asked her more questions; they would have pleaded with her to change her mind.

But Joshua Lapp was not an ordinary man.

He'd just been making friendly conversation, and she'd been so rude. But he'd asked so many questions, and if she'd answered any of them truthfully, he probably wouldn't have wanted to get to know her more.

If she told him that she hadn't spoken to her parents in years, how she'd been addicted to drugs and living on the streets, or how she'd met her Amish friends, he would have run for the hills.

No, she couldn't tell him. She actually liked him, and she was so afraid to scare him off. That's why she'd said she couldn't say those things, not to him, but it had come out all wrong.

Alexis sighed in frustration. She'd blown it. This man had affected her in a way no other man had.

She was not the type of girl who believed in love at first sight.

Alexis believed that the process of love was gradual and not spontaneous. She likened it to a plant. It needed watering, nurturing, and care; it didn't just sprout up from the soil.

Then why did she feel this way; a way she'd never felt before? Her heart pounded, and her stomach was in knots. She couldn't decide if she felt nervous or excited, in addition to feeling guilty for snapping at Joshua. What was happening to her?

Alexis pulled off her gloves as a stream of sunlight pierced through the trees around the church, bringing her warmth and comfort. She took in a deep breath of the fresh, frigid air.

Some guests were milling in the parking lot, talking before lunch. The reception was about to begin, a potluck-style meal where everyone brought their own food to share, held on the first floor of the church. Alexis had brought brownies made from a box mix, one of the few things she could bake.

"Are you okay?" Freya asked behind her.

Alexis jumped, turning around.

"Sorry," Freya said. "I didn't mean to scare you."

Alexis shook her head. "I was just deep in thought. I'm fine, why?"

Freya could read her friend like a book. "I can tell when you are happy and when you are sad. What's bothering you?"

Why couldn't her friends leave her alone? Then guilt stung her for feeling annoyed. She was so blessed to have such wonderful friends.

Liz hurried outside to join them.

"I don't want to be a nuisance on Maria's special day," Alexis said, waving her hand dismissively. "Please, I'll be fine."

"You're feeling guilty again, aren't you? No one holds anything against you, Alexis," Liz reminded her. "We all love you."

Alexis couldn't help her lip from quivering as a tear rolled down her cheek. "I don't deserve you all." She told them about her conversation with Joshua. "I completely overreacted. He was just being nice, trying to talk to me."

"Joshua is very understanding. Don't worry." Liz looped her arm through Freya's. "I'm sure he will forgive you." She gave a mischievous grin. "I saw the way he looked at you."

They all chuckled, which lifted the burden from Alexis' shoulders. "I hope I get the chance to apologize."

"You will," Freya assured her. "For now, let's eat lunch. I'm starving."

They went inside through the back door to the first floor, which was populated with wooden tables and more backless benches. Alexis felt lousy for only bringing box mix brownies which had been set on a long table covered with several other decadent, homemade desserts like pies, cakes, and pastries.

The bishop got everyone's attention and said a prayer over the food, and then everyone got in line to fill their plates. Finally, they sat down to eat, and a few minutes later, Alexis saw Joshua go outside with another man as they were conversing.

"I'll be back in a bit."

Her friends followed her gaze, then smiled with understanding. Alexis wandered outside and breathed in the cool, crisp autumn air.

When she saw Joshua outside still speaking with another Amish man, Alexis walked toward the edge of the woods where she would be somewhat hidden until she gathered the courage to talk to him again.

If Joshua knew about her past, he wouldn't give her a second glance. And this was why she could never get close to anyone new who didn't already know what she'd gone through.

Maybe that was how it was meant to be.

Memories of her time with the sex traffickers rushed into her mind—the torture, the guilt, the killings. She stumbled toward a tree and leaned on it for support.

Would she ever go one day without a flashback or one night without a nightmare?

"Alexis?"

She turned around and found Joshua looking into her teary eyes.

The memories cut deep into her. She fought so hard to control the tears, but she couldn't, and it was even more embarrassing because Joshua was there.

"Alexis? Why are you crying?" Joshua sounded worried. "Did something happen just now? What's wrong?" He touched her arm lightly.

She licked her lips and swallowed. "No, nothing happened just now. I'm fine." She nodded and drew in a deep breath to calm her nerves.

Joshua stepped closer to her. "Fine? You don't look fine to me. Look, I know we just met, but can I help you?" He quickly pulled out a clean handkerchief and handed it to her. "Here, take this."

"Thank you." She grabbed the piece of cloth and ran it over her eyes, fighting with herself not to let more tears trickle down her cheeks. She wished she could share with him what was making her cry, but she couldn't. How could she? Alexis barely knew the man and it would only scare him off.

She doubted that her friends here had told him about what she'd done—they were good at keeping her secrets and wouldn't want to paint her in a negative light. Most people here had no idea what her true role had been in Anna, Liz, and Maria's capture. They probably just assumed Alexis was like them—also a victim.

How could she ever tell him what she'd done to them? That part of her was very delicate. It wasn't something she was proud of, and she wasn't prepared to share it with anyone just yet.

"Thank you." She returned his handkerchief after wiping her eyes, noticing black smearing the white linen. "I'm sorry I've ruined your handkerchief with my mascara."

Joshua chuckled. "I have no idea what that is, but that's okay."

She couldn't help but give a small smile, but then the sorrow immediately returned. Would this guilt and shame ever leave her?

Joshua liked Alexis, but she was a hard one to figure out. She seemed like a good person with a beautiful heart.

"Alexis! There you are," Freya said, walking toward her.

"We are going to see Derek and Maria privately since Anna, Isaac, and Olivia can't speak to them in the church," Freya said. "Want to come? It means we'll miss dessert."

"Definitely, I want to come. Let's go," Alexis said with a smile. "Thanks again, Joshua. See you later."

"I hope so." Joshua flashed her a smile and walked back to the church.

Alexis hadn't been able to talk to them all day because they'd always been surrounded by so many wedding guests, but she was grateful she'd get the opportunity to spend some time with her friends on this special day.

6

The lingering loneliness that drifted within Alexis' soul made her feel empty as she stepped into her bedroom after the wedding. Yet, at the same time, her heart fluttered and soared when she thought about how she'd been able to visit the bride, Maria, and ask for her forgiveness.

Maria had told Alexis she'd already forgiven her.

Sweet Maria had been so understanding, and Alexis had the feeling they'd become good friends. Anna had even insisted that Alexis had saved their lives, but Alexis wasn't sure about that.

Alexis had told Maria, "That day in the warehouse, I wasn't going to tell them about your cell phone, but I needed something to distract him so that he would not kill Anna. When Sebastian threatens something, he does it, even if it costs him. I knew he might kill one or both of you. So, I came in and told them about the phone, thinking maybe he'd start packing everyone up to move. But I was hoping enough time had passed for CPDU to track the phone after I called 911 and get there before they loaded all the girls into the vans. And I was right.

CPDU got there in time. I just wanted to tell you I am sorry I spied on you for them."

"Alexis, you saved my life. If it weren't for your intervention, Sebastian would have probably killed me," Anna said with an appreciative smile, wrapping her arms around Alexis' shoulders.

"Thank you, Alexis. If it wasn't for your quick thinking... We owe you so much." Maria's voice cracked with emotion at the thought of how close Anna was to death. "I had no idea at the time that you were being forced to spy for them."

Alexis sighed. "All that matters is that we are all safe now, and those men have been put away."

Now that Alexis had made things right with all three of the Amish women she'd spied on, and they had forgiven her—Anna, Liz, and Maria—a weight had been lifted off Alexis, and she felt as though she could breathe.

Like she could finally move on with her life.

Except... There were two more people she had to make amends with first.

Her parents.

And she would...once she mustered up the courage to do it.

"Please, Jesus, give me the strength to apologize to them and find the right words to say," Alexis whispered.

Right now, she just felt...drained. Exhausted.

Alexis buried her face in her palms as she wondered what she'd say to her mom on the phone. Then she remembered what had happened with Joshua and how she'd treated him.

She rubbed her eyes, which were swollen and painful from too much crying. She'd acted out of character today and felt deeply ashamed for her reaction.

Alexis untied the ribbon that held her long black hair, allowing it the freedom to cascade down her back. A small smile played at the corners of her lips as she remembered how nice Maria, Anna, and Liz had been to her when they had first met, forgiving her even before she'd apologized.

Alexis squeezed her eyes shut, trying to block out the memories of her time in captivity. She still always wore long sleeves to hide the burn scars on her arms and still flinched if anyone moved too quickly around her.

But they saw beyond her past and loved her unconditionally.

"Beautiful souls," she whispered. Her friends were truly incredible women.

But when would she rid herself of this guilt? When would she forgive herself and move on like her friends? Her guilt went deep. There were so many other girls and women she spied on over the months who had already been sold and would never be rescued. Where were they now? How could she ever reach them and apologize to them? One of them had even been murdered partly because of her.

Alexis peered at herself in the mirror, wanting to be normal. She wanted to fall in love and live happily ever after, but a frail voice kept whispering negative words to her.

What if Joshua finds out about my past? He'll think I'm a horrible person. A monster.

Her lips began to tremble as she pondered on a suitable answer, but she couldn't find any.

Tears soaked her pillow, and she fell into a restless sleep before the sun even set.

Alexis awoke when she heard the knock. Confused, she looked around the room. It wasn't dark yet. She hadn't meant to take a nap.

At first, she wondered who it was, and then reluctantly, she crawled out of her bed and walked toward the door.

Joshua Lapp had come to her house! Shocked, she ran a hand over her hair and hoped she looked okay, then opened the door.

"Good evening, Alexis," he said.

Alexis blushed and wiped a hand over her face, stifling a yawn in the process. "What are you doing here?"

"I'd like to take you out tonight. I was thinking we could leave my buggy here and take your car, if that's all right. The Amish don't own cars, but we can ride in them. We could go get ice cream a few towns over. If someone from the community sees me with you, I could get in trouble. I hope you understand," Joshua replied. "I want to apologize to you. I'm really sorry if I pried too much earlier."

Alexis raised a brow. "No, I'm the one who's sorry. You were just trying to make conversation, and I was rude to you."

"If there are things you don't want to talk about, that's all right."

How could she ever make him understand? "There are some things I'm still sorting out in my life. I don't like to talk about it."

He flashed a charming grin, and she couldn't help but smile. "It can't be that bad. You must be a great person if you're a friend of Anna, Freya, and Maria. They are good judges of character."

Alexis smiled. "They're wonderful."

"So, what do you say?" he asked, hands outstretched with his palms up.

"Yes, I'd love to go out with you. Give me a minute. Come on in while I get ready. I'll be quick."

"Okay, great. No problem." He grinned. "Sorry I didn't call first. I don't have a cell phone."

"That's okay. I'm just glad you're here," she said and headed to the bathroom. After brushing her hair, she went to the sink to wash her face and realized in horror that her mascara had been smudged while she was crying. Joshua had seen her like this, but it was too late now to do anything about it, and he had been too polite to mention it. She quickly washed her face and changed clothes.

Was this a date?

She pulled her hair into a quick bun, then threw on a simple black dress and a pea coat. This was as good as it was going to get.

She walked out of her room to the entryway.

"Wow," Joshua said, looking her over from head to toe. "You look amazing."

"Thanks," Alexis said shyly.

Joshua opened the door. "Shall we?"

Alexis took his arm, and they walked to the car. She drove them to a small ice cream shop about twenty minutes away.

"I love riding in cars. For me, it's fun because I don't get to do it very often," Joshua said from the passenger seat. "The Amish believe owning a car is prideful, but I don't see it that way. I bet for you riding in a car is nothing special, just an ordinary thing."

Alexis nodded. "Yeah, it is. I can't imagine not having a car."

Joshua patted the door. "I wish I had one sometimes. Riding in a buggy is so slow, and it takes a while to hitch up the horse. We can't go very far with it. If we want to go somewhere far, we hire a driver or take a bus."

"You wish you had a car? Really?"

"Well, yes. Sometimes. But no one knows that. We're supposed to be content with the way things are."

"Your secret's safe with me. Oh, look, we're here." Alexis pulled into the parking lot, and they walked inside the fifties-themed ice cream parlor with checkered floors and a jukebox.

She laughed. "I guess I should have worn my poodle skirt."

"Your what?"

"It's something women wore a long time ago that used to be in style. At least, I think they wore it in the fifties."

"Sounds really funny-looking. What would you like to have?" Joshua asked once they were both seated.

She bit her lip, feeling kind of nervous, and looked down at her hands folded in her lap. "Nothing." Her stomach was doing somersaults. Why was she feeling this way?

"What, you don't like ice cream?" He grinned, and Alexis realized he had a wonderful smile.

She almost complimented him but couldn't find the right words.

"Oh, you probably had dessert at the wedding. I'm sorry. I didn't even think of that. I was so busy helping clean up that I didn't have any," he said.

"No, actually, we went to see Derek and Maria instead of having dessert. I don't feel like having anything." She shrugged.

"I guarantee I can change your mind. I'll get us mint chocolate chip, one of my favorite flavors." He rose swiftly, strolled toward the sales counter and talked casually with the workers behind the counter as if he knew them well.

Alexis' fingers were trembling as Joshua returned with two cups of delicious-looking ice cream. Why did Joshua make her feel this way? She'd never felt this way before. She was nervous and giddy, yet felt like she could say anything to him—if she could only find the words. Her heart was pounding as if she'd just run a mile.

She was impressed by the way Joshua carried himself. A smile played on her lips as he set the bowl of ice cream before her.

"What's that sweet smile about?" He lifted a brow and settled in his seat.

"Nothing." She blushed.

"Why were you crying earlier?" he asked, leaning forward with concern.

She just wasn't ready to share her past with anyone. Especially not with a man like Joshua, who seemed so innocent, like nothing bad or difficult had ever happened to him in his life. What if he didn't understand that she had to make difficult choices? What if he stopped talking to her after learning of her involvement with those criminals?

"Can we not talk about that?" She smiled politely.

Joshua exhaled sharply. "Sorry. That's okay. If you want, you can tell me when you're ready."

She was learning things about him fast. He had a sensitive spirit and a tender heart.

"I am sorry for the terrible way I acted earlier. You were just trying to make conversation, and I was overly sensitive. I overreacted."

"Accepted, but only on one condition."

"What would that be?" Alexis eyed him warily.

"We forget the whole thing and have fun." Joshua circled a finger in the air, wagging his eyebrows jokingly.

Alexis laughed and made the promise.

After all the niceties, they fell quiet, but Joshua didn't let the silence dominate them for too long.

"You're not Amish, but you live near the community. Tell me about yourself." Joshua pushed his empty bowl aside. "So, did you grow up around here? Do you have family nearby?" Joshua asked, watching her face and wondering if he'd again asked too much.

"Well, my parents live in Augusta, but we haven't spoken in years," Alexis admitted.

"Why is that?" Joshua blurted out. "Sorry. You don't have to tell me."

"That's okay. I did something that hurt them deeply, and we haven't spoken since then."

"Have you forgiven each other and apologized?" he asked.

"Well..." Alexis twirled her spoon around in her bowl. "Not exactly. I haven't had the courage to call them up and apologize. Or maybe it's my pride... Or both."

Joshua furrowed his brows. How could he get her to open up to him? "Life is so short, Alexis, and you can lose loved ones in the blink of an eye, and then all those things you wish you could say to them, you can't. Trust me... You should call your parents and make things right while you can. God calls us to love one another and always to forgive others. And to even forgive ourselves, which can sometimes be the hardest."

Alexis sighed. He had no idea.

"I'm sure they miss you terribly, and they'd be so happy to hear from you," he added.

"Maybe," Alexis murmured. Was it too much to hope for?

"So, I know I asked this before, but if you don't mind me asking, how did you get to know Maria, Freya, and Anna?" Joshua asked.

"You know, I live close by, and it's a small town. Everyone knows everyone." She shrugged. While that was true, Alexis wasn't ready to answer fully. She was still avoiding his question. She quickly changed the subject. "How about you? Tell me everything about yourself."

"There's not much to say. There's nothing interesting or fascinating about my life. I've spent all my life on the farm, and that's how I developed a passion for animals."

"It is good to do what you love." Alexis saw something in his eyes when he spoke about the farm. Joshua was comfortable there. It was home to him. "I'm afraid of cows," she confessed.

"You're kidding, right? But we're eating ice cream," he teased.

"No, I am just afraid of their long tails and fierce-looking eyes. And their long tongues. I got licked by one once, and I was never the same," she said, and Joshua burst into laughter.

Joshua's joy was infectious. Alexis hadn't had this much fun in a long time—in fact, she couldn't remember when she'd had so much fun. The Alexis she'd been at the wedding was already quite different from the woman who sat across from Joshua, with tears of laughter streaming down her cheeks.

"Let's do this again." He leaned closer and reached across the table to touch her wrist lightly.

His touch was like a wave of electricity. This time, she didn't pull away.

Joshua said with a grin, "I enjoy your company and would love for us to go on another date."

"Date? Was this a date?" She blushed.

"Well, I thought it was. Wasn't it? Do you want to do this again?"

Alexis enjoyed Joshua's company too. He had been open with her, but she was not yet ready to tell him about her past.

"We can definitely do this again," she agreed, but a guilty feeling clouded her mind.

Friends didn't keep secrets from each other. But were they friends, or was this quickly turning into something even more?

7

A month had passed since Joshua first took Alexis to the ice cream shop. They continued to meet secretly, getting to know each other while bowling, getting more ice cream, and going to an indoor ice-skating rink.

Joshua had grown fond of her during these meetings, and he couldn't stop yearning for more.

Usually, Joshua was awakened by the bleating of sheep and mooing of cows; sometimes, he could tell what hour it was by listening to the rooster crow or the other animal sounds. He had not slept very well, as his thoughts had been focused on Alexis. He liked her; he couldn't deny what he was feeling. There were definitely sparks of attraction between them.

All of his life, he'd grown up on this farm. He knew everything about it. He knew when the animals were hungry and when they needed to rest. His experiences had given him his love for animals and his desire to study veterinary medicine.

Joshua often spent hours reading books on animal health, anatomy, and new medicines and treatments for animals. He'd often stay up late and read in his room by the light of his battery-operated lamp when he should have been going to bed early in order to rise early. But being sleepy the next day was worth it.

He wanted to break out and attend college more than anything, but what about his parents? They'd be devastated.

It wasn't just about going to college for Joshua. He was also stifled by the conservative ways and strict rules of the Amish community. He secretly disagreed with many of their rules, like how children were not allowed to go to school beyond eighth grade and how they were not allowed to play instruments, not to mention that electricity and modern conveniences were taboo.

But there were also so many good things about being Amish, like how the community always helped each other, even rebuilding homes or barns after fires. They even pitched in to pay for a neighbor's medical bills if needed. He loved their wholesome values, the slower pace of life, and how faith and family always came first. It was for these things that he had decided as a young man to be baptized into the Amish faith, but now he wasn't so certain he made the right choice.

He knew he would miss those things about this life.

Joshua heard his mother bustling around in the kitchen. He looked up. What time was it? He'd spent too long reading again.

He bolted off the bed and hurried out of his room towards the barn.

The wind welcomed him, ruffling his hair while the golden morning sun smiled on him like an old friend. After his chores were finished, he went inside for breakfast.

"Good morning, *Maam*," he said to his mother.

"You woke up late today. What happened?" his mother, Dorothy Lapp, asked.

"Sorry, I guess I was just really tired and overslept." Blushing, he hoped she wouldn't realize he was lying.

"Is that something to blush about?" His mother set a pot of oatmeal on the table, then cut up fruit and some homemade bread.

Joshua shrugged and lowered himself into a chair. He imagined what it would be like to marry Alexis. If he decided to stay right here with his parents, she would have to become Amish and live on the farm with him. Would she even consider that?

He quickly banished the thought. It was way too soon to be thinking such things.

Then he imagined them living in the city together, which was his dream. There was so much to see and do in the city—so many cultures all in one place. He had a feeling they'd make a great team.

Mrs. Lapp leaned in closer and put her hands on her hips, smiling wryly. "I've seen that look before. Someone is obviously smitten by a lovely girl. Care to share? Does she live in this community?" She winked. "So that explains why you've been acting so *ferhuddled* lately."

"Who's acting *ferhuddled*?" Adam's father, Abner Lapp, walked into the kitchen from outside, kicking the mud off his boots.

"I think Joshua is smitten with a girl," Joshua's mother said.

"Oh, who is this girl? Tell us all about her," Mr. Lapp asked enthusiastically. "It's about time you get married, son. We want grandchildren."

Joshua chuckled. He couldn't answer them. He knew his parents had expectations of him, but they would be very disappointed when they found out the girl who'd stolen his heart wasn't Amish.

"Wait, is it the *Englisher* girl who was at Maria's wedding? She must be one of Maria's *Englisher* friends," his mother said.

How on earth had she guessed it?

"I saw the way you looked at her at the wedding, and I saw the two of you talking. Who is this girl? Are you in love with her?"

Avoiding the conversation, Joshua walked toward the door. "I really have to get back to work outside—"

"Stop right there, Joshua!" his father commanded. Joshua halted. "You know you could be shunned if you get too involved with that girl."

"I know, I know. I'm being careful. She's wonderful, I promise. But I do have to go. I'll be back later." Joshua hurried out the door.

Mr. Lapp shook his head. "That boy needs to get his head out of the clouds."

Maria, Freya, and Alexis sipped tea at Freya's small kitchen table, where they ate Maria's homemade banana bread.

"Okay," Maria said, leaning forward in her seat eagerly. "I have to ask you something, Alexis. Do you like Joshua? You know, romantically?"

Alexis' brows furrowed, feeling like she was on a stage and the lights were on her as her two friends peered at her curiously. She bit off a huge piece of the banana bread to buy her a few seconds.

Of course, she liked Joshua. She had never felt so relaxed with any other man. He was so easy to talk to. Maybe she was imagining things, but being around Joshua made her feel safe.

Freya pushed her bread away and clasped her hands together. "So, do you like him?"

Alexis couldn't deny what she felt. They definitely shared a powerful connection, even if they'd only known each other for a very short time.

"I do like him. The truth is that I can't stop thinking about him," Alexis confessed.

"I knew it!" Maria cried.

"So, what is stopping you?" Freya glowed with anticipation.

Again, Alexis' eyes filled with unshed tears. "Other than the fact that he's Amish and I'm not? That alone is a problem."

"There's more to it than that, though, isn't there?" Maria asked.

"You think it's easy for me to live with the fact that I worked with those people to spy on the other kidnapped girls? That is something that I am deeply ashamed of. I don't know if I can ever get past that." Alexis' voice wobbled. "When he finds out, he'll think I'm a monster. How will he still want to be with me then?"

"What happened wasn't your fault. They would have probably killed you if you hadn't, and we both know the price you paid when you first refused them and how they killed that woman, Caroline, in the warehouse. Also, if it wasn't you then they would have chosen someone else, who might have been less likely to help others when possible. And you most definitely would have been shipped somewhere else, never to be found. It was a bit of self-preservation, choosing the lesser of two horrible scenarios. It was beyond you, and you did the best you could. You survived, and so did Liz, Anna, and many others." Maria wrapped Alexis in a hug and rubbed her back as Alexis continued to sob, and Freya got up and stood beside them, also wrapping her arms around Alexis.

"There's no way you could understand. No offense," Alexis choked out once her crying slowed a bit.

"How could you even say that?" Freya asked, tears shining in her own eyes. "At least you haven't killed anyone. I have, even though it was an accident. Do you think it was easy to live with the fact that I took a life? He was my husband's brother and Maria's first husband. I was depressed for months, and lived in perpetual fear until I made the decision to tell the truth. My husband still grieves for his brother, who is dead because of me." Freya turned to Maria. "Maria, I know a part of you will always miss him, even though you are happily remarried now."

Maria's eyes glistened with tears as she reached for Freya's hand.

"You were offered two options; life and death; you chose life. And life meant survival, not just for you but for many others. Alexis, I understand more than you think," Freya continued.

"She's right," Maria added. "When Freya first came here, I did and said horrible things to her because I was unable to forgive her back then. I hated her for accidentally hitting my husband with her car. I did those things to her because I wanted to. You had no choice, Alexis."

"I know it's not at all the same as being kidnapped and held captive by traffickers, so we will never fully understand that, but we do understand what it's like to regret," Freya added. "I don't think any of us will ever know what you truly went through when you were with them."

Alexis swallowed and nodded, unable to speak. No, they had no idea, and she wasn't sure if she'd ever be able to tell anyone the extent of what the traffickers had done to her. Not to mention all of the victims she'd met who had been sold, never to be seen again. She still remembered their faces, and she'd been forced to betray many of them.

"Believe me. It wasn't easy telling Adam, Maria, and the Lapps the truth. But they are good people, and they forgave me." She sighed. "So, believe me when I say that I think Joshua will understand when you tell him about your past. He already knows a little about what happened. You should tell him the whole story. Don't let your past hold you back from living your life and making a future for yourself."

Alexis felt stronger, having been reminded that someone else had walked down this road and came out the other end with a positive future. She felt better knowing she wasn't alone.

"So, I have to tell him? When?" Alexis asked.

Maria leaned closer and took Alexis' hands. "You already know the answer to that, Alexis. The longer you wait, the harder it will be. You are a good person, and good people tell the truth. The foundation of any relationship should be honesty and truth."

"You're completely right. Thank you both. You're such good friends."

"We just want you to be happy," Freya replied. "We've got your back. No matter what, we support you."

"Thanks." Alexis smiled. "Do you think I should meet him at his home?"

"I don't know. His parents might not like that. Maybe you should meet in a public place," Freya advised.

"How can I reach him? He doesn't have a phone, right?" Alexis asked.

"Well, no. The Amish only have phones in their businesses. Adam told me Joshua often goes to the coffee shop shortly before noon. Maybe you'll get lucky and run into him," Freya said.

"Okay. I feel nervous. Is that normal?" Alexis pressed a shaky hand against her chest.

"Yup. If you have butterflies in your stomach, it means you care," Freya teased.

A trickle of excitement poured over Alexis as she thought of Joshua's handsome face and smile. She couldn't wait to see him again.

Then dread filled her as she realized the next time she saw him, she would tell him the truth about her past. Alexis thanked Freya for all her advice and decided to find a way to reach Joshua while she was feeling so brave and encouraged.

8

Joshua strolled into the local coffee shop, hoping the friendly, familiar environment would help him clear his head.

He waved at some customers he knew, went to the counter to place his order, then moved to an empty table and sat. He couldn't think of anyone other than Alexis, and he was dying to tell her about how he was thinking about leaving the community. After spending some time here thinking, he'd head over there.

Joshua pulled out one of his scientific magazines and began to read it until his coffee was ready, and he went to the counter to get it. He sipped it while thinking about the next step to take.

When the door chimed and opened again, he looked up. Alexis walked into the coffee shop. His gaze locked on her dark eyes.

Alexis' heart raced, and blood pumped in her ears as she stared into his gorgeous eyes.

What was happening to her? She'd never felt this way about anyone before.

Joshua stood up and called her to his table. He looked so handsome in the white shirt and suspenders he wore.

"You look lovely." He ran his eyes swiftly over her flowery dress.

"Thank you." She blushed.

"Would you like anything?"

"No, thanks," Alexis replied, then sat down, and so did Joshua.

"I'm actually really glad you're here. You're a very beautiful person, Alexis, and I would love for us to be friends. I mean..." he started, then trailed off.

Friends? Her heart sank. She'd hoped he would want more.

"Sorry, I'm not sure what to say. I guess I'll just say it. I have feelings for you, and I want to get to know you better. And maybe one day we can be more than friends," Joshua said, smiling.

Her heart filled with joy.

"You aren't saying anything," Joshua said nervously.

Alexis cleared her throat and looked him straight in the eye. "You don't know me that well. There are some things you should know about me first." She bit her lip, and shame washed over her anew.

Joshua looked stunned.

She told him everything.

Tears sprang up in her eyes as she pulled up the sleeves of her cardigan, and Joshua's face paled when he saw the scars on her arms. "They did this to me and told me they'd do it to some of the other girls too if I didn't do what they asked. But I still regret what I did."

She hoped one day she could forgive herself.

"I regret all of it. I wish I could take it all back." She fought hard to hold back the tears, but one tear managed to trickle down, followed by several more. "After we were rescued, I helped the Covert Police Detectives Unit by giving them information on the sex trafficking ring that put several traffickers away, so I never went to jail or prison. It was obvious I'd been forced to do those things against my will. If you want to validate the story, just have Adam look it up. Liz, Maria, and Anna could have told you all this, but I guess they were giving me the chance to tell you myself. That was kind of them."

"You'd been kidnapped and taken advantage of. It was the only way for you to survive and come out alive, to work with those men, and work against them, by giving the police information," Joshua reassured her.

"That was how I became friends with Freya and the others. They forgave me and moved on." She wiped tears from her face. "So, I can only hope you don't think I'm a terrible person."

"You were only trying to survive. A lot of people have done worse things and been forgiven. I don't think you're a terrible person at all." He leaned closer and grabbed her slender hands in his. "I think you're strong, beautiful, and amazing. You were a victim, too. There is nothing to forgive."

His words were like balm to her wounds.

She smiled shyly. "Thank you."

Joshua seemed to be struggling with something. "So there's something I need to tell you. I plan to study to become a veterinarian," he blurted out.

She lifted a brow in surprise. Joshua was not just handsome. He had dreams and concrete plans for his future, but from his tone she could tell there was a barrier.

"But if I do, I'll be shunned like Anna, but I've decided that I'm leaving to go to college."

"It's not going to be easy, but I'm so happy for you, and I'm proud of you," she said. "Speaking of a new life, I have some good news. I found out today I got into nursing school. My program starts in four months."

"That's fantastic! Congratulations!" Joshua jumped out of his chair and pulled her up before wrapping his arms around her. Alexis breathed in his woodsy scent, smiling with contentment as she rested her head on his chest.

"Thanks."

Joshua grinned and held her at arm's length. "You know what? Why beat around the bush? Life's too short not to say what we feel. Alexis, I'm falling in love with you. I think we have a special connection, and I want to see where this goes."

Alexis' heart danced in delight. "Really?"

"You heard me." He gave her hands a squeeze.

"Well, it just so happens I'm falling in love with you too." She smiled.

"Why don't we travel together then? Share some adventures? There's nothing I want more than to get to know you better." He leaned closer until she could see the golden flecks in his eyes.

Alexis thanked God for this moment.

Her response was a delightful laugh. “I would love that.”

A few months later, Joshua walked home and stepped through his front door after spending the afternoon with Alexis, who was waiting for him in the driveway.

Today was the day he would leave his Amish community behind forever to pursue his dreams and marry the love of his life.

“That young woman is not Amish, so what were you doing with her? Who is she?” Abner asked, looking out the window to see Alexis sitting in her car, waiting for Joshua.

“You cannot be with a girl that is not Amish. You cannot bring shame to us by turning your back on our beliefs as your cousin did,” his mother said with sadness in her voice.

A sting of indignation bit into Joshua. His mother was talking about Adam. They didn’t speak his name anymore, as if he had never existed.

Adam was Joshua’s hero for leaving to pursue his dreams, and hearing his mother talk about his cousin like that wasn’t right. He had been forcing himself to live with values he wasn’t comfortable with, but he was ready to move on with his life.

“If I find a girl who isn’t Amish, I could still love her because she is human. And humanity transcends beliefs.”

"You will do no such thing!" his mother flared, then her voice softened. "Don't leave us like your cousin left his family, please. I just couldn't bear it."

Now was the time to tell his parents of his plans. Joshua took a deep breath and said, "*Maam, Daed*, I have to tell you something. I want to leave the community so I can go to college and become a veterinarian. I don't agree with some of the Amish rules. Most of all, I've fallen in love with an *Englisher* woman."

"No!" his mother cried, falling onto a chair. "This can't be happening."

"You cannot leave the church! You will be shunned, just like your cousin," his father warned.

"His name is Adam. My cousin's name is Adam, and it's not right that you never talk about him. And he is doing well for himself. He's a police officer, helping people and making a difference, and he is happily married to his wife, Freya. If finding the path to my destiny will make me an outcast here, then so be it."

Dorothy sobbed, her shoulders shaking. "Joshua, please don't leave us. You were already baptized years ago. Why are you changing your mind now?"

"I've been thinking about this a lot the past year. I've made up my mind."

"I just couldn't bear it if you were shunned," Dorothy choked out. "We wouldn't be able to talk to you."

Guilt and second thoughts assailed Joshua as he looked at his parents. Could he really do this to them, especially his poor mother?

He walked over to her and wrapped his arms around her shoulders.

"Please, Joshua. Don't do this. Don't you love it here? This is your home," she whispered.

"Of course, I love it here, but I love Alexis and want to marry her."

"She's right, Joshua. You could build a wonderful life here." Abner gave Joshua a knowing look, his long gray beard bobbing as he nodded his head. "It would mean everything to us if you stayed. Please, son."

"I've made up my mind. I'm sorry." He ignored the mounting guilt of abandoning his parents. They were getting older, and who would take care of the animals once they were too frail? Who would run the farm?

If he left, everything would fall apart for them. And maybe that was too high of a price to pay for following his dreams.

What about his community, which was like one giant family? Could he really leave everything and everyone he loved behind for a world full of the unknown?

"Maybe you can hire someone to replace me. I can try to send money to help whenever I can," he said, hoping it would ease some of his guilt. He ignored the rising doubts in his mind.

"You must earnestly pray about this, Joshua," his father added. "God will show you the way."

"I have," Joshua insisted. "As I said before, I've made up my mind. Alexis is here to drive me to the city." He looked out the window to make sure she was still waiting, then hurried to grab his bag from his room. There hadn't been much to pack, just the essentials—clothing, toiletries, and his Bible. Even though he was leaving the Amish, he was taking his faith in God with him.

He went back downstairs where his parents were waiting.

"I want you to know I love you and you are the best parents in the world to me," Joshua said in a cracking voice, hugging both of them.

A sickening feeling filled him as he realized he might never see his parents again, but he turned and walked toward the door even though every step was agony.

"Don't leave, Joshua!" Dorothy cried, chasing after him. Abner followed her out the door, catching up to her and placing a hand on her arm, murmuring something to her.

"I'm sorry, *Mamm* and *Daed*. I love you both," Joshua said, giving them each another hug on the porch before turning and hurrying toward the car.

Alexis rolled down her window and parked, her heart aching when she saw the look on his parents' faces.

"He's made his choice, Dorothy," Abner told her. "There's nothing we can do."

"But he will be shunned!" Dorothy cried. Then they both set their eyes on Alexis. Instead of the hateful glares that Alexis had expected, Abner and Dorothy's eyes were only filled with pain and sorrow.

"Let's go," Joshua blurted as he opened the back door of the car and threw his bags onto the seat. He quickly got into the passenger seat.

"Are you sure you want to do this?" Alexis asked for the hundredth time.

"This is what I want, Alexis." Joshua looked into her eyes. "I love you. I want to be with you and be a veterinarian. I'm sure. Now let's go."

Alexis backed out of the driveway and drove away, leaving Dorothy and Abner on the front porch, crying.

9

Alexis and Joshua were married in a courthouse soon after. It was simple, and there were only a few people in attendance, but Alexis didn't care that there was no cake, music, or expensive wedding dress.

Alexis found out a few months later she was pregnant. Because she was so sick during her pregnancy, she put nursing school on hold as Joshua continued attending college to be a veterinarian. After their daughter Sophia was born, the three of them couldn't have been happier. A few years later, Joshua became deathly ill with stage four cancer.

Dorothy and Abner came to say goodbye to their son for the last time.

Alexis had called them to let them know he was sick as soon as she found out, and they had been visiting him in the hospital, not caring that they could be shunned for it. They'd hired a driver to take them back and forth several times. Alexis never told anyone from the community that they had done so, not wanting to get them in trouble, and she wasn't sure if they had ever told anyone to this day. She admired them for putting their son first during that trying time.

"Thank you for coming," Alexis said as they entered the hospital room. She sat beside her husband, holding his hand as usual, with Sophia on her lap. Alexis and Sophia had been practically living at the hospital at that time, trying to spend every minute they could with Joshua.

"*Mamm... Daed...*" Joshua murmured, almost inaudibly, in a cracked voice.

"We're here, Joshua." Dorothy turned to Alexis. "Thank you for letting us know," she said, choking up as she covered her mouth with her hands.

What she meant was that Alexis had called to tell them this could be Joshua's last day.

Dorothy grasped Joshua's hand gently. "We're here, dear. We love you." Her voice crumbled into a sob.

Abner put his arm around his wife's shoulders, doing his best to comfort her, but there was nothing he could do to ease her pain. He cried tears of his own though he was clearly trying to be strong for Dorothy, who continued to sob.

"I'll give you time with him alone." Alexis bent down to kiss her husband on the forehead before walking out of the room with Sophia to wait in the hallway. Finally, Abner and Dorothy emerged from the room.

"We want you to know we are not angry with you at all about Joshua leaving the community," Abner told her gently. "He was going to leave anyway. He had his mind set on it."

"I encouraged him," Alexis said. "I would understand if you were mad at me."

"Not at all," Dorothy said. She smiled at Sophia, who was coloring as she sat in the chair in the hallway. "Clearly, he loves you and Sophia very much. You've made him very happy. We thank you for that."

"You are welcome to stay with us after..." Abner cleared his throat and bent his head. "Our home is always open to you."

While Joshua had been shunned for leaving, Alexis and Sophia were not because they weren't Amish. Alexis pictured the swaying fields of green corn and tall grass and the sounds of horses' hooves clip-clopping on the pavement. The last time she'd been there, she'd helped Joshua leave the Amish behind, and before that, that community was where she'd had to face some of the women she had betrayed.

Joshua had asked her to take Sophia to visit his parents, but he had understood when Alexis didn't want to return.

"I'm not sure I could ever go back there," Alexis murmured, her eyes downcast at the speckled linoleum floor. "I'm sorry. It's too painful. I think it would only remind me of him. I hope you understand."

"Of course, dear," Dorothy said, then reached out and touched her arm. "If you ever change your mind, just call the number we gave you. If you lose it, just look up the number for one of the nearby businesses, like the Unity Community Store. They'll connect you to us."

"Thank you for the offer. I appreciate it," Alexis said, glancing at Sophia. Should she take her daughter back to the place where her father grew up? Surely, she would love it there, and it would be good for her to see her grandparents.

But Alexis knew guilt would overcome her if she ever went back to Unity.

"We will let you be with him now," Abner said, twisting his black hat in his hands. "Please call us if you ever need anything at all. I do hope you come to visit us, at least. We would love to see both of you."

"Thank you. I'll try," Alexis said, but she knew she didn't sound convincing.

"Goodbye, Sophia," Dorothy said. Sophia looked up and waved.

"Can you give your *Mammi* and *Daadi* a hug?" Alexis asked.

Sophia nodded, slid off the chair, and hugged each of them.

"Be good for your mommy," Dorothy said. "And remember that your daddy loves you very much."

"We will miss you," Abner added.

"Goodbye, dear," Dorothy said, giving her one last tearful glance before breaking down into sobs as they walked down the hallway.

Alexis never returned to Unity to visit. She just couldn't bear to go back to Joshua's childhood home and face his parents again, though she wasn't sure if that would be worse than the guilt of knowing she was breaking her promise to him. Not only that, it reminded her of her time with the traffickers.

After Joshua's death, everything they had built together shattered. Just when Alexis was starting to really put her past behind her, just when she started to think she could be happy, everything she knew was ripped from her.

As a single mother, Alexis didn't know how to cope with the shame of her past along with how to raise her young daughter alone, so she ignored the phone calls from her friends and in-laws in Unity, shutting everyone out, including her own family.

Maybe I'm better off alone, Alexis thought to herself as she sat at the kitchen table alone one night after Joshua's death, thumbing numbly through a stack of unpaid bills. *I caused so much pain in their lives. Why should I go back to Unity? It would only bring back terrible memories that I'd rather forget. I need to focus on making enough money to pay the bills.*

"Mommy?"

Alexis turned to see three-year-old Sophia walking toward her slowly, rubbing her eyes with one hand and holding her blanket in the other.

"What's wrong, baby?" Alexis asked.

"I had a dream about Daddy," Sophia said groggily. "I wet the bed."

This was a regular occurrence ever since Joshua had died, but Alexis had found out it was normal for young children to do that after a big change in their lives.

"It's okay," Alexis said. "Let's go change your sheets." Alexis got up and wrapped her arms around her daughter. "I dream about Daddy, too. It's good to remember him."

Maybe I should follow my own advice, she thought to herself glumly.

"Can we go see *Mammi* and *Daadi*?" Sophia asked, referring to Joshua's parents. "I miss them." During their visits at the hospital, Sophia had bonded with them.

Alexis knelt down to her daughter's eye level. "I don't think so, sweetie."

"Why not?"

Alexis sighed. How could she explain to her daughter that visiting Joshua's parents in Unity and seeing Joshua's childhood home would only break her heart?

"Let's go change your sheets," Alexis said, guiding her daughter back to her room.

God, help me get through life without Joshua and be the best mom I can be for Sophia, Alexis prayed.

I can't do this without You.

10

PART TWO

Three years after Joshua's death, Alexis rushed around the diner where she worked, trying not to mix up any orders as she sometimes did.

"Here's your sandwich, and here's your salad," she said, setting the plates down in front of a couple dining together. "Is there anything else I can get you?"

"I asked for no croutons and the dressing on the side. There are croutons on this," the young woman spat, pointing to the offending squares of carbs. "And there's dressing on it. Get me a new one."

"Oh, I'm sorry about that. I will right away." Alexis' face heated both in embarrassment and anger, and she snatched up the salad bowl, her other hand in a clenched fist. In her sweeping motion, she knocked over the young woman's coffee. The dark liquid dripped off the table and seeped onto the customer's expensive-looking dress.

"Watch what you're doing!" the woman shrieked, grabbing handfuls of napkins from the dispenser on the table and dabbing at her dress. "Do you know how much I paid for this dress?"

The man the woman was dining with looked down at his lap, ears red. "Tasha, please."

"The only reason we came here instead of a nice restaurant is because we are on a *road trip*," Tasha said with an eye roll. "We shouldn't have even gone on this trip. I hate road trips, but our therapist said it would be a good bonding experience. I knew this would be a terrible idea to come here to this dump." She looked Alexis up and down. "The service is terrible."

"I'm so sorry; it was my mistake," Alexis said, eyes stinging with hot tears. "I can pay to have it dry cleaned."

"I'm sure you can't afford it. You're a nobody. Just worthless and completely incompetent." The woman glared at Alexis, then furiously blotted her skirt. "You should be ashamed of yourself."

"Worthless? That is not true," Alexis said fiercely, slamming the salad down on the table.

The young woman's head popped up, and she stared at Alexis in shock. Other customers looked up too.

Alexis continued, "I have seen things that would scare you straight. I have been tortured, and I have seen people killed. I was kidnapped and sold into sex slavery, and I survived. Yes, I still have nightmares, and yes, I still feel shame. They told me I was worthless trash, but now I know that's not true. I am stronger because of it. And most of all, I am a child of God, made in His image. And you should never speak to another human being like that ever again. You are the one who should be ashamed of yourself."

Alexis stood tall as she looked into the woman's eyes, who only continued staring at her with her mouth hanging open.

Alexis took a good look around the diner, confidence filling every cell of her body. A few of the other customers began clapping slowly, and within a few moments, the entire diner was clapping for her.

"Alexis!" The owner, Bill, stormed over. "She is sorry, ma'am. And the cost of cleaning your dress will come out of her paycheck. She'll get you a new salad now. We apologize." Bill grabbed Alexis' arm, his face red with anger, and took her to the kitchen. "What was that? Never in my life have I been so embarrassed!"

"That woman was extremely rude to me. She called me worthless," Alexis snapped.

"I don't care. You know what? She was right. You are worthless. You'll never make anything of your life. And you're a lousy waitress. And if you ever talk that way to a customer again, you're fired." He pointed at her, his hand right in front of her nose. "I would fire you right now, but we're short-staffed."

Alexis smacked his hand away. "Yeah, maybe I am a lousy waitress, but I'm not worthless. I quit!" She yanked off her apron, threw it on the floor, and stormed out of the diner.

Alexis stepped outside, breathing in the air as if for the first time. And as she looked around the town, she felt as though she was seeing the world for the first time as well.

"I can be whoever I want to be. I am capable of anything," she told herself and marched to her car. She'd find a new job, and a better one at that. She'd figure it out.

All that mattered was that she'd stood up for herself and spoken her mind. She refused to let people treat her wrongly and walk all over her as she had before.

No, this was a new Alexis.

Never in her life had she felt so empowered.

But now she had no source of income. How would she support her daughter as a single mom?

"How was your last day of kindergarten?" Alexis cried as she wrapped her arms around her six-year-old daughter while picking her up at school. Alexis savored the scent of her daughter's bubblegum-scented shampoo as she squeezed Sophia tightly.

Sophia pulled away, brushing a strand of brown hair out of her face and lifting a drawing. "Great! We drew pictures of our families." Her brown eyes lit up in a smile.

"You did? Let me see." Alexis held the paper in her hands. Sophia had drawn her mother, herself, and her father, Joshua. Even though he had died three years ago, Sophia still remembered him.

"Even though Daddy is in heaven, he's still a part of our family, so I drew him."

"Of course, baby," Alexis choked out, hugging her again. "Daddy will always be a part of our family, no matter what."

Sophia's smile returned, warming Alexis' heart.

"This is so good, Soph. You're so good at drawing. I think you're even better than me," Alexis gushed. "You're definitely better than I was at your age." She meant every word. Sophia was very artistically talented for her age.

"Thank you," Sophia said, taking the drawing back and tucking it into her backpack. "I'll put it on the fridge when I get home."

Home—their small, dingy apartment was all Sophia had ever known since Joshua had died, and now Alexis couldn't even afford that. What was she going to do? She had already been living paycheck to paycheck, and the diner hadn't paid much. Now she didn't even have a job. How would she pay her bills and put food on the table?

Visions of swaying cornfields and buggies rumbling down the road flashed across her mind. Joshua's parents had always told her to let them know if she needed anything at all, and it had been a while since she'd seen them.

Three years, in fact. She just hadn't had the heart to return after Joshua's death. Maybe it was time to take Sophia back and see them.

"What's wrong, Mom?"

Alexis blinked. "Remember *Grossdaadi* and *Grossmammi*? Daddy's mom and dad?" They lived in Unity, Maine, about an hour and a half away.

"*Daadi* and *Mammi*?" Sophia asked, using her shortened names for them. "Yeah. We haven't seen them in a long time."

"Would you like to go see them?"

"Yes! I miss them."

"I'll call them and leave a message. We can see if they would like to have us over soon at their farm." Alexis opened the backdoor of the car, and Sophia climbed in.

"They live on a farm? With animals? I want to go!" Sophia cried.

It had been so long. Alexis just hoped they would be happy to see them. They had left her messages over the years and she had listened to them, she'd ignored their calls. Just hearing their voices broke her heart, reminding her of her late husband and how she had been part of the reason why he had left them.

Her parents had also called her and left voicemails, but she'd ignored them as well. The last time they'd spoken, they said things to each other that still made Alexis' heart ache. So, she would move without even telling them.

How would she manage going back to her husband's childhood home? It would shatter her, but she had no other choice at the moment if she wanted to take care of her daughter.

Maybe they'd let her stay until she got back on her feet—if that wasn't too much to ask after how she'd treated them.

What about her friends? At Maria's wedding, she had promised to visit but had been a failure as a friend.

Would Joshua's parents be upset that she had stayed away for so long? Would they turn her away?

As Alexis drove home, her mind churned with questions.

Later that evening, after Sophia went to bed, Alexis dialed Joshua's parents' number with shaking fingers. She knew they wouldn't get her call tonight since she was calling Abner's business phone, and they might already be in bed by now. She would have to leave a message.

When she heard the beep, she said, "Hi… It's Alexis. I'm sorry I haven't called in so long or responded to your letters. I got your voicemails, but I just…" She cleared her throat. This was even harder than she thought it would be. "I feel so bad about how we left things, and after Joshua…" She took in a deep breath. "That's no excuse. I should have at least called, and I'm sorry about that. So, well, I was wondering if Sophia and I could come to visit you. We've hit some hard times, and we need a break. Sophia's out of school for the summer. Anyway, if you would like us to come up, just call me back and let me know." She left her cell phone number and ended the call.

She let the phone drop from her hand onto the couch and sank back into its cushions. Well, that was the worst voicemail she'd ever left, but it was too late to change it now.

Dorothy and Abner would want to see them, wouldn't they?

What if they didn't? What if they didn't even call her back? Well, she wouldn't blame them if they didn't. She'd pulled their son away from them and then abandoned them after his death.

She wasn't exactly going to win the daughter-in-law of the year award.

11

Alexis jumped when her cell phone vibrated next to her. She was still on the couch, but the sun was up. Had she fallen asleep here last night?

The phone continued to vibrate, and she fumbled to grab it and read the caller ID. It was Abner and Dorothy calling early in the morning. To them, it probably wasn't early.

Alexis took a deep breath and answered the phone. "Hello?"

"Good morning, Alexis," came Abner's voice. "I got your message this morning when I came in to check the messages, and I wanted to call you back right away. We would love to have you and Sophia come to visit. You can stay as long as you'd like. We've missed you and Sophia. In fact, if you want to move in, we'd love to have you."

Alexis' eyes widened. "Move in?" She stammered.

"Well, of course. I know it must be hard for you, and Dorothy and I aren't getting any younger. The house is so quiet. We would love to fill it with laughter again. It would mean so much if you came to live with us."

Alexis blinked, her mind rapidly going through all the things she would have to do before moving. "I'll do my share. I will help with the chores and pull my own weight."

"I'm sure Dorothy would love your help. So, will you come?"

"Yes," Alexis blurted, not even taking time to think about it. Sophia deserved more than this dingy apartment. Sure, Sophia might miss her friends from school, but she could make new friends in the community. This could just be a temporary move until she got back on her feet, or maybe it would be permanent. Only time would tell if they would feel at home there or completely out of place.

"When can you get here?"

"It might take me a few weeks. I will give my landlord notice today, but I need to pack up and take care of some things before I come," Alexis said, getting up off the couch and stepping into the kitchen. Sophia was just walking out of her bedroom, rubbing her eyes. She waved to Alexis, and Alexis waved back.

Sophia gave her mother a curious look.

"Take all the time you need. We look forward to seeing you. We've missed you both so much."

"We've missed you too," Alexis said. "I'll be there as soon as I can."

Sophia poured herself a bowl of cereal and sat at the small kitchen table as Alexis ended the call. "Where are we going, Mom?"

Alexis sat in the chair beside her. "Well, you know how I said we are going to visit *Daadi* and *Mammi* in Unity?"

Sophia nodded enthusiastically and took a big bite of cereal.

"How would you like to go live with them?"

"You mean leave here?" Sophia asked.

"Yes. Would that be okay with you?" Alexis asked, unsure of what her daughter thought of the situation. "Their house is much bigger than our apartment."

"Yes!" Sophia cried. "Yes, I want to move. The kids at school aren't very nice to me except for Monica. I'll miss her a lot. Can I still see her?"

"Of course. We aren't moving that far away. Maybe we can meet up with them sometime this summer. Or maybe they could come to visit us at the farm in Unity." Alexis knew once they moved that Sophia would quickly make so many new friends with the Amish children and would soon probably forget all about Monica, but she would still take her to visit her friend if she wanted to.

"Yay! We're moving!" Sophia cried, jumping in her seat and causing droplets of milk to fall from her spoon onto the table.

Alexis chuckled. "Yes, sweetie, but we have a lot to do. We better get started."

Ben Banks stared at the blank screen before him, drumming his fingers on his desk. Just like that screen, his mind was blank. He was hoping to write ten thousand words before his daughter came home from school, but once again, that wouldn't be happening today. No, not even close.

Yes, what he had was a terrible case of writer's block.

When his phone rang, he jumped, then grabbed it to read the caller ID. It was Margaret, his agent. He groaned, but he'd been avoiding her calls for the past few days.

Reluctantly, he answered it. "Hello?"

"Ah, so he lives," Margaret joked. "Where have you been, Ben?"

"Right here," Ben muttered.

"Why haven't you sent me those pages yet? The publisher wants to know that the fourth book is in the works. They want some proof."

"I'm working on it."

Margaret sighed, her breath crinkling into the earpiece. "That means you haven't started yet."

"I'm sitting at my desk right now," Ben insisted. "I just can't seem to write anything good. I did write something, but then I deleted it. It was terrible."

"Couldn't have been that bad."

"No amount of editing could have improved it. I'm starting over."

Silence lingered on the other end of the line. "You do this every year."

"What?"

"It's almost the anniversary," Margaret said sympathetically. "Maybe you need some time off. I think I could talk them into giving you more time. We should have given you more time to begin with. It can't be easy, being a single dad and having such a demanding full-time job besides writing. And with the anniversary of—"

"I don't want to talk about it," Ben interjected firmly. "I'll be fine."

"No, Ben. What you need is a break from your everyday life. Get some time off from work and take Nichole out of town. Go somewhere nice and clear your head until the date passes. Maybe when you get back, you'll be able to write something worth sending to the publisher. When was the last time you had a vacation?"

Ben used his thumb and forefinger to rub the bridge of his nose. "I'm not sure. The thing is, I'm not sure I can get time off from CPDU."

"How long have you been working there? Come on. Don't you have vacation days saved up?"

"Maybe."

"So, ask them."

Ben sighed. Sure, he got royalties from his books, but it wasn't enough for him to be able to quit his job and write full-time. He'd been naïve in thinking that once he got published, he'd be able to quit his job as so many people assumed. So, as he wrote his books, he continued working as a field agent for the Covert Police Detectives Unit in Kennebunkport, Maine—one of their many locations throughout the state. He'd been an agent for years, but the job was wearing him down. The things he'd seen ate at his soul, from protecting people from dangerous stalkers to rescuing survivors of sex trafficking. Some of the faces of those he'd helped would forever be ingrained in his memory.

He'd wanted to quit for a few years now, but the job was a part of him that he couldn't seem to let go of. He needed to help people, and he felt as though he might be incomplete without it.

"It's been three years, Ben, but it's still okay to grieve, especially at this time of year. Call me when you get back, okay?" Margaret said.

"Fine," Ben said. "If I can get the time off, I'll go somewhere."

"Good. Take care."

Ben ended the call and then glanced at the clock. Nichole would be getting off the bus and home from school any minute. This was her last day of school, so he wanted to do something special for her, but he'd lost track of time staring at that blank screen.

He pushed back his chair and hurried downstairs. Nichole loved pancakes and usually wanted a snack after school, and Ben had seen an idea online that he wanted to try. He mixed up pancake batter from scratch and cooked the pancakes, then put two on a plate. He sliced up a banana, using slices for the eyes and chocolate chips for the smile. He also put chocolate chips on the eyes. When he was done, two pancakes for his daughter were smiling up at him.

Before he'd met Estella, he hadn't been able to cook at all, but Estella had taught him well. It was a good thing she had because neither one of them had ever suspected that Ben would end up raising Nichole alone, especially since Estella's parents had both passed away as well as his. Estella did have a brother, Jeff, but he was often busy with his own wife and children, and Ben hadn't been very good about being in touch ever since Estella died.

A few minutes later, he heard the bus stop in front of his house, and Nichole came through the door a moment later.

"Hi, Daddy," she said, hanging up her backpack on the wall.

"How was your last day of kindergarten?" he asked, wrapping her in a bear hug. Nichole looked so much like her mother that it made his heart ache whenever he looked at her. She had the same bright eyes and smattering of freckles across her nose as Estella once had.

Nichole shrugged. "Pretty cool. We got to watch a movie in science class, and all my friends signed my yearbook."

"Well, look. I have a surprise for you." Ben led her to the kitchen and showed her the pancakes. "Ta-da."

Nichole laughed. "Thanks, Daddy."

"Is it lame?" he asked.

"No, I like it." She smiled up at him. "One for me and one for you?"

"They're both for you."

"They kind of look like us. Don't you think so?"

Ben laughed. "I didn't mean for them to look like us."

"You should have made one more to look like Mom," Nichole said, then frowned. "Sorry. I know you don't like it when I talk about her."

Ben sat at the table and patted the seat beside him, and Nichole sat down. The table was situated in the corner of the large, white kitchen in front of a wide glass window that overlooked the ocean. His large beach-front home often led people to assume he was wealthy, but Ben had inherited this house from his parents, who had passed away.

"It's not that I don't want you to talk about Mom," Ben said. "Yes, I miss her, and I know you miss her, and we should keep talking about her to keep her memory alive. Right?"

"Even if it makes you sad?"

"Yes," Ben said. "Because she would want us to remember the good times."

"But you always get so sad in June. That's because the day that Mom died is coming up, isn't it?" Nichole asked.

"Well, yes, sweetie," Ben said. "It reminds me of that. But I have an idea. How about we go on a vacation?"

"Vacation? Really? Yes!" Nichole grinned. "That would be fun."

"We could go visit my friend Derek and his wife, Maria. We haven't seen them in a long time, huh?"

"Yeah. I remember Rachel and Carter. I liked playing with them."

"Well, let me give them a call and see if we can go visit them. If we can't go there, we can go somewhere else."

"I don't want to go anywhere else," Nichole said. "I really like it there. I hope they say yes." Nichole took the plate of pancakes. "These are good, Daddy. Thanks."

"You're welcome. While you're eating, I'll call Derek." Ben kissed his daughter's head and dialed Derek's number on his cell phone. It had been almost a year since he'd visited his friends, so it was long overdue.

Ben dialed Derek's number, and he was surprised to hear someone answer.

"Derek? It's Ben."

"Ben? Wow," Derek said. "It's been a long time. How are you?"

"I'm okay," Ben said. "I was thinking it's been too long since we've seen each other."

"It sure has," Derek agreed. "Can you come?"

"I am going to call work and make sure I can get the time off, but I do have vacation days saved up. To be honest, I have been throwing myself into work at CPDU, and I've had writer's block lately, so I definitely need a break."

"Well, you're welcome to come up any time. Branson better give you that time off. You're one of their best, and you deserve it," Derek said.

"Thanks. Do you think Maria would be okay with us staying there?"

"Of course! She would want to see you and Nichole too, I'm sure, and so would the kids. They'll be so excited. When can you get here?"

"I will find out if Branson will give me the time off, then I will let you know. It could be a week or two."

"Sounds great."

12

Two weeks later, as Alexis and Sophia drove to Unity, Alexis tapped the steering wheel anxiously. It had taken her several days to pack up their belongings and sell or donate most of what they no longer needed, only keeping the bare necessities. Though she was looking forward to seeing family and friends, she was filled with apprehension. What would they say after she hadn't come in so long, ever since Joshua died?

Three years. A lot could happen in three years.

Alexis turned the car onto the dirt lane, where the Community Store sat near the main road. She passed it, her stomach in knots. Sophia was still sleeping in the back seat, leaning against a pillow.

"We're here, Soph," Alexis said, and Sophia slowly opened her eyes and looked around.

"We're here!" She stretched her arms, smiling at the fields and houses passing them by. "I'm so excited!"

"Me too." Alexis smiled at her over her shoulder as she approached Dorothy and Abner's house and pulled into the driveway. Sophia got out immediately, running to the door. Before she could knock, the door swung open, and Dorothy came out, followed by Abner.

This place brought back memories. Being here once again caused Alexis' mind to go back to the day she had picked up Joshua and helped him leave the community. She could still remember him walking out the front door with his bag in his hand as though it had happened yesterday.

As Alexis heard her in-laws talking to Sophia, she was quickly jerked back to the present, her heart wrenching. She'd had a major role in breaking Abner and Dorothy's hearts the day their son left, shattering their entire world.

Yet, they had invited her back into their lives as though nothing had happened. How could they forgive her for such a thing?

"Look how big you are!" Dorothy cried, bending down to give her granddaughter a hug. They hadn't seen her since they'd spent time with her while visiting Joshua at the hospital. "Hello, Sophia."

"We're so glad to see you," Abner said, also hugging her. "I'll go help your mom with the bags."

"I'm going to make some snickerdoodle cookies. Do you want to help me?" Dorothy asked, and Sophia nodded enthusiastically, following her inside.

Abner came over and gave Alexis a hug. She felt her eyes prick with unexpected tears, then quickly blinked them away. "Hi, *Daed*," she said, still feeling strange calling him the Amish word for father when she hadn't seen him in so long, but Dorothy and Abner had insisted on it the last time she had seen them.

"It's so good to see you, Alexis," Abner said, reaching for a bag in her trunk. "I'll help you carry these inside."

"Thank you," Alexis said. "It's good to be back." And she meant it. The sweet summer air was so much cleaner here than in downtown Portland, even if it did smell like manure here. She actually preferred it over the smog of the city.

"Dorothy made us all a lunch fit for kings." Abner chuckled. "We're so happy you're moving in. We have plenty of room, and it's felt so empty for so long. We want you to stay as long as you want, and if you want to stay permanently, we would love that."

Alexis blinked. "I don't deserve that. I don't want to impose."

"It's no imposition. It's a blessing to us to have you here. You're our daughter now, and we want you and Sophia to have a nice place to live."

"Thank you," Alexis murmured, stunned. "I don't know what to say."

Abner smiled. "We're family, Alexis. We take care of each other. That's what families do. Now, let's go inside."

They walked into the house, where Dorothy was showing Sophia how to measure flour with the measuring cup. Alexis wished she had baked with her daughter more, but she worked so much that by the time she got home, she was usually exhausted. Besides, the extent of her baking skills was making brownies from a box mix or putting store-bought cookie dough into the oven, and even that she often burned.

Baking from scratch was just one of the many new things they would learn here.

Alexis had sold her furniture, which she had bought second-hand at a thrift store, and didn't have much to begin with anyway, so it didn't take long for them to unload the car. She and Abner put the bags and boxes in a bedroom.

"This was Joshua's room growing up," Abner said, his voice cracking slightly.

"Really?" Alexis looked around at the simple room that contained a full-size bed, dresser, desk, and nightstand, all probably handmade. She hadn't exactly had a tour of the house yet because when Joshua had left the Amish to marry her, Alexis had avoided his parents, knowing they didn't approve of her because she was an *Englisher*, and he was being shunned for leaving.

"We always thought we'd have more children to fill this house, but it wasn't the Lord's plan for us." He sighed sadly. "Sophia can have the spare room."

"Thank you. She might end up sleeping in here with me, but she also might like to have her own space." Alexis' heart ached for the couple. Perhaps if they'd had other children, Joshua's leaving and death wouldn't have been quite so hard on them.

Then again, nothing could ever lessen the pain of losing a child.

"Of course. Well, I'll go see if Dorothy needs anything. When you're ready, we'll have lunch." Abner nodded and walked out of the room.

Alexis looked around at her late husband's childhood bedroom, imagining young Joshua drawing pictures or doing homework at his desk. She opened the closet to see a few boxes on the high shelf. One was full of wooden blocks, probably homemade by Abner, and one had children's books, a marble game, and wooden blocks. It was sweet that they had kept Joshua's old toys.

She turned to the bed which was covered with an intricate quilt covered in colorful triangles. Had Dorothy made that quilt for her son? It was certainly more beautiful and vibrant than the ghastly white sheets that had covered Joshua as he lay dying in the hospital.

Alexis squeezed her eyes shut as her mind went back to the day that Joshua had asked her to visit his parents as he lay dying in the hospital.

"Promise me you will go visit them," Joshua asked her, his voice cracking.

Alexis blinked back tears. "I'll try."

"They need you," he whispered. "You need each other. Sophia needs them."

She nodded. "I know... But it would be so hard to go back there. It will just remind me of you."

"So, remember me," Joshua said.

"But the last time we were there, your parents were so upset because you left the church," Alexis cried.

"You'll make new memories," Joshua said. "I want Sophia to have her grandparents in her life. Please, promise me you will bring her there to visit."

"I promise," Alexis choked out.

Joshua closed his eyes and sighed. "Good."

Now, here in Joshua's childhood bedroom, tears streamed down Alexis' cheeks. She'd broken her promise to Joshua for three years.

How could she ever make up for that?

As Ben drove to Unity with Nichole coloring in the back seat, he let his mind wander to the day he'd married Estella on the beach in front of his house. She'd looked so beautiful in her white dress with a flower in her hair. She'd been so full of life, always laughing, smiling, and joking. And sassy, so sassy. Not to mention bossy. She had known what she wanted and wasn't afraid to go after it.

He should have said no when she'd insisted they go mountain climbing on their anniversary getaway, but she'd begged to go. She was always living life on the edge, never afraid of anything, while he was the cautious one.

"I'm going to beat you to the top," Estella had cried while scaling the mountain.

No one had realized that Estella's climbing equipment was faulty. She'd plummeted to her death while climbing up the side of a mountain.

Ben had been completely helpless, unable to do anything as she crashed down the steep incline, hitting every boulder and tree on her way down. He could still hear her screams, which had suddenly stopped before she had even reached the bottom.

"Estella!" The guttural cry had torn through him, and even though he descended as quickly as he could, he could still recall how it was not nearly fast enough. He had just wanted to jump after her, but then he would have left Nichole without both parents.

No, there was nothing he could have done to save her in that moment. He should have just gone with his instinct and refused when she'd told him she wanted to go rock climbing. Why hadn't he just said no?

But who was he kidding? Estella did what she wanted, and even if he had said no, she would have climbed that mountain with or without him.

A tear leaked from his eye, and he quickly swiped it away, not wanting his daughter to see.

"Are you okay, Daddy?"

"I'm fine, baby."

"No, you're not. I miss her too," Nichole said.

His eyes filled with tears again.

"So, are we almost there?"

"Yes, actually." Ben drove down the dirt lane that led to Derek's house. They passed several plain, large Amish homes before reaching his friend's house, where two children bolted out the door, followed by their parents. Maria was pregnant with their third and kept a hand on her round belly as she approached the car, her long skirt and prayer *kapp* ribbons trailing in the breeze.

"Nichole!" Carter, Maria's oldest, cried as he reached the car. Carter's biological father had been killed in an accident before he was born, before Maria had met and married Derek. "Hi, Nichole! Want to go play tag?"

"After, let's play hide and seek!" Rachel, their younger daughter, said enthusiastically.

"Sure." Nichole smiled and ran off with them.

Ben chuckled, amazed at how children just picked right up where they left off as though it hadn't been months since they'd seen each other.

"They'll have so much fun together while you're here," Derek said, giving Ben a hug. "How have you been?"

"I'm okay." Ben shrugged with his hands in the pocket of his jeans.

"I know it's hard for you this time of year," Maria said with understanding. "I hope being here helps ease the pain a little, if that's even possible."

Maria had lost her first husband while pregnant with Carter, so she knew how Ben felt.

"So, you're still a field agent at CPDU?" Derek asked, who used to work with Ben for the branch of police before he decided to marry Maria and join the Amish.

"Yeah," Ben sighed. "But I think I'm getting too old for it."

Derek chuckled. "There's no shame in giving up chasing criminals for a simpler life, you know. You've done your part, and Nichole needs you to be safe."

Ben watched Nichole running around with the other children as his heart clenched. His job was dangerous, and he didn't even want to think about what would happen to her if he was caught in the line of fire. Yes, he had a will saying Derek and Maria would take care of her if that ever happened, but he never wanted it to come to that.

"Maybe you're right," Ben agreed. "Maybe I should retire and focus on my writing."

"*Ja*," Maria nodded enthusiastically. "Speaking of writing, how is it going? Are you working on a new book?"

"Well, that's part of why I'm here, to be honest. I have major writer's block. My publisher wants to see pages, and I've got nothing to show them. So, my agent told me to get out of town for a while. I thought this place might give me some inspiration."

Derek smiled. "Then you've come to the right place. This place can be very inspiring."

Maria smiled. "You'll be writing again in no time."

13

Alexis didn't want to keep the others waiting, so she took a deep breath and went to the kitchen, where Dorothy and Sophia were setting the table.

"Wow, Sophia, those look delicious!" Alexis exclaimed as she noticed the cookies cooling on the counter. "Good job."

"I made them with *Mammi*," Sophia said proudly.

"She did most of the work. I just showed her what to do," Dorothy said with a smile. "She's a natural. You'll be baking cookies all by yourself in no time, dear."

Alexis smiled. Maybe Dorothy was right. This place would be so good for both of them.

Maybe it would help them heal.

"Let's eat," Dorothy said. "I have chicken stew on the stove, and the biscuits are ready." She pulled a tray of biscuits, probably made from scratch, out from the woodstove. She also set the pot of stew on the table, resting it on a hot pad.

"It smells amazing," Alexis said.

"And I'm hungry!" Sophia said, eagerly sitting at the table.

Alexis also sat down. Where did Joshua sit at the table growing up? She wanted to know but didn't want to ask and ruin a happy moment.

"We normally share a silent prayer at meal times," Abner said after Dorothy brought the biscuits to the table in a basket. "But since you are here, this is a special occasion, so I will pray over the food this morning," Abner said, bowing his head. "Lord, thank You for sending Alexis and Sophia to us. Thank You for the wonderful time we have already had and all the times we will share together in the future. Thank You for our family and our community and our church. Thank You for this food, and bless it to our bodies. In Your name, amen."

"Amen. This is delicious," Alexis said, knowing it was much better than anything she could cook. "I can't cook very well, but I'd like to learn how."

"Thank you, dear," Dorothy replied. "I'd be happy to teach you how to cook."

"That would be fun," Sophia interjected.

"Thank you. We'd love that. We're so glad you invited us to stay here, but we intend on helping out a lot and pulling our own weight. Right, Sophia?" Alexis said.

She nodded and smiled, her mouth full of buttered biscuit.

"I intend to get a job as soon as I can so I can start saving," Alexis said.

"I would be happy to look after Sophia while you are working, if that is fine with you," Dorothy offered.

"Wow, that would be great. I'd really appreciate it," Alexis gushed. "Thank you. The diner where I worked barely paid enough to cover our bills, especially our rent. So, I would really like to start saving as soon as possible." She was sure her car would need repairs soon, and Sophia needed new clothes and shoes. "I want to pay for our own groceries, and I can pay you rent."

"Nonsense!" Abner cried. "We don't want you to pay us any rent."

"And we don't want you to pay for any groceries, so that will help you save," Dorothy said.

"I really want to pull my own weight. I don't want to be a burden in any way," Alexis insisted.

"You are not a burden. We want you here. You're our family," Dorothy reminded her. She looked to Abner. "Did you tell her about the house?"

Abner nodded.

"Thank you so much," Alexis said to Dorothy. "To both of you. That's honestly the nicest thing anyone has ever done for me."

"What? What is it, Mom?" Sophia asked curiously.

How could she explain it to her daughter now, in front of them? She didn't want Sophia to even think about the fact that one day her grandparents would pass away after she'd already lost her father.

"It's just that... You're going to get your own room here. Isn't that great?"

"Wow! Yeah!" Sophia grinned. "Our apartment was small, so Mom and I shared a room," she explained to her grandparents. "This house is so much nicer."

"We want you to feel at home," Dorothy said.

"We can set it up later." Alexis smiled, then turned to Dorothy and Abner. "So, do you know if there are any places hiring around here? I can do most anything that doesn't require a college degree."

"Hmm. I think the general store is hiring cashiers," Dorothy said.

"I'm not really much of a people person. I realized that with my last job," Alexis admitted.

"Sid Hoffman is hiring stable hands at his horse ranch," Abner said. "You could work with horses instead. Sometimes horses are easier to talk to than people." He chuckled.

Alexis set down her fork, fully interested. She leaned forward. "Wow, that would be my dream job."

"Mucking stalls is your dream job?" Abner chuckled.

Alexis smiled. "Well, I know that's part of it, but I've always loved horses. When I was young, I used to ask my parents for a pony every year for my birthday and Christmas. Of course, they were very expensive, and we couldn't afford it. I went to a horseback camp in the summers and I loved it."

"Well, then, it might be just the right job for you. I'm good friends with Sid. If you want, I can bring you by and introduce you to him," Abner offered.

"That would be great. Can we go today?"

"Sure. I don't see why not."

"Can I come? I like horses, too," Sophia piped up.

"Of course, baby. That will be fun, won't it?"

"We can ride over in the buggy," Abner said. "You can meet our horse, Daisy."

"Aw," Sophia cooed. "I like that name."

"Joshua picked it out." Dorothy gave a sad smile. "He loved that horse so much."

A pang shot through Alexis' heart, and she wondered if Joshua had first wanted to become a veterinarian because he took care of the animals here in their barn, especially that horse. She remembered him talking about Daisy many times in the past.

"Daddy had a horse?" Sophia asked.

"Oh, yes. He loved caring for Daisy and all the animals," Dorothy explained to Sophia. "He'd spend hours in the barn, taking extra care of them and reading them stories when he was younger."

Sophia giggled. "He read books to the animals?"

"Oh, yes. It was one of his favorite places to be, summer or winter," Abner said proudly. "He took very good care of the animals."

A thick silence fell over the table, and Alexis felt as though she had to say something to break the tension. "When you're done, I'll go show you your room, Soph."

"Then we can go see the horses?" she asked eagerly.

"*Ja,* I will take you when you're ready," Abner said.

After they finished eating, Alexis and Sophia helped Dorothy clean up and wash the dishes.

"Let's go see my room!" Sophia cried and hurried down the hall. Alexis gave Dorothy an apologetic look, who only shrugged and smiled. Alexis went down the hall after her daughter.

"Wow, it's so nice," Sophia said, turning slowly to look at the room similar to Alexis'. "Can I set it up how I want it?"

"Sure, but we aren't going to paint the walls or hang pictures or anything like that. Let's unpack your things, okay?" It wouldn't take long. Since Alexis hadn't been able to afford to give her daughter a quarter of the things she would have liked to, Sophia didn't have many toys or clothes. When they had everything unpacked, it looked a bit strange to see Sophia's pink comforter on the bed over the quilt that had been there and her colorful clothes hanging in the closet in contrast to the plain atmosphere of the room. But Alexis figured if they were staying here, they might as well make it feel like home.

Seeing Sophia's colorful belongings in the simple room struck Alexis with a thought—if Sophia and Alexis lived here permanently, would Dorothy, Abner, and the rest of the community expect them to become Amish? Could they live here if they weren't Amish?

Alexis had seen non-Amish homes interspersed between Amish homes on the way here, so she knew that non-Amish people lived here, but their situation was different. They were moving in with Amish relatives.

What exactly would be expected of her? Alexis pictured herself wearing the white prayer *kapp* and simple, long dresses that Dorothy, Maria, and the other women here wore. It wasn't like Alexis planned on moving back to Portland.

"If you're ready, we can go to the stables," Abner said from the doorway.

Alexis jumped and turned. "Okay. We can go now."

"Yay!" Sophia clapped her hands, and they all put on their shoes and went outside, out to the barn.

"This is Daisy," Dorothy said as they walked up to a stall with a brown mare, stroking the horse's nose. "Do you want to pet her nose, Sophia?"

"Okay." Sophia held out her hand, and the horse sniffed her. "That tickles!" She giggled, then patted the horse's nose.

"Now she knows what you smell like," Abner said. "Let's get her hitched to the buggy." He opened the door and led her outside.

As Abner took the horse out, Alexis looked around the barn. The scent of manure was strong, but she didn't mind. A few sheep bleated in a pen, and Sophia hurried over to lean over the railing and look at them, laughing. "They sound like babies when they make those funny sounds."

"That's what you sounded like as a baby," Alexis joked.

"I did?"

"A little."

"Many of our animals have passed away. Now that Abner is retired and getting older, we don't have as many as we used to," Dorothy told Alexis softly.

"Sorry to hear that," Alexis said.

"We do enjoy retirement, but I think Abner gets bored. He likes to be doing something all the time. I'm the same way," Dorothy said as they watched Sophia pet the sheep. "It's so good to have you here. The two of you have brought joy into our lives once again."

"So have you," Alexis said, turning to her. "I have a question I thought of earlier. I really do appreciate you letting us stay here. Thank you so much for that. I was just wondering, if we stay here permanently, do we have to become Amish?"

"That's completely up to you," Dorothy said. "Joining the Amish is a very big decision. Not many *Englishers* join the Amish and actually stay Amish, but we have had it happen here. We aren't a gated community, shutting out the rest of the world as some people think. There are people living on this lane who are not Amish, and many of us have *Englisher* neighbors. In fact, Adam, Joshua's cousin, left the Amish and married Freya, an *Englisher* woman. You know her, don't you?"

"Oh, yes, I do know her."

"Well, they live just down the lane even though they aren't Amish. So, you wouldn't be the only one."

"Okay. I wasn't sure since we are moving in with you. You won't get in any trouble, will you?"

"No, no, dear. We already spoke with the bishop, and everyone is happy you're here. You're family, after all. No one here is going to force anything on you. Of course, if you do decide to join the Amish, that would be wonderful, but no one expects that of you, dear."

Alexis sighed in relief. "That's good to hear. You're right; it's no small decision. I honestly hadn't even thought of it very much until it struck me earlier."

"Who knows?" Dorothy gave her a knowing smile. "People have come here not expecting to stay, let alone become Amish, but some have. This place has a way of growing on you. You might surprise yourself in time."

Once again, Alexis pictured herself in plain Amish clothing, baking from scratch and doing laundry with a Maytag washer. She would already be mostly living an Amish lifestyle anyway, but could she really make that type of lifelong commitment?

"Also, there are many young, single men here. You never know. You might find love again," Dorothy said softly. "And if you did, we would be happy for you, whether he is Amish or not."

Stunned, Alexis blinked, unsure of what to say. "Oh, I'm not sure I'm ready for that."

"The Lord has a plan for you, dear. You don't need to worry." Dorothy patted her hand as Abner returned to the barn.

"Daisy is all hitched up. Let's get going."

Sophia hurried to join him, and he helped her up into the buggy. They all piled in, then drove down the lane toward Sid Hoffman's ranch.

14

"This is so fun!" Sophia cried, clapping her small hands together as they rode in the buggy. Alexis couldn't help but smile at her daughter's enthusiasm and zest for life.

Yes, she knew deep in her heart she had made the right decision by coming here.

When they pulled into Sid's long driveway, Alexis spotted the large horse barn and fenced-in pastures where several horses were roaming and grazing.

"They're so pretty," Sophia chirped.

"They are, aren't they?" Alexis agreed.

"I want to know all their names."

Alexis chuckled. "Well, if I get a job here, maybe we will find out what all their names are."

Abner parked the buggy, and they all got out.

"Hello, Sid!" Abner called out when Sid walked out of the barn.

"Well, what a nice surprise," Sid said, grinning widely. "And who do we have here?"

"This is Alexis, our daughter-in-law, and Sophia, our granddaughter," Dorothy said proudly.

A quick flash of surprise registered on Sid's face but was quickly replaced with his former grin. "So nice to meet you. I'm Sid." He shook Alexis' hand. "Nice to have you here in town."

Alexis was sure the entire community knew the story, but perhaps some people would still be surprised to see her after all this time, unless word spread quickly and everyone already knew she was here.

"Thank you. Nice to meet you as well," she said.

"I like your horses," Sophia said.

"Thank you, Sophia, but actually, most of these horses aren't mine," Sid explained, gesturing to the horses in the pasture. "I take care of other people's horses for them."

"Why don't they take care of their own horses?" she asked.

"Well, some people don't have barns on their properties, but they still want a horse, so they have the horses stay here, and come to visit them whenever they want."

"Oh, wow. Mom said she always wanted a horse growing up."

Sid chuckled. "A lot of kids do, but they are quite expensive. Do you want to say hi to them?"

"Yes!" Sophia cried, and they all chuckled and made their way over to the fence.

Sid pointed out each one. "That's my horse, Zeke. That one is Ladybug, and that one is Chestnut. That one over there is Pecan Pie."

"Pecan Pie?" Sophia laughed out loud. "Those are funny names."

"I once boarded a horse named Cinnamon Roll," Sid added.

Sophia laughed even harder. "That's so funny."

"So, are your clients all Amish or some *Englisher*?" Alexis asked.

"My boarding clients are mostly *Englisher*, but I also breed horses, and both Amish and *Englisher* buy from me," Sid explained.

"Are you still hiring stable hands?" Abner asked.

"Oh, yes. I just took on several more new horses, so I need more employees to help with the workload."

"I want to apply for the job," Alexis said. "I don't have much experience except for going to horseback camp as a kid, but I'm a hard worker and a fast learner. I can do whatever you want me to do—mucking the stalls, feeding the horses, getting the hay... I don't know what the other responsibilities would be, but I can do it all, I promise."

"She worked at a diner before this and raised Sophia here all on her own. She's a hard worker," Abner added proudly.

"Well, then, you're hired, Alexis," Sid said with a smile.

"Really? That's it? Don't I have to fill out an application?" Alexis asked.

"No need. I care more about someone's character than their job history. If Abner recommends you, then you have the job. I have respect for single moms. That shows dedication and hard work." He gave her a knowing look, probably thinking about Joshua's death.

"I appreciate this so much. Thank you, Sid. I won't disappoint you."

"You're going to work here, Mom?" Sophia asked, stepping away from the fence.

"Yes, so now you'll learn all the horses' names."

"Can I help take care of them too?"

"Of course!" Sid agreed. "First, we will teach you all the safety rules, and then I will teach you both how to take care of them."

"Can I learn to ride too?" Sophia asked, jumping up and down.

"I'm not sure if we will have time for that," Alexis said, not wanting to take advantage of Sid's kindness.

"I would be happy to teach both of you how to ride Western," Sid offered. "That way, you can eventually help me exercise the horses."

"Wow, thank you. We would love that, right Sophia?" Alexis said.

"Yes!" Sophia cried, giggling. "I can't wait."

"When can you start, Alexis?" Sid asked.

"Now. Today. Or tomorrow. Whenever you want me to."

"How about tomorrow morning at six?"

It was earlier than Alexis was used to since she used to go to work after Sophia went to school in the mornings, but she wouldn't complain. "Sounds great. Thank you so much, Sid."

After spending some more time getting to know the horses, they returned to the buggy.

I really should go see my friends soon, Alexis thought to herself as they climbed in and said goodbye to Sid. *I just hope we can pick up where we left off, and they can forgive me for abandoning them for so long.*

As the kids played outside, Derek, Maria, and Ben sat on the porch, talking and laughing. Ben felt a bit of anxiety lift from his chest. It was so good to be around old friends again. Because they had worked together so closely at CPDU, Derek knew him better than almost anyone else.

A buggy rumbled down the lane, and they looked up to see Sid Hoffman riding by. He tipped his hat toward them. "Hello, Derek and Maria. Ben! How are you? It's been a long time, hasn't it?"

"Yes. I'm visiting for a few days," Ben said. "It's good to be back."

"You're welcome to stay as long as you want," Derek interjected.

"Thank you, but I'll have to go back to work after my vacation days are up," Ben said.

"You know who else is here? Abner and Dorothy's daughter-in-law, Alexis," Sid said. "She just arrived with her daughter today to stay with them."

"She did?" Maria gasped. "Dorothy mentioned it, but I didn't know exactly when she was coming. I need to go see her right now."

"Go ahead, dear," Derek said. "We will look after the children."

"Thank you. Oh, I can't wait to see her." Maria was already heading to the barn to get the horse.

"I just gave her a job at my stables," Sid said. "I think she's staying a while. Maybe permanently. I didn't want to pry."

"Really? That would be wonderful!" Maria called, then headed into the barn. "I have to find out."

"Alexis? Alexis Fernandez?" Ben asked, feeling as though someone had doused him with a bucket of ice water. Could it be her, the woman he had helped rescue from that dingy warehouse with the other trafficking survivors? Her dark eyes had haunted his dreams more times than he cared to admit.

He had rescued many people in his career, but none of them had ever etched themselves into his mind as she had, and that had been years ago.

"Yes," Derek said. "She became friends with many of the women here, but we haven't seen her since her husband died."

"Well, I need to go pick up supplies. I'll see you all later," Sid said, then drove off.

"Thanks, Sid," Derek called, and they waved.

"Her husband?" Ben asked Derek with concern.

"She married a young Amish man named Joshua, who left the church to become a veterinarian and marry her, but he died of cancer three years ago," Derek explained as they turned and walked toward the barn. Derek helped Maria lead the horse out, and he hitched it up to the buggy for her.

"Three years ago?" Ben repeated, stunned. His wife had died three years ago as well.

"That is quite a coincidence," Maria said softly. "Well, the two of you have a lot in common. She has a daughter around Nichole's age, too."

Ben's heart jumped in his chest. He had felt a connection to her that day he had spoken to her outside the warehouse, seeing the burns on her arms and the pain in her dark eyes. All this time, he had ignored it, saying he just felt sympathy toward her.

Could it be more than that? And if it was, was his heart ready for what that might bring?

"I'll get her to come over so you two can get reacquainted," Maria said, a twinkle in her eye.

"Maria, don't go playing matchmaker again," Derek warned with a smile.

"What? I want my two good friends to meet. What harm is there in that? Besides, the kids will have so much fun." She shrugged innocently, and Derek chuckled as he helped her up into the buggy.

"See you later." Derek waved and turned to Ben. "She could be gone for hours, catching up. Or she might drag Alexis over here immediately. You never know with Maria."

Ben hoped it was the latter.

15

Not long after Alexis, Dorothy, Abner, and Sophia arrived home, there was a knock on the door.

Dorothy opened it to see Maria standing on the porch. "Hello, Dorothy," Maria said. "I heard Alexis is here."

"Yes, she is," Dorothy said, letting her inside.

Alexis hurried from the kitchen to the front door. "Maria!"

"Alexis!" Maria cried, running to hug her. "It's so good to see you."

"You too," Alexis said. "You look amazing. I didn't know you were pregnant. Congratulations."

"Thank you," Maria said, smiling.

"I'm so sorry I haven't visited in so long," Alexis said. "For a long time, the thought of coming back here was too hard."

"I understand," Maria said.

"Come sit down, ladies," Dorothy said, ushering them into the kitchen. "I'll make some tea."

Maria and Alexis sat down at the kitchen table while Sophia played a game with Abner in the living room.

"Is that Sophia?" Maria gasped. "You got so tall!"

Sophia smiled, and Alexis wasn't sure if she remembered Maria or not from the funeral. "This is my friend Maria," Alexis told her.

"Hi. My name is Sophia." She smiled shyly and gave a small wave.

"Hi, Sophia. Nice to see you again. We are so glad you both are here. I have two kids—a boy and a girl. I think they would love to play with you." Maria turned to Alexis. "In fact, I'd love it if you came to our house for dinner tonight. I think Sophia would have fun with Carter and Rachel, and we could catch up."

"That would be great," Alexis said.

"I want to meet them!" Sophia cried.

"Well, I can take you to my house in my buggy," Maria offered.

"Okay! After our game," Sophia said, turning back to Abner as he continued to explain the rules to her.

Alexis laughed, her heart warming at seeing her play with her grandfather. If she had come here sooner, Sophia and Alexis would have had the support of Dorothy and Abner after Joshua had died.

They wouldn't have been so alone.

Thanks to me, Sophia missed out on spending time with her grandparents here, Alexis thought glumly. *Maybe it would have helped her heal after losing her father.*

"That would be fine," Maria said, leaning forward. "So, how have you been, Alexis?"

"To be honest, I was barely getting by before coming here," she admitted.

"It can't be easy, being a single parent out there and paying for everything yourself," Maria said. "I don't know how you did it for so long."

"The diner didn't pay much. I quit and gave the owner a piece of my mind. He didn't treat me right at all, and neither did some of the customers."

"Well, good. It's good to stand up for yourself. Remember, I also worked as a waitress after I left the community for a while. That was before I came to my senses and came home. It seems like so long ago. Anyway, we're here now, and that's all that matters. So, how long are you staying?"

"We want her to move in permanently," Dorothy interjected as the teapot whistled. She took it off the woodstove and poured the hot water into three mugs. "Sid gave her a job today at the stables."

"That's great news! So, now that you have a job, will you stay?" Maria's eyes widened as she grabbed Alexis' hand.

Alexis looked over at Sophia laughing with her grandfather and sighed happily. "Even though we have only been here a day, I haven't seen Sophia this happy since before..." She sighed. What did she have to go back to? Her empty apartment was now being occupied by someone else. She hadn't spoken to her parents in years—which she knew was entirely her own fault and was something she had to remedy.

Once she got the courage. But would they even want to talk to her? They didn't live very far from here.

"Yes, I think we will stay." Alexis smiled as Maria clapped her hands together.

"What?" Sophia whirled around and ran toward them. "We are staying?"

"Yes, baby. We're moving in with your *Mammi* and *Daadi*. We're going to live here."

"Forever?"

"Well, as long as possible. What do you think of that?" Alexis asked.

"Yay!" Sophia cried, throwing her arms around her mother's neck.

Alexis laughed as her daughter squeezed her tightly.

"Thank you, Mom. You're the best. This is the best day ever!" Sophia let go of her and twirled around, running to her grandparents one at a time. "We are going to live with you!"

"And that is so wonderful," Dorothy said, her eyes gleaming with tears. "That is the best news we've had in a long time."

"We're so happy," Abner said as Sophia hugged him. "We are so glad you're staying. We're going to have a lot of fun together."

"Can we play games and go see the animals every day?" Sophia asked him.

"Of course!" Abner patted her head.

"Who knows? Maybe she will meet a nice young Amish man and join the church to marry him," Maria said to Dorothy.

"That's what I was thinking." Dorothy chuckled. "But don't worry. You don't have to join the church if you don't want to."

Dorothy took her tea into the living room and chatted with Sophia and Abner as they finished their game, giving Alexis and Maria some privacy.

"Well, the thought has crossed my mind, but it's a big decision," Alexis admitted. "I wonder what Sophia would think of the possibility."

"You're considering it?" Maria asked.

"I don't know. I'll think about it. I do love it here, and since we will be living here, I'm sure the simple way of life will grow on me."

"And what if you met a nice *Englisher* man? Do you think you could consider starting a relationship with someone new? What if you want to join the Amish but he's an *Englisher*?" Maria asked in a rush.

Alexis laughed nervously. "What? Why are you asking that?"

"I'm sorry. That's none of my business." Maria waved her hand dismissively.

"No, it's okay. You can ask me whatever you want to, Maria. It has been three years, and even though I still miss Joshua, I think I could love someone again someday if I met the right person—Amish or *Englisher*," Alexis explained.

Maybe being here really would help her heal, which in turn would help her open her heart up to the possibility of loving someone again.

"Unity is a place full of second chances," Maria said. "This is where I met Derek after I lost Robert. You could find love again too."

Alexis sighed. Could that really happen? She had only ever been able to imagine herself being married to one man—Joshua. How would he have felt about her moving on after his death and falling in love with someone else?

"You know, Joshua would want you to be happy," Maria whispered.

"You're probably right, but it's still so hard to see myself with anyone else. That seems like a distant dream."

"But it could happen." Maria smiled.

"You're not going to play matchmaker on me, are you?"

"Me? No!" Maria stood up, a mischievous glint in her eye. "It looks like they're done with their game. Want to leave?"

"I won!" Sophia cried, hopping up and down.

Abner smiled. "I didn't go easy on her, either. She's good at this game."

"Thank you for playing with her," Alexis said, then turned to Sophia. "Great job."

"It's my pleasure. You all go on and have some fun now," Abner said.

"Do you want to come too?" Maria asked Abner and Dorothy.

"I have dinner cooking for us, and I'm sure you young folks want to catch up. Go on, and we will see you later," Dorothy said with a smile, waving them off.

Sophia, Maria, and Alexis climbed into the buggy. As the buggy started down the road, Alexis asked, "How are Liz and Anna?"

"Liz is happily married to Simon, her true love." Maria smiled.

"What about Anna? Last I'd heard, she got into nursing school. Did she go?"

Maria nodded. "She did, but that means she left the Amish church, as you know. She married the love of her life and now works at a hospital. She's happy, but we miss her."

"I'm happy for her," Alexis said. "She followed her dream."

"And what about you? You were going to go to nursing school. Did you change your mind? I remember you said you wanted to work with horses."

"Well, I got in, but I never went. When I got pregnant, I decided not to go to nursing school because I was so sick. But it wasn't just that. I just had the feeling it wasn't going to be right for me, like I was meant to do something different," Alexis explained.

"Like work with horses?" Maria suggested.

As they arrived at Maria's house, Alexis' eyes narrowed at the car in the driveway. "Who else is here?"

"Derek's friend," Maria said innocently, keeping her eyes on the road as she drove the buggy.

Three children ran around the barn, playing tag. Two were Maria's children, but she didn't recognize the young *Englisher* girl who was Sophia's age. Maria's husband Derek ran around the yard with them along with another man who looked familiar, but it was hard to tell from this far.

"Oh! I want to go play with them!" Sophia cried.

"Sure, you can, sweetie. Let me help you down from the buggy once it stops."

"Do you remember Ben Banks? He works for CPDU. He was part of the team who rescued us that day," Maria said.

"Ben Banks?" Alexis turned to Maria. How could she forget? "Is Ben married? Is his wife here too?"

"No, his wife passed away. Three years ago, actually," Maria explained, stopping the buggy and turning to Alexis.

"Agent Ben Banks?" Alexis asked, her mind reeling back to the day when CPDU had stormed the warehouse, arresting all the traffickers and safely extracting all the survivors. Agent Ben Banks had taken the time to talk to her outside afterward, making sure she would be okay. He was the one kind and caring agent who stood out in her mind. He had given her a blanket, asking her if she needed anything at all.

She'd never forgotten his kindness and his warm, sincere brown eyes.

"You do remember him, don't you?" Maria asked.

"Yes, I do. He was hard to forget."

Maria smiled mischievously again. "Oh, really?"

"Stop it." Alexis swatted at her playfully. "You said you weren't going to play matchmaker."

"I'm not! My two friends just happen to be here at my house for dinner at the same time, they happen to have a lot in common, and I care about both of them very much," Maria said sweetly, feigning innocence.

"You didn't think to tell me he would be here for dinner?" Alexis crossed her arms.

"Why does it matter? Come on, let's go talk to them. It'll be fun."

"They're already coming over here." Alexis gulped as Derek and Ben approached the buggy. As Derek helped his wife down from the driver's side, Ben came around to Alexis' side and held out his hand.

"Let me help you down." He looked up at her, and when her eyes met his, her heart jolted in her chest, and butterflies danced in her stomach. Yes, she remembered the way he looked, but she had forgotten just how lovely his eyes were—dark and mysterious, yet warm and sincere. She blinked, unable to look away as her heart pounded in her ears. His square jawline was framed by a short beard, and his brown hair was a bit unruly from chasing the children around, giving him an appealing, approachable look. He was so incredibly handsome—even more handsome than she remembered.

And he was still holding out his hand to her.

16

"Thanks," Alexis said, taking Ben's hand and quickly climbing down from the buggy, ignoring the way his warm hand had felt when it touched her skin. She turned around and helped her daughter down.

"Alexis, this is our friend Ben," Derek said. "His daughter Nichole is over there running around. She's about Sophia's age."

"Can I go play with them, Mom?" Sophia asked.

"Of course, sweetie," Alexis said, and Sophia took off running.

"Nice to see you again," Ben said, turning to her. "I wasn't sure if you'd remember me. We met very briefly, and I'm sure there was a lot going on for you that day. Besides, you probably met dozens of CPDU agents and officers."

"No, I remember you," Alexis blurted out. "You talked to me after the rescue. You gave me a blanket, got me a drink, and asked if there was anything you could do for me, making sure I was okay until I gave my statement and went to the hospital. Thank you. I appreciated that."

She hadn't intended to say that much, but he was looking at her so tenderly and now she was glad she had.

"You had been through so much already," Ben said. "It was the least I could do. I wish I could have done more, really, but it all happened so fast. You went to the hospital, and I had to go back to CPDU, then I lost touch. I'm sorry about that. I meant to check in on you."

He had? Alexis' stomach flipped, but she ignored it, shrugging casually. "I'm sure you help lots of people. There's no way you can check in on everyone. Don't worry about it, really."

Alexis realized that Derek and Maria had quietly moved away from them and were now playing with the children, leaving Ben and Alexis alone.

"I know it's no excuse, but I got really busy after that. Actually, I got married not long after, then Nichole was born." Ben looked over at the kids chasing each other around the barn and chuckled.

"Maria told me about your wife. I'm really sorry," Alexis said. "Actually, my husband died three years ago too."

"Maria mentioned that," Ben said. "I'm sorry for your loss. And I see you have a daughter Nichole's age. I guess we do have a lot in common."

"We do," Alexis agreed, nodding slowly. "So, how long are you here for?"

"We're just visiting Derek and Maria for a few days; then I have to get back to work. I have a deadline coming up, and my agent told me to take some time off. I couldn't think of a better place than here to clear my head. There's just something about this place, isn't there?"

"Yeah, there is. Did you say your agent?" Alexis asked curiously. "You work for CPDU, right?"

"Well, yes, I work for CPDU, but I have always loved writing. I was referring to my literary agent. After several years of pitching my book to agents online and at conferences, I finally got one." Ben scratched his head. "But I have some writer's block. I'm supposed to be writing my fourth book, but I can't come up with anything good. That's why I'm here. I guess I'm hoping for some inspiration to strike."

"Well, you were right about coming here. I've only been here less than a day, and I already feel like a whole new world is opening up to me. I'm considering things I would never have thought about before. I'm realizing I should have come here much sooner. We've been missing out."

"What new things are you considering, if you don't mind me asking?"

"Well, first of all, I decided earlier today that Sophia and I are moving here," she explained. "Sophia clearly loves it here, so we're staying."

"Wow. You decided that today?" Ben stuck his hands in his pockets.

Alexis nodded. "Like you said, there's something about this place."

"You've got that right."

"The other thing is I was wondering if I would have to join the Amish church now that I'm living here. Abner and Dorothy said I don't have to, but I've been thinking about it. If you had asked me a week ago, I would have said no, but the idea of a simpler life is growing on me."

Ben gave her a sidelong glance. "Really? You think you might?"

"It's a huge decision. I have no idea, but I have been thinking about it. I wouldn't want to join and then change my mind. If I join, I would join for life."

Ben nodded.

"So, you still work for CPDU, right?" she asked. "That must be a lot, working two jobs and being a single parent."

"Yes, but I'm thinking about resigning and writing full-time, or maybe finding another job if I don't get enough writing work. I've loved working for CPDU, but that type of job wears on a person, you know?"

"I can only imagine," she agreed.

"Besides, Nichole needs me," Ben said. "I don't want her to worry about me. My job with CPDU is dangerous, while writing gives me flexibility to work from home and be more available to Nichole."

"What kind of books do you write?" she asked.

"Crime thrillers." He shrugged. "They say write what you know, and I know crime. So, what about you? Sid told us when he was driving by that he hired you. That's great."

"He's such a nice man," Alexis agreed. "I love horses. I've always loved them, and I always wanted one, but of course, my family could never afford one. Actually, I have this crazy dream..." She waved her hand, laughing self-consciously. "It's silly."

"What is it?" he asked, turning toward her and peering into her eyes.

"I have always wanted to get certified and offer equine therapy, a place where people can come and learn to ride and care for the horses to help them heal from past traumas. There is something about being with horses that is so healing for the heart and soul. There's nothing else like that around here." She shrugged, smiling. "Maria says this place is full of second chances."

"Of course, it is," Ben agreed. "And that's not a crazy dream. That's a very realistic dream that could happen. Sid knows everything about horses. Maybe he could help you open your own business."

"Maybe. I mean, I wouldn't want to compete with him or anything."

"It's not the same thing. He breeds and sells horses. I don't think that would be competing with him. Maybe you could even add it to his business and open it with him. His expertise would be so invaluable," Ben offered.

"Hmm." Alexis nodded slowly. "Maybe. Everything has changed in the past few days."

"And a lot more could change even over just the next few days." Ben gave a playful smile, and Alexis' heart fluttered.

What is wrong with me? she wondered. *I haven't felt like this since Joshua and I were dating.*

She never thought she'd feel this way again, especially about a man she barely knew at all. Maybe her hormones were all out of balance from the new changes in her life.

Maybe tomorrow she would feel completely different after getting some rest.

Wow, Ben thought to himself as he talked with Alexis, who was so much more confident and self-assured than the terrified woman he had spoken to all those years ago. Her dark eyes still held a thousand secrets, questions, and painful memories, but her smile lit up her entire being. Her long, dark hair gently blew in the breeze, and he let himself stare at her for a moment as she smiled at the children running around in the yard.

"They look like they're having fun," she said. "I'm just glad to see Sophia so happy. She seems to be loving it here."

"How could she not? This is a child's dream to be around farm animals and have all this open space to play."

"And she's with her grandparents here. I feel terrible for not coming here with her sooner." She shook her head. "I just couldn't bring myself to come back here and face his parents. I was part of the reason why he left the Amish—so he could marry me. I felt guilty about that, and I knew being here would bring up memories of when I met him. It was selfish of me to stay away, though. If I had brought her here sooner, she would have their love and support."

"Don't blame yourself," Ben said. "Grief affects everyone in different ways. I understand that, believe me. When Estella died, I shut everyone out too. I've barely seen Derek and Maria since. That's part of why I'm here, to make up for lost time."

"Really?" She looked over at him.

"When I needed my friends the most, I ignored their calls and letters. I just couldn't face anyone for a while. I used to come here with her to visit them, so I knew coming back here would bring up memories too." He sighed. "We're only human, Alexis. All that matters is you're here now, and now she gets to live with her grandparents. She'll be okay, and you're doing your best, which means you're doing a great job. It's not easy being a single parent."

"You can say that again." Alexis chuckled humorlessly.

"You know, there's something I want to tell you," he said. "I should have let you know sooner. CPDU worked with a joint task force from the FBI to gather records at the criminals' other locations and from their phones and computers. They were able to track down and rescue many of the women that had been sold by the trafficking ring, and your testimonies helped tremendously. It wouldn't have happened without your help."

"Really?" Alexis asked, tears shining in her eyes as relief swept over her. "Also, after CPDU went through the criminals' computers, they showed me photos of the survivors and asked me if I knew anything about them, like when they were taken, when they were sold, or who had bought them." Alexis shivered, a sick feeling roiling in her stomach. She would always hate using those terms when it applied to people, and it would never get easier. "I told them everything I remembered. I hope it helped."

"Yes, you did help them tremendously. You were so brave to testify in court against all those traffickers. It must have been exhausting and painful for you," he told her with admiration.

"It was, but I had to do it. I had to do something to make up for what I did," Alexis said, wrapping her arms around herself as she turned toward the playing children. A gentle breeze lifted a lock of long, dark hair off her shoulder, and it was such a lovely sight, he had to force himself to stop staring.

"You were a victim too, Alexis. No one blames you for anything," he reminded her, but her expression told him she didn't agree with him.

"You said many of the women were rescued. Do you think they will be able to find all of them?" Alexis asked. "Or is that wishful thinking?"

"Unfortunately, it's unlikely. Most victims of trafficking are never rescued. But we can keep praying," he said somberly.

Maria walked over to them. "I'm going inside to finish up dinner. It's been cooking, but I just have a few more things to do."

"Let me help you," Alexis offered, following her inside.

"Thanks," Maria said, giving her a knowing smile. "But I've got it."

"No, no. I want to help." Alexis followed her into the house, then Derek walked over to Ben.

"Maria's trying to play matchmaker with you two," Derek said, chuckling. "Obviously. Sorry about that."

"Don't apologize." Ben waved a hand. "It's just Maria being Maria. She's a really caring person—not a bad quality."

"That's why I married her." Derek grinned. "So, how's it going with Alexis? We saw you chatting quite a bit over here."

"She's incredible," Ben said in awe. "She's been through so much, yet she's persevering."

"Sounds like someone else I know. Clearly, you two have a connection. It seems like you hit it off."

"I think we do have a connection, unless I'm imagining things." Ben sighed. "She mentioned she's considering joining the Amish. If she's serious about it, maybe I should stay away from her. I wouldn't want to get in the way of that."

"So, you think this could lead somewhere, then?" Derek asked, eyebrows raised.

"I don't know." Ben shook his head. "Is it crazy to feel so close to someone after talking to them for only a few minutes? I didn't think I'd ever feel this way about someone again."

"You like her." Derek grinned.

"Yeah, I do," Ben admitted. "I want to get to know her. Too bad I'm only here for a few days."

"That can easily change. You can write from anywhere, and you said you wanted to resign from CPDU, right? There's no time like the present," Derek said. "Besides, I could give you a job at my cabinet shop."

"I do appreciate the offer," Ben said, smiling. "But you don't have to do that. I would have to move here to work here."

"You like it here, don't you?" Derek asked.

"Well, yes, I do. And you're here."

"Nichole likes it here too. Our kids could play together all the time."

"I don't have much experience with carpentry."

"Don't worry about that." Derek waved his hand. "We'll train you on the job. Actually, it's better this way. You don't have any bad habits. We can teach you the right way the first time."

So, you think I should just call my boss and tell him I'm resigning over the phone?" he asked, chuckling. "And then sell my house and move here? Just like that?"

"Why not?" Derek patted him on the arm. "You said yourself you never thought you'd feel this way about a woman again. To me, that's a sign this could really lead to something special. I think you should stick around, get to know her, and see where this leads."

"I'm so sorry I stayed away for so long," Ben said. "Either way, I'll be back to visit more, I promise."

"All is forgiven. We completely understand," Derek said. "But seriously, if you ever need a job, I would love to have you come work for me."

"Thank you. I appreciate that."

"Ben, a woman like that in a town like this won't stay single for long. Don't pass up this opportunity. At least see where this goes," Derek said.

Ben nodded, taking in his friend's words. "You're right, Derek. After I first met her, I meant to check in on her, and I never ended up doing it. I always regretted that. I don't want to lose touch with her again and regret that too."

17

"So, how's it going out there?" Maria asked as she stirred a pot of homemade chicken noodle soup on the woodstove. Her eyebrows moved up and down playfully. "We saw you talking for a while out there. It seemed like you were comfortable with him, and I know you don't have long conversations with just anyone."

"It's strange," Alexis said as she sliced a loaf of Maria's homemade bread. "I do feel comfortable with him even though we have only briefly met. Is that crazy?"

"No, not at all. I think sometimes we meet people in life, and we just know we like them right away. Immediately, we feel a connection to them, like we know we can trust them and talk to them about anything." Maria smiled. "I felt that when I met you. I knew we would be good friends."

Alexis smiled, tears pricking her eyes. "I don't know how you could feel that after what I did to you." She looked away, brushing her tears away with the back of her wrist.

Maria walked over to her. "How many times do I have to tell you that you had no choice and nothing was your fault? We all love you so much. I'm sure the other women would also hate to see you feeling guilty about this."

"Ben just told me CPDU and the FBI were able to use my testimonies and the traffickers' phone records to track down and rescue many of the women that had been sold by the trafficking ring," Alexis told Maria. Just knowing that gave her a sense of peace and closure.

"Wow!" Maria cried. "That's wonderful. You helped them."

"But he also said many of them will never be found," Alexis added in a cracked voice, feeling her eyes sting with tears again. "So, I will never be able to ask them to forgive me."

"That is out of your control. All we can do is pray. God forgives you, and that's really all that matters." Maria touched the wrist that Alexis had wiped her tears with. "Besides, you are not the one who kidnapped and sold them. The traffickers did that. It was all out of your control. It's time to put that part of your life behind you and forgive yourself."

"I have," Alexis argued, gently pulling away, feeling unworthy of Maria's compassion and understanding.

"You think you have, but you haven't. Not really. I can tell. We've been friends long enough for me to be honest with you, right?" Maria asked, trying to peer into her eyes.

"Of course, Maria. You know you can tell me anything."

"So, have you truly forgiven yourself?"

Alexis shifted under her wise gaze. "I don't know. I guess maybe I haven't, but I've convinced myself I have."

"God forgives you, Alexis, so you should too. I know it's easier said than done. Have you talked to your parents yet?"

Alexis sighed. "No. I just can't bring myself to call them. I'm so afraid they won't want to speak to me that I've been letting it hold me back."

"I am sure they'd be happy and relieved to hear from you. They must be worried sick."

"I walked out on them to live on the streets when they needed me most. I said horrible things to them when I left. I don't think they'd be exactly thrilled to hear from me."

"They know you're safe at least and that you were rescued, right?"

"CPDU alerted them about my capture and that I had been rescued because they're my next of kin, yes. I consented to that and was glad CPDU was going to let my parents know I was safe. I even provided my parents' phone number, but I made it clear I didn't want any personal contact with them. My parents didn't even know I'd been trafficked until after CPDU got us out. They thought I was still living on the street as a junkie." Alexis sighed.

They might think I went back to doing drugs again to deal with the trauma, she thought.

She knew she should call them and let them know she was doing well, but she didn't even want to think about it.

"Well, this is a place of second chances. Remember I'm here for you. We are all here for you when you want to talk about any of this.

You carry heavy burdens, Alexis. I can see it in your eyes. I hope while you're here you can find the strength to let go."

Alexis looked up at her friend's sweet smile. Clearly, Maria could tell Alexis wasn't ready to open up about that part of her past yet, but Maria wouldn't push her. "Thanks."

"I've seen many people get close to God here when they thought things were hopeless. It happened to me. After Robert died and I came back home, I thought I'd never love or laugh again. I realized God had never left me, but I had run away from Him. I grew close to Him again here, and this is where I got to know Derek, even though it was under dangerous circumstances."

Maria was referring to when Derek had been her bodyguard, protecting her from the trafficking ring that had been stalking her.

"That was pretty miraculous," Alexis admitted, smiling.

"See? Even when everything is falling apart around you, God can use that to create something beautiful—even a whole new life for you. And sometimes that doesn't happen until we've hit the bottom."

Alexis stopped slicing the bread to ponder her friend's words. "I've pushed everyone away until there was no one left. I lost my job and had nowhere to turn. Maybe this is my rock bottom, even though I've been through much worse."

"I think you're here for a reason, Alexis. You've already reunited with Joshua's family, and I think one day, you'll have the courage to reunite with your own family. And one day, maybe you'll create a family of your own." Maria winked at her knowingly.

"Still, that seems like a far-off dream. I have to admit it sounds nice, though. Almost too good to be true."

"It's not too good to be true. It happened to me. I was a single mom raising Carter alone, and now Derek and I have children of our own." She rubbed her belly. "I can't wait to meet this one."

Alexis grinned, a fleeting pang of jealousy tearing through her. If Alexis was honest with herself, she wished she could let go of her haunting past, get remarried, and start a new family with a nice man like Maria had.

Could that ever really happen to her? How could she move past what she'd been through when nightmares still plagued her every night and flashbacks ate at her mind?

The front door flung open, and all the children poured in, followed by Derek and Ben.

"When is dinner ready? I'm starving," Carter asked, kicking off his black sneakers.

"Me too!" Rachel cried as the rest of them removed their shoes.

"It's ready. I was just about to go get you all," Maria said with a chuckle. "Come sit down."

Nichole and Sophia were lost in conversation, discussing Alexis' new job.

"My mom just got a new job at a horse barn, and I get to learn all the horses' names," Sophia boasted proudly.

"I've always wanted to learn to ride a horse, but Daddy won't let me," Nichole complained, then lowered her voice to a whisper. "He says it's dangerous."

"It is?" Sophia asked. "Horses seem so nice."

"People fall off or get kicked," Nichole said.

"Oh." Sophia frowned. "Sid said he is going to teach us how to ride."

"Really?"

"I hope we don't fall off."

"Sid will teach us all the safety rules," Alexis said, walking over to them.

"Even knowing all the safety rules, you could still get hurt," Ben said to Nichole.

Wasn't he the one with the dangerous job?

"The Amish know horses very well. I'm sure Sid won't let anything happen to us," Alexis argued.

"Some things are out of one's control," Ben contradicted, crossing his arms. "What if a horse throws you? Would he be able to stop it?"

"I'm new to all of this, but I think he wouldn't let it come to that," Alexis said.

"Sid's horses are very gentle," Derek interjected. "I don't think you have to worry about that."

"It's always good to be cautious," Ben added.

"As long as it doesn't prevent you from living life," Alexis countered.

"Okay," Maria interrupted, clearly trying to break the tension. "Everyone, come sit down and have some soup."

The kids scrambled to the table, and Sophia and Nichole continued to chatter on about various topics throughout the meal. Alexis smiled at how well they were getting along as they enthusiastically discussed horse names, their favorite foods, and what they thought of kindergarten.

After the meal, Ben approached Alexis as she helped Maria clean up from dinner.

"I'm sorry about earlier," Ben said, sticking his hands in his pockets. "I didn't mean to dampen the mood."

"It's okay," Alexis said, seeing Maria leave the room from the corner of her eye, following Derek and the children out the front door to play outside.

Once again, they were alone.

"Ever since Estella died, I've been overly protective of Nichole." Ben sighed. "She's all I have left. I don't want anything bad to ever happen to her."

"Well, we both know you can't protect her from everything," Alexis said, turning away from the sink of dirty dishes.

Ben picked up a plate she had just washed, dried it, then put it in the cabinet. "I know. But I wish I could. I wish I could put her in a bubble so nothing can ever hurt her."

"I feel the same way about Sophia, but we also need to let them experience life, right? If we become too cautious, then where's the fun in that? They'll only want to do the things we don't let them do even more."

"I guess that could be true. I'm just trying to find the balance."

"I totally understand what you're saying." Alexis continued to wash the dishes and hand them to Ben so he could dry them. "After what happened to me, I don't want Sophia to ever experience anything like that. Whenever we go anywhere, I always make her hold my hand the entire time, and I never let her out of my sight. My worst fear is that she will be taken like I was. But that doesn't mean I don't take her out to the park, the beach, or the library. I'm not just going to keep her in our apartment until she's an adult."

Ben gave her an understanding look. "I guess you, of all people, would understand."

Alexis nodded. "Keep her safe; just don't wrap her in bubble wrap." She smiled. "You'll figure it out."

"I sure hope so. I do want to prepare her for the real world someday. I don't want her to be shell-shocked when she goes out on her own." He shook his head. "I don't even want to think about that."

"We still have time, right? Although, everyone says it goes by so fast."

"And they're right. She just finished kindergarten, but to me, it feels as though we just brought her home from the hospital as a newborn. Sometimes I wish I could just slow time down and keep her little forever."

Alexis laughed. "I feel the same way sometimes."

Before they knew it, the dishes were washed and put away. "Thanks for helping me," Alexis said.

"That went by quickly. We're already done?"

Alexis nodded. "Want to join them outside?"

"Sure. I promised the kids another game of tag, and I plan to smoke them."

Alexis laughed as she watched Ben and Derek chase the kids all around the yard. They squealed and laughed with delight as the two men growled and pretended to be bears as they tried to run and hide. She sat down next to Maria on the porch swing.

"I just love seeing her have so much fun," Alexis said as she watched her daughter. "I think she worries about me too much. It's good to see her being a kid."

"She's gone through more than many kids her age have," Maria agreed. "You've done a great job raising her so far, you know. What a sweetheart."

"Thanks. It's not me, though. Sometimes I feel like she's the one raising me. She's just naturally a sweet, caring kid. She gets it from Joshua."

"She gets it from you, too. You don't give yourself enough credit."

Alexis smiled. "Thanks, Maria. Your kids are wonderful too."

"Thank you. We do adore them. I hope to have as many as I can." Maria rubbed her belly lovingly.

Alexis knew it was common for the Amish to have large families, and though it was hard for her to imagine, she hoped to have more children of her own one day if she ever met the right man.

"I need to get Sophia home," she said, standing up. Calling Dorothy and Abner's house 'home' felt surprisingly natural on her lips. "It's getting late, and I'm working early tomorrow. Thanks so much for dinner."

"Come by anytime, Alexis." Maria hugged her. "Remember what I said. We're all here for you."

"Thank you." She smiled gratefully, then called Sophia over. "We need to get home, sweetie."

"Already?" Sophia frowned. "We're having so much fun."

"I have to be at work really early tomorrow, and you need to get to bed soon." Alexis realized Maria had driven them here in her buggy and she hadn't brought her car. "I'm so sorry, but I just realized we have no way to get back."

"I'll drive you home in my car," Ben offered.

Alexis hesitated. "Are you sure? I don't want to be a bother. We could just walk back."

"Nonsense. It's no trouble at all. Come on, let's go," Ben said, already walking toward his car. Alexis and Sophia said their goodbyes, and they followed him.

As they drove out of the driveway, Alexis said, "Thank you. I appreciate the ride."

"No problem at all. I'm happy to help. I wouldn't want you to walk back."

"It's not that far."

"Still, I don't mind, really." Ben glanced over at her with a smile, making Alexis' heart trip. Only a few minutes later, they pulled into Abner's driveway.

"Thanks again for the ride," Alexis said, putting her hand on the door handle.

"Actually, before you go, there's something I want to ask you."

Alexis gulped.

"Would you go on a picnic with me on Saturday?" he asked, his eyes hopeful.

Alexis blinked in surprise. They had only spent the afternoon together, and he was asking her on...a date?

Was it a date?

"We can bring the girls, too. I'm sure they'd have fun together," he added in a rush, noticing her hesitation.

"That would be so fun!" Sophia cried in the back seat, kicking her legs excitedly.

"Sure," Alexis stammered. "We'd love to."

"Great." Ben grinned. "Have a good night."

"Thanks. You too." Alexis scrambled to get out of the car, not wanting him to see how nervous and flustered she was, as she opened her door and stepped out, then opened Sophia's door. They walked toward the door, waved to Ben, and he drove away.

"He's nice. I like him." Sophia smiled widely, clasping her hands together. "He played with us a lot. It was fun."

"He did, didn't he?" Alexis watched his car disappear down the lane. It was sweet of him to play outside with the children.

"I can't wait for the picnic!"

Dorothy opened the door and let them inside. "Did you have a nice time?"

"Oh, yes!" Sophia cried. "We played tag and bear hunt and all kinds of games outside; then we ate chicken noodle soup. I got to play with Rachel, Carter, and Nichole."

"Oh, did you?" Dorothy chuckled. "That does sound fun."

"You made some new friends," Abner observed, walking up behind his wife.

"Yeah." Sophia yawned and rubbed her eyes. "They're nice."

"Time for bed, kiddo." Alexis took her hand and led her down the hall. "You get to sleep in your new room tonight."

"Yay!" Sophia's fatigue finally eclipsed her enthusiasm, and she yawned again. After brushing her teeth and putting on her pajamas, she climbed into bed.

"I like it here, Mommy," Sophia said softly as Alexis pulled the blanket up to her chin and tucked her in. "I'm glad we're staying forever."

"So am I."

"Do you think we'll be a family again?" she whispered.

"We already are a family—you and me," Alexis told her. "We only need each other."

"But now we have *Mammi* and *Daadi* too. They're our family, right?"

"Oh, yes, baby. Of course."

"Most kids at my school have two grandmothers and two grandfathers. Why do I only have one *mammi* and one *daadi*?"

Alexis hesitated. She'd never talked with Sophia much about her own parents.

"Don't you have a mommy and daddy?" Sophia pressed.

"Yes, sweetie, I do."

"How come we don't see them?"

"It's complicated."

"I want to see them. Are they like *Mammi* and *Daadi*? Or are they not nice?"

"Oh, they're very nice," Alexis sighed. "I just haven't seen them in a long time."

"Why not?"

"We have so much going on right now. Maybe one day I will take you to meet them, okay?" she said, then realized Sophia would take that as a promise Alexis would need to keep.

"Okay." Sophia smiled and snuggled up under the blanket. "I always wanted grandparents like the other kids at school, especially since I have no daddy."

Her daughter's words shot Alexis straight through the heart. What had she done? She'd deprived her daughter of two sets of grandparents all because of her own fear, shame, and selfishness. Alexis had wasted so much time that Sophia could have spent with them.

And Sophia had no idea.

"Goodnight, Mommy."

Alexis kissed her daughter's forehead, guilt washing over her. "Goodnight, Soph."

18

The next morning before Sophia woke up, Alexis drove to Sid's stables.

"Good morning!" he called cheerily.

"Good morning," she replied. "So, what do I do first? I'm sorry, I don't know anything about this. It's all new to me."

"Don't worry. You'll learn as we go," he said. "Let's go introduce you to the other employees." They walked into the stables where two teenage Amish boys were mucking stalls and filling water troughs.

"Alexis, this is Sam and Jacob," Sid said. "Sam and Jacob, this is Alexis, our new stable hand."

The two young men waved and smiled.

"Hello," Sam said.

"Nice to meet you, ma'am," Jacob said.

"Now, Alexis is new to the horse business, so I'd like you to give her pointers as she is learning on the job," he told them, then turned to her. "Just ask any of us for help any time."

"Thanks," she said. "I appreciate it. I'm excited to start."

"Well, good. We have a lot of work to do. Come on. I'll teach you the safety rules as we muck the stalls." Sid smiled.

For the rest of the day, Sid taught her as much as she could learn about feeding, brushing, and caring for the horses. She put down new bedding, cleaned bridles and saddles, and filled water buckets.

She loved every moment, knowing that her work had meaning.

Even mucking the stalls and shoveling manure was therapeutic for her, giving her the sense of helping one of God's creatures. It gave her a feeling of purpose and peace—so distant from her previous life with the traffickers.

At lunch, Sid took the employees inside where Alexis met his wife, Brenda, who made them all a large lunch.

"One of the perks of the job is that I will feed you lunch every day, dear," the plump woman said as she scurried around the kitchen. "We like to keep our workers well-fed."

"A full worker is a happy worker," Sam joked, and they all laughed.

"Especially when we get to eat Brenda's delicious food every day," Jacob added as he took a portion of chicken pot pie from the center of the table. "Thank you, Brenda."

By the time the day was over, Alexis' feet and back ached even though she was used to working long, busy shifts at the diner.

"You're using muscles in new ways," Sid said as she rubbed her shoulders. "Don't worry. You'll get used to it."

"I sure hope so."

"Later on, I will eventually teach you how to exercise the horses, but for now, caring for them is enough for you to focus on. Exercising them is a whole new skill set. I also do basic training with them. Maybe one day you can help me with that as well, but it will take a while for me to teach you how. We would have to both train them the same way, so the horses don't get confused. So, we can worry about that later."

She nodded. "It's a lot to take in." She felt as though her mind was on overload as she tried to remember everything she had learned that day.

"You're doing great. And remember, just ask if you have questions or need help. It's a lot to learn, so you're not going to master it all in one day." He gave her a friendly smile with one tooth missing, framed by his long white beard. "We're here to help you learn every step of the way."

"Thank you," she said gratefully. "You have no idea how much I appreciate this job."

"Abner is a good, old friend of mine, and since you're his daughter-in-law, I wanted to help. You've proven yourself to be a good worker today, so I know I made the right decision." He gave her a thoughtful look. "I am very sorry about Joshua. He was a good man."

"Thank you." Alexis rubbed her upper arm. "He was."

"How are you doing?"

Alexis sighed. "The past few years, I've been just trying to keep my head above water, you know? I was barely getting by. Now that I've moved here and reunited with Dorothy and Abner, I already feel at home, even though we just got here. I feel like I can finally breathe." She smiled. "I just wish I had come here sooner."

"All that matters is you're here now, dear." He grinned. "Have a nice weekend, and get some rest. We'll be right back at it on Monday. Once I start teaching you how to ride, you can bring your sweet daughter over for some lessons. Brenda will just adore her. I have to warn you that she might spoil her a bit."

Alexis chuckled. "Can't wait. Thank you, Sid." She waved goodbye and drove home, eagerly anticipating a hot shower to wash away the smell of the barn and ease her sore muscles.

As soon as Alexis walked through the door, Sophia ran up to her. "How was it? How are the horses?"

"It was great," Alexis said, kicking off her boots. "The horses are doing well. I got to know all of them today. Sid said you can come for riding lessons soon after I learn how to take care of them a little better."

"Yay!" Sophia clapped her hands excitedly.

"What did you all do today?"

"We baked cookies, a pie, a loaf of bread, and we swept the floor. We fed the goats, and I brushed Daisy. Then I played games with *Daadi,* and he read me some books," Sophia said in an exhilarated rush, her eyes wide with delight. "It was so much fun!"

"Wow! Your day sounds as busy as mine was!" Alexis laughed, grateful Sophia was able to have all of these new experiences and learn new skills. "It sounds like you learned a lot today."

"We had a great time." Dorothy patted Sophia's shoulder. "She was a big help."

Sophia grinned. "I like helping."

"She beat me at Old Maid again," Abner said with a chuckle. "We did have fun. You don't have to worry about her being bored at all when you're at work."

"I guess not," Alexis said, grateful it went well on her first day. "Can I help with dinner?"

"Thank you, but it's all ready. I'm sure you're exhausted, dear," Dorothy said.

"Stable work isn't easy," Abner added.

"You can say that again." Alexis rubbed her back as she walked over to the counter and took a basket of bread to the table.

"That's the bread we made," Sophia said proudly.

"It looks delicious. You're already a better baker than I am." Alexis wrapped her in a hug, then they sat down to eat. Over the meal, Alexis told them all about her first day. After they cleaned up from dinner, Alexis went straight to the bathroom for a shower.

After putting Sophia to bed, she went to bed early herself, remembering that she was going on the picnic with Ben tomorrow, and her stomach flipped in anticipation.

A smile spread across her lips as she fell into a deep sleep that her body desperately needed.

Ben sat at the desk in the spare room at Derek's house, staring at the blank screen of his laptop. The small vertical line blinked, mocking him and his unwritten words. He wanted to bang his head on the keyboard. He needed to write something before his laptop died in a few hours. The only place he could charge it was the coffee shop down the street, which was closed at this time of night.

What on earth was wrong with him? Why couldn't he think of anything good to write in his next crime thriller?

His cell phone rang, causing him to jump. It was Margaret, his agent.

"Hello?"

"Ah, you're still up. I thought the Amish went to bed around eight o'clock at night."

"My friends are in bed, but I'm not Amish. You know I'm a night owl. I usually do my best writing late at night."

"And how is that going for you?" she asked.

Ben sighed.

"That bad, huh? I thought going to a new place might spark some inspiration."

Images of Alexis smiling in the summer sun danced through his mind. Memories of Nichole and Sophia tucking wild daisies and buttercups into each other's hair made him smile.

"Or has it?" Margaret asked.

A new realization came over him. "I do feel inspired to write something, but it's not my next crime thriller."

"What? Ben, the publisher is expecting book four in your series. You can't just up and switch genres, especially with the book launch party for book three coming up."

"Don't authors ever switch genres?"

"Not ones who want to make money," Margaret retorted. "You stick with your genre. When you make a million dollars, then you can branch out, I suppose."

Ben stared at the blank screen again, but this time, the words were already flowing through his brain. "But what if I feel like I have to write this story?"

"You write what the publisher tells you to write, Ben," Margaret said, and he could hear her long fingernails clacking on a countertop or table. "Now stop this nonsense and get back to writing your thriller."

"What if I wrote a romance instead? A clean, inspirational romance about second chances? A romance that features an Amish setting and Amish characters?" he rushed to say, the storyline already coming to his mind.

The story he shared with Alexis from how they met, how much they lost, and how they found each other again.

"What? A romance? An Amish romance?" She laughed out loud. "You want to write an Amish romance?" Her laughter slowly faded. "Hmm. Actually, I've heard Amish romance is a very popular genre."

"Of course, it is. What if I combined my crime stories with an Amish romance? What if I wrote about two characters with tortured pasts, both affected by sex trafficking, who lose their spouses and then get a second chance at love?"

"Hmmm," Margaret said again, clearly deep in thought. "That sounds good to me, actually, but it's not about what I think. I just don't think the publisher will go for it. Either way, you're still under contract to write book four in your crime thriller series. Maybe after this series is completed, they might consider it, but it's unlikely. Even if they did publish you with a different genre, they would probably want you to use a pen name."

"A pen name?" Ben wrinkled his nose. "But it's my work. I want my name on it."

"That's how this business goes, sweetheart. Anyway, I have to go. Put that Amish romance on the back burner and get me those pages for book four, okay? I want something to show the publisher before the book launch party for book three. I'll check in soon."

With that, Margaret hung up, and Ben smacked his phone on the desk.

The book he was originally going to write just didn't seem good at all to him anymore—it felt overdone and stale. This new story that was unfolding in his mind about him and Alexis felt so much more real and inspiring to him.

He had to write it. If he didn't, he knew it would eat away at him. Maybe he could write this one and also work on the other one at the same time. He'd written two books at once before. Hopefully, the inspiration for the story he really wanted to write would help ease his writer's block for the book he was under contract to write.

With that newfound idea and a surge of creative enthusiasm, he began typing away on the laptop's keyboard late into the night.

19

"They're here!" Sophia cried from the window, hopping up and down.

Alexis took one last look in the mirror, tucking a few black strands of hair behind her ear. She wore a yellow sunflower printed dress and sandals with simple hoop earrings she had bought on clearance at a department store. She smoothed down the front of her dress, hoping she looked okay.

"This is as good as it's going to get," she muttered before rushing to the front door. Dorothy had already let Ben and Nichole inside, and Ben stopped when he saw Alexis.

"Wow, you look amazing," he blurted out, and a fierce, hot blush crept into her cheeks.

"Thanks," she said shyly, not missing Dorothy's knowing smile.

"You all have some fun," Abner said, waving from his chair in the living room, where he read a book.

"Yes, go on and have a good time," Dorothy said, practically shooing them out the door. "Bye!"

"It's like she wants to get rid of us," Alexis joked as they made their way to his car. "So, where are we going?"

"There's a beautiful spot with a pond near the woods, just down the lane," Ben said. "Derek told me about it."

"Oh, did he?" Alexis grabbed Sophia's booster seat from her car and put it in the back of Ben's car.

"Well, yeah. I wanted to take you someplace nice." Ben smiled and scratched behind his ear, which only made him appear even more humble and appealing to her. "Let's go!" he said to the girls, who cheered before getting into the back of the car.

A few minutes later, they parked near the edge of the woods, where a sparkling blue pond shimmered in the sunlight. "Wow, this is beautiful."

"Sure is," Ben said as the girls scampered out of the car. "And you look beautiful," he added shyly.

"Thank you again," she said, smiling before quickly turning away and busying herself with getting out of the car before he could see how deeply she was blushing. She wished her cheeks would stop turning so red, giving her away.

Get a hold of yourself, Alexis, she chided herself.

"Let's eat over here," Nichole said, pointing to a spot on the grass near a small dock. Ben carried a blanket and picnic basket over and spread out the blanket. The girls immediately plopped down, giggling and chattering. Sophia's long, light blonde hair shone in the sun while Nichole's short brown hair just grazed her shoulders, and they whispered into each other's ears with their heads together.

"What are you two talking about?" Alexis asked them, hands on her hips.

"Oh, nothing," Nichole said, and Sophia only giggled mischievously.

Ben shrugged, smiling. "The mysteries of little girls. Who knows what they talk about?"

As Ben took food out of the basket, Alexis sat on the blanket, staring at the spread in awe. "Did you put this together all by yourself?" she asked, eyeing the sandwiches, cookies, cheese, crackers, and containers of sliced fruit and vegetables.

"Maria and Nichole helped me," Ben said. "They knew I'd be helpless without them."

"Yeah, and we wanted it to be good," Nichole added.

"Hey, I can cook," Ben argued. "I'll make you a real meal some time, Alexis, and I'll prove it to you."

Alexis smiled. "I'd love that. This looks delicious. Thank you, Nichole."

Nichole smiled proudly and went back to whispering with Sophia. Every so often, the girls would look over at Ben and Alexis, giggling. What in the world were they talking about?

"We're done!" Sophia cried as she set down the crust of her sandwich on her plate and stood up.

"Can we go play?" Nichole asked.

"Just stay away from the water," Alexis warned.

Sophia said, "Can we just put our feet in?"

"No!" Alexis cried louder than she'd intended. Sophia looked at her quizzically. "I mean, I don't want you to fall in. You can't swim."

A young girl's lifeless body floating on the water resurfaced in Alexis' mind, and she squeezed her eyes shut to block out the memories.

"Nichole can't swim yet, either," Ben said. "I don't want her to fall in. How about you girls go play in the grass and pick flowers?"

"Yeah!" they cried, running off into the field.

"You look a bit pale," Ben said. "Are you okay?"

Alexis nodded and forced a smile. "I'm fine. I'm just protective of Sophia. You really are protective of Nichole, too," Alexis observed.

Ben sighed. "I can't help it, I guess, ever since Estella died."

Alexis tilted her head to one side, wanting to ask how Estella had died, but wasn't sure how to ask.

"What?" he asked, noticing how she was looking at him.

"Sorry." She averted her eyes, picking up a few slices of cucumber.

"You're wondering how my wife died, aren't you?"

Alexis looked up at him in surprise. "How did you know that?"

"Just a guess." He shrugged. "I figured you might want to know why I'm so overprotective of Nichole." Ben stared off into the field after the girls, watching them as they happily picked wildflowers, tucking them into each other's hair. "She was killed in a rock-climbing accident."

"Oh, I'm so sorry." Alexis put a hand over her heart.

Ben explained, "We were out hiking on a mountain, and she started climbing a rock near the edge. I had a bad feeling about it, and I told her to stop, but she insisted. She was always so playful and spontaneous. I tried to tell her it was dangerous, but there was no talking her out of something once she set her mind to it."

"I'm sure there's nothing you could have done."

"As I watched her fall, there was nothing I could do except watch and hear her screams." He squeezed his eyes shut. "It should have never happened. I regret it every moment of every day."

Alexis leaned forward and found herself touching his hand. "I know the feeling, but I'm not going to pretend like I understand how you feel. I hate it when people try to tell you they know how you feel when they clearly don't, even if they mean well."

When Alexis touched his hand, Ben felt a pleasant tingling fill his body. Just being with her was so peaceful, and surprisingly, talking to her was easy—even though he had been shutting everyone out since Estella died.

"But you do understand," Ben said. "So, may I ask how your husband died?"

"Cancer," Alexis said. "He had a rare form of brain cancer. It happened so fast." Still, Alexis' heart went out to Ben because while there was nothing Alexis could have done to save her husband, Ben clearly felt as though his wife's death was his own fault. She didn't have to live with that, but he did.

Instead, she lived with other regrets and guilt.

"I'm sorry," he choked out. "That must have been horrible to see. I hear the end is the worst. I can't imagine knowing your spouse is not going to make it. Those final weeks must have been so difficult.

I'd rather not know when it's going to happen." He shook his head. "I'm sorry. I shouldn't have said that."

"No, you're right. It was awful, knowing I only had a few weeks left with him. I was by his side every moment, trying to make the most of the time we had together. The worst part was Sophia seeing the cancer progress so quickly. I hated for her to see him like that, but she wanted to be with him, and how could I tell her no? I wish those weren't her last memories of him. He looked so pale, thin, and helpless in that hospital bed."

"You did what you thought was best, and that's all that matters."

"Dorothy and Abner came to say goodbye to him. That was the last time I saw them before I came here," Alexis admitted. "I called them when we found out, and they also came and spent as much time with him as they could, hiring a driver to take them back and forth those last few weeks. I still remember when they said goodbye to him the day the doctor told us it could be his last night. Dorothy just sobbed and sobbed."

Alexis shivered at the memory, remembering the way Joshua's mother had held his hand, telling him how much she loved him. The memory of Dorothy and Abner crying and holding each other near Joshua's bed still ripped her heart apart.

"After his funeral, they called me several times, leaving messages and inviting me to come over and see them. I should have come. I should have called back, but I ignored their calls. It was too painful." She wrapped her arms around herself, watching the girls play in the grass as a breeze ruffled their hair. "Joshua wanted me to come, but I didn't, and I regret it so much. I keep thinking about all that Sophia missed out on these past three years."

"We all have regrets. There's nothing we can do to go back and change things," Ben said understandingly. "All we can do is move on and do the best we can today with the time we have now. Dwelling on the past gets us nowhere. I'm a hypocrite. I guess I should take my own advice." He finished his sandwich and brushed his hands on his jeans. "After Estella died, I ignored Derek and Maria's calls too. I get it. It was too painful. I regret it, but I guess we both need to let go of the past."

Alexis nodded. "I know we don't know each other that well yet, but I haven't been able to talk about this with anyone, and I can easily talk about it with you," she blurted, then wanted to smack her forehead. Why had she said that? Would it scare him off?

"I feel the same way." Ben smiled. "I feel like I can be myself when I'm around you and tell you things I haven't told anyone."

She breathed a sigh of relief. He felt the same way.

But did his heart pound like hers did when they were together?

Ben couldn't help but stare at Alexis as she watched the girls play. When a breeze lifted the long, dark strands off her neck, it took his breath away. She was so mesmerizingly beautiful, and she seemed to have no idea, which made her all the more appealing.

"So, what did you do before you came here? This is your first time working with horses, right?" he asked.

"Oh, yes. I was going to go to college to become a nurse, but then I got pregnant with Sophia. I was so sick during my pregnancy, I decided not to go. After Joshua died, I worked at a diner. It was terrible. The boss was a mean bully. I should have never let him disrespect me for so long, but I needed the job, and there wasn't anywhere else hiring at the time in town. Also, I needed a place to work without a college degree during Sophia's school hours. Since then, I've vowed not to let people disrespect me."

"That's good." She deserved to be treated like a queen, to be loved and cherished every day of her life. "Don't let people walk all over you."

"I used to," Alexis admitted. "Then, one day, I had enough. I spilled coffee on one of the customers, and she told me I was worthless. I told her I wasn't worthless, and how I'd been through terrible things and that she should be ashamed of herself. Then my boss was rude about it, as usual, so I quit."

"Wow!" Ben grinned at her. "I wish I could have seen that. I'm glad you stood up for yourself."

"The owner has always been so disrespectful to me. I wish I had quit sooner, even if it would have taken me a while to find a new job. I'm not going to let people treat me like that anymore."

"Good. No one should treat people like that." Ben gazed at her, a slow smile spreading across his face. His brown eyes searched hers, causing a shiver to snake down her spine as butterflies leapt in her stomach. "Alexis, you're amazing. I've never met anyone like you. You've been through so much, yet you're so strong and full of determination. Nothing could ever stop you."

She laughed nervously at his unexpected compliment. "Thanks."

"I'm serious. You faced your fears when you came back here. You got a job, and you're starting a new life. That's admirable."

"I'm just doing my best." She shrugged.

"Here's to being single parents and doing our best even when it's hard." He lifted his cup of water, and she lifted hers to clink against his.

"Cheers to that." She took a sip.

Ben also took a drink, then rubbed his eyes and yawned.

"Am I boring?" Alexis laughed.

"No, not at all! I'm so sorry. I was up really late last night writing. I got some new ideas, and I just had to get them written down before I lost my inspiration. I stayed up too late, but it was worth it," he explained.

"What's your new book about?" she asked curiously. "I used to read all the time when I was younger. I loved it. I really should get back into it."

"You should, now that you're here. So, I'm supposed to be writing the fourth book in my crime thriller series about a secret agent who works undercover as someone who cleans homes for wealthy criminals and listens to their conversations. But now, that idea just seems lame to me."

"That sounds interesting to me! People who clean houses must hear all kinds of conversations. That would be a great cover for a secret agent," Alexis marveled.

"Thanks. My series is about secret agents who go undercover while working normal jobs." He sighed. "But I think I want to go in a different direction."

"What kind of direction?"

"I was thinking...inspirational romance." He winced. "Don't laugh. I know that sounds silly for someone like me to write."

Alexis shook her head. "I don't think that's silly at all. I think it's a great idea. If you want to write this new story, then why not just write it?"

"My agent told me to forget about it, basically, saying I have to stick to my genre. I did sign a contract to deliver this crime book, so I do have to finish it, but I want to write this new story."

"Can you write both?"

"I'm going to try, but I do have a deadline for the crime thriller."

"I think if this new romance story is in your heart, then you should do your best to write that one too. Otherwise, you might end up losing your inspiration for it eventually. Could that happen?" Alexis asked.

"It could," he agreed.

Alexis stared off into the distance, her eyes suddenly wide. "No... It can't be," she murmured gravely, her skin as white as the crochet trim on her dress. "Sophia! Come here!" she screamed.

"What is it?" Ben asked, already whirling around to see what she was looking at, but nothing was there.

20

"I thought I saw... Never mind. It's impossible." Alexis shook her head, her long dark hair swishing over her shoulders.

Sophia and Nichole ran over immediately.

"What's wrong, Mommy?" Sophia asked with concern, running to her and putting her arms around her shoulders.

"Tell me what you saw, Alexis. I want to help you," Ben urged. What had she seen to make her so terrified?

"I thought I saw Sebastian, the trafficker who kidnapped me and made me spy for him," Alexis said to Ben, her hands now trembling in her lap as fear tore through her. Despite the summer heat, an icy chill snaked down her spine. "It's impossible. He'll be in prison for years. It can't be him."

"Who's Sebastian?" Sophia asked.

"No one, baby," Alexis murmured. Sophia gave her a confused look.

I said too much in front of her, Alexis realized. "He's gone, and he won't ever come back. We don't have to worry about him, Sophia."

Sophia nodded, her eyebrows drawn together in concern.

Ben tenderly grasped her hands. “You’re right, Alexis. Sebastian will be in prison for years. There’s no way a criminal with a rap sheet that long would ever get out of prison early. You’re safe, Alexis.”

“I swear I saw him. Am I seeing things?” she asked, her eyes full of terror.

“Sometimes we see things after a trauma. That doesn’t mean you’re crazy. Our minds can play tricks on us sometimes. After Estella died, I thought I saw her walking on the beach once. I ran outside, but there was no one there.” He slowly shook his head. “Don’t worry. He’s not really there, Alexis.”

“I remember that,” Nichole said softly, sitting next to Ben. He gave her a sad smile.

The sight was touching, and Alexis tried to slow her breathing and her heart rate. Ben’s warm hands tenderly holding hers brought a soothing comfort to her soul, and his nearness brought her a peaceful calmness.

“You’re right. I was just imagining it,” she said, mostly to herself.

“To be safe, I’ll call my friend Elijah at CPDU right now and check the status of Sebastian’s prison sentence,” Ben said, already lifting his phone to his ear.

“That would give me peace of mind,” Alexis agreed. “Thank you.”

While Ben was on the phone, Sophia hugged her mother. “Are you okay, Mommy? You looked scared.”

“I’m okay now, sweetie,” she said. “I just thought I saw something, but nothing was there.”

"Okay," Sophia said. "I don't want you to be scared."

"Don't worry. There's nothing to be afraid of," Alexis assured her.

"Ben will protect us, right?" Sophia asked.

Alexis chuckled. "Well, if we were in danger, I'm sure he would, but nothing bad is going to happen. Don't worry."

"Daddy wouldn't ever let anything bad happen to anyone," Nichole said proudly. "He's really strong and fast. He keeps people safe."

"Yes, he does." Alexis smiled. "See, Sophia? We're safe."

Ben clicked off his phone. "My friend Elijah at CPDU looked into it personally. Sebastian is serving life without parole. So, there's nothing to worry about."

"Thank you so much for checking," Alexis said, breathing a sigh of relief. Not only had he trafficked hundreds of girls and women, but Sebastian had also committed murder, which gave him a life sentence.

"Of course." Ben gave her a concerned look. "You still look shaken up. I understand if you want to go home."

Alexis furtively glanced over at the tree line again, where she had thought she'd seen the trafficker. Of course, no one was there.

"I don't want to ruin this beautiful day. I want to stay," she said as the girls ran off to play again.

"You're sure?" he asked.

"I'm sure." She smiled, looking up at the clouds. "The picnic was wonderful, and the girls are having so much fun. Let's just enjoy this peaceful afternoon."

"Sounds good to me." Ben grinned, sitting down next to her, which pleasantly surprised Alexis.

They sat side by side, watching their children play as they talked late into the afternoon under the summer sun. Slowly, Alexis felt all of her worries melt away like an ice cream cone on a hot day.

The morning sun crept through the windows, along with the sounds of birds chirping. Alexis had left the window open the night before, so their singing woke her up. When she heard pots and pans clanging in the kitchen, that told her Dorothy was already making breakfast. Alexis hated not helping, so she swung her legs out of bed and got dressed for church.

This would be her first time going to church since moving here, and though she was looking forward to seeing her old friends, she also felt anxiety gnawing away at her insides. What would they think of her after staying away for so long? She knew they had already forgiven her, but she hadn't seen them in so long. What had she missed in their lives?

After dressing in a long, modest dress and thin cardigan, she checked on Sophia, who was still sleeping in her bed, then went to the kitchen.

"Good morning," Dorothy chirped.

"Good morning," Alexis replied, rubbing her eyes. "The birds were up early."

Dorothy chuckled. "It's like that every day in the summer. They start singing at four-thirty in the morning some days."

"That's still nighttime to me," Alexis said. "What can I help with?"

"I'm making biscuits with sausage gravy," Dorothy said. "Here, you can cook the sausage on the woodstove."

As Alexis stirred the meat around in the pan, she fell silent, thinking about each of her friends she would hopefully see today.

"Is something troubling you, dear?" Dorothy asked.

Alexis turned. "I just haven't seen my old friends in so long. I hope they forgive me for staying away so long."

"Of course, they will. Everyone understands."

"I could have had their support and your support, but I chose to push everyone away." Alexis turned back to the stove. "I'm sure I missed out on so much, and I know I caused Sophia to miss out on bonding with you."

"We all grieve in our own ways. We've already forgiven you, so I hope you will soon forgive yourself, dear." Dorothy patted her shoulder. "What matters is you're both here now. Perhaps God had you live on your own for a reason all this time."

"Maybe." Alexis sighed.

Abner came inside from the barn, where he'd been feeding the animals. "Looking forward to church this morning, Alexis?"

"I am," she said.

Sophia wandered down the hallway, rubbing her eyes. "We have church today," she said with a smile.

"Yes, we do, and there are many children your age you will get to meet there," Dorothy said. "After, you can play outside with them during the potluck."

"That will be fun." Sophia sat at the table as Dorothy pulled the biscuits out of the oven.

"Oh, I forgot about the potluck!" Alexis cried. "I didn't make any food to bring."

"Want me to help you make something?" Dorothy offered. "We still have time."

"If we have time, I would appreciate that. I'd hate to show up empty-handed," Alexis admitted.

"First, let's finish making breakfast." Dorothy showed Alexis how to mix the sausage into the gravy, and they sat down to eat.

Abner said, folding his hands, "Let's bow our heads." They all bowed their heads in silence and said a silent prayer over the meal. Abner began dishing food onto his plate, and the others followed suit.

After breakfast, Dorothy helped Alexis make homemade snicker-doodle cookies, and Sophia stood on a chair next to them, helping mix the batter. They laughed almost the entire time, and Alexis felt the weight lifting off her shoulders.

"They look delicious," Alexis said as she pulled them out of the oven. "Thank you for teaching me. I only know how to make the ones that come from a can."

"You and Sophia did the work. I just guided you." Dorothy smiled. "Everyone will love them."

Once everyone was ready, they rode over to church together in the buggy. The summer sun illuminated the green fields of corn and the tall grass which would be cut into hay. As the buggy rolled down the long stretch of road, the horse's hooves clip-clopped on the pavement in a soothing rhythm. Alexis closed her eyes and savored the sounds.

Oh, I wish I'd come here sooner. This place is paradise—the way life should be, she thought.

"We're here!" Sophia cried as they pulled into the parking lot. The wooden church building was sturdy but plain, built into the side of a hill.

As they walked through the front door that led to the top floor, Alexis carried the large container of snickerdoodles. Just before they walked through the door, her heart pounded in anticipation.

"I'll introduce Sophia to some of the other girls," Dorothy offered, taking Sophia's hand and walking toward the sanctuary.

"Alexis!" Maria called as soon as she stepped inside, and Alexis immediately spotted Liz, who was right behind Maria.

"It's so good to see you!" Liz cried, throwing her arms around Alexis despite the container. "I missed you so much."

"I missed you too," Alexis said. "All of you. I am so sorry I stayed away for so long. And I'm so sorry I didn't come to your wedding." She lowered her eyes to the floor.

"Please don't feel bad." Liz smiled sympathetically. "I know that was a difficult time in your life. We know you've been through so much. We're just really glad you're here now."

"Thank you." Alexis looked around. "I was looking forward to seeing Anna. I wish she were here too." Since Anna was shunned, anyone Amish was not allowed to talk to her, but that rule didn't apply to Alexis.

"We all miss her," Maria said. "But she's pursuing her dream and has found the love of her life, so we're happy for her." Maria pointed to Alexis' container of cookies. "Let's take those downstairs."

They walked down the stairs to the first floor. Two long tables stretched out on one end of the room holding food that women had brought for the potluck, including savory pies, sandwiches, casseroles, soups, salads of all kinds, and desserts.

"That's my husband, Simon," Liz said, pointing to a young bearded man who was speaking with some other men across the room. Among them were Derek and Ben, and when Alexis met Ben's eyes, her heart leaped in her chest as memories of their lovely picnic came rushing back to her. He wore a light blue button-up shirt with gray pants and looked so handsome.

"Are you okay?" Liz asked, then followed her gaze. Liz smiled knowingly. "Ah, I see."

"It's nothing," Alexis said, placing her dessert on the table.

"Hmm. Okay." Liz smiled.

"They went on a picnic together yesterday," Maria whispered to Liz.

"Oh, did you now?" Liz raised her eyebrows, intrigued.

"Yes, we did, and thank you for the food, Maria. It was delicious."

"He was so worried about making everything just right. You should have seen him all flustered. I knew I had to help him, and Nichole helped too. I heard you had a great time," Maria said. "He put a lot of thought into it."

"He did, didn't he?" Alexis glanced over at him, catching his eye once more before turning away. Her cheeks heated in a fierce blush.

"You're blushing like a schoolgirl," Liz chuckled. "You must really like him."

"We've been on one date, if you can even call it that," Alexis countered.

"Oh, it was a date to him. Trust me." Maria laughed. "He talked to Derek about it for a while after."

"Well, I'm so happy for the two of you, Alexis. Oh, look." Liz pointed out two young children, a boy and a girl. "Those are my children, Hope and Peter."

"They are adorable." Alexis smiled. "I am sure Sophia would love to play with them sometime."

"Of course!" Liz said.

"All of our children will be the best of friends." Maria grinned.

"That would be wonderful. Sophia needs some good friends. She had one friend at school, but she often told me about how the other kids either didn't talk to her or even bullied her. I think here she will have a much easier time making friends."

"Oh, you won't have to worry about that. All the children here will love her," Liz said.

"We need to all get together soon," Maria suggested. "Freya will love to see you too. They go to the small non-denominational church down the road."

"I'd love to see her and catch up with all of you," Alexis said.

"We will plan something soon, then. We could go to the coffee shop down the street," Liz said.

"How about tomorrow evening after dinner?" Alexis asked.

"That would be great. My husband can put the children to bed while I go," Liz said.

"Same for me," Maria agreed. "It's about to start. Let's go upstairs and sit down."

Upstairs, they walked over to the backless benches. The right half was where the men sat, and the left half was where the women sat. Alexis could feel Ben's eyes on her as he entered the room with Derek.

Dorothy walked over with Sophia and Nichole. "I just introduced Sophia and Nichole to many of the children."

"We made a lot of new friends, Mommy," Sophia chirped. "They're all so nice."

"That's wonderful," Alexis said, putting her arm around her daughter.

"My daddy asked if it would be okay if I sat with you," Nichole asked shyly.

"Of course!" Alexis said, then looked over at Ben, who nodded his thanks from across the room. The way he smiled at her made her face heat, and she quickly turned away.

"There are mats in the back of the room where the children often go to sit together or even take naps. So, if you want, you can go back there later. It's going to be about three hours long," Dorothy explained to the girls. "So just let me know if you want to go to the back."

"Okay," Sophia said with a smile, and Nichole nodded.

The bishop, Bishop Byler, came to the front of the room and opened the service, then they opened their *Ausbund* songbooks and sang slow German hymns for about an hour. Alexis didn't know German, and since they were singing so slowly, she often lost her place during the songs. Near the end of the singing, Dorothy offered to take Sophia and Nichole to the back of the room to sit with the other children.

The service then transitioned into the sermon, which was surprisingly in English.

"Last time I was here, the sermons were in German," Alexis whispered to Dorothy.

She nodded. "Recently, they decided to change it to English," she whispered back.

Alexis was grateful because she didn't know any German at all, and she would have been lost through the entire sermon. Her back ached from sitting on the hard bench, but she listened intently to the bishop's words about devoting one's life to God and not just going through the motions.

After the service, everyone went downstairs for lunch. Alexis noticed that the men and women continued to remain separated, so even though Ben would smile at her every now and then and she wanted to go over and talk to him, she kept her distance.

After getting their food, Alexis, Nichole, and Sophia sat down with Maria and her daughter Rachel along with Liz and her daughter Hope. The four girls were all relatively the same age, so they chattered amongst themselves in lively conversation.

"I helped make the snickerdoodles," Sophia said proudly. "My *grossmammi* taught me, and my mom helped."

"They're yummy," Nichole said.

"We like to bake a lot at my house, too," Rachel said.

"Me too," Hope added. "You should come over and bake cookies with us."

"That's a great idea," Maria said. "We can plan that soon."

The girls continued discussing what other fun things they could do together, and the sight of her daughter smiling and laughing with the other girls warmed Alexis' heart.

After the potluck, they all went outside. Alexis carried her container, which was now empty.

"Your cookies went so quickly," Liz said with a laugh.

"Dorothy deserves all the credit," Alexis said. "I had no idea what I was doing."

"I think you don't give yourself enough credit," a voice behind her said, and Alexis turned to see Ben standing there, smiling at her with his hands in his pockets. "Thanks for watching over Nichole."

"You're welcome," Alexis stammered.

Another young Amish man walked up to them with Derek.

"Alexis, this is Simon, my husband," Liz said, and Simon shook Alexis' hand.

"Nice to meet you," he said.

"You too," Alexis said. "Ben, have you met Liz?"

He had briefly met her on the day of the rescue, but he didn't want to bring that up. "It's been a long time," Ben said, shaking her hand. "Nice to officially meet you."

"You as well," Liz said. "Well, we are going to visit my parents today, so we need to get going." She turned to Alexis. "It was so nice catching up with you. I'm so happy you're here."

"Thank you." Alexis smiled. "Me too."

Simon, Liz, and their children walked toward their buggy, then Derek and Maria also left to go spend time with family, as was common on Sundays. Sid approached them, tipping his black hat.

"Hello," he said. "Alexis, Ben. And who is this little lady?" he asked.

"This is my daughter, Nichole," Ben said. "Nichole, this is Mr. Hoffman."

Nichole waved to him. "Sophia told me you have really nice horses."

"Yes, I do," Sid said with a grin. "Would you like to come by and see them?"

Nichole turned to Ben with a pleading look. "Daddy, could we go see the horses tomorrow?" Nichole asked Ben. "Sophia told me about them, and I really want to go see them."

"Tomorrow would be fine with me," Sid said.

Ben drew his eyebrows together in thought. What if something happened to Nichole at the stables? A horse could kick her or—

"We will be really careful," Nichole said, giving him her best puppy-eyed look. "Please?"

"I will make sure you know all the safety rules," Sid added. "Stop by anytime tomorrow."

"Okay, we can go, but just to look at them," Ben said. "No getting too close."

Nichole grinned triumphantly. "Thank you, Daddy!"

"Feel free to bring Sophia, too," Sid said, "As long as she has a way to get home after."

"Of course," Alexis said with a nod. "I won't let her being there interfere with my work. Thank you, Sid. They will love it."

Sid smiled and nodded.

"I can bring them in the afternoon so she can go home with you when you leave," Ben offered. "Or I can bring her home after."

"Thank you," Alexis said. "Well, then I guess we will all see each other tomorrow."

"That will be so fun!" Sophia cried, throwing her arms around Nichole.

Alexis and Sophia waved goodbye, then they walked to the buggy where Dorothy and Abner were waiting. As they rode home, Sophia went on and on about how excited she was for the next day, and Alexis couldn't help but smile—her daughter's enthusiasm was contagious.

21

The next day, Ben picked up Sophia and drove the girls over to the stables after lunch. They talked the whole way about the horses.

"I wish I could learn to ride," Nichole said with a sigh.

"It's dangerous, sweetie," Ben said, glancing in the rear-view mirror. "Besides, we don't own horses, so you would only be able to ride here."

Because we are leaving soon, he added mentally, but didn't want to say it out loud.

Nichole sighed and crossed her arms, but Sophia didn't seem to notice as she continued to chatter on about the colors of the horses. A few minutes later, they arrived, and the girls scrambled out of the car as soon as Ben parked it.

"Hello," Alexis called, coming out of the barn. She looked beautiful in her straw hat, faded jeans, and t-shirt, holding a rake. Her long, dark hair was tied back in a braid that fell over her shoulder. "Thanks for bringing them here."

"No problem," Ben said, keeping an eye on the girls as they scurried over to the fence, where Sophia taught Nichole the names of all the horses in the pasture.

"I'm surprised she remembers all their names," Alexis said, smiling as she watched them. "I shouldn't be, though. She has a great memory when it's something she cares about."

"Hello, there," Sid called, coming out of the barn. "Do you want to feed the horses?" he asked the girls.

"Yes!" they cried.

"Here's some hay. Now hold it out on your hand, but keep it flat," Sid told them, then clicked his tongue to call the horses over.

"Nichole—" Ben said, about to stop her. What if the horse bit her finger?

"Ben, it's okay," Alexis said, briefly touching his arm. "Sid won't let anything happen to them."

Two horses walked over, one eating from each of the girls' hands. They giggled with delight, and Ben couldn't help but smile.

"See? They're loving it." Alexis smiled.

"You're right," he admitted. "I just don't know much about horses, so it makes me nervous having Nichole near them."

"These are very gentle horses," she assured him.

Ben watched the horses skeptically. "If you say so."

"Hello!" a voice called behind them, and Ben turned to see a plump Amish woman walking toward them. "I heard you were visiting today. I'm Brenda." She stuck out her hand, and Ben shook it.

"Nice to meet you. I'm Ben," he replied.

"I made cookies for the girls if they want to come inside and have some," Brenda offered.

"Cookies?" Sophia asked.

"Thank you, Brenda. That's very kind of you. I'm sure they'd enjoy that," Ben said, secretly thankful his daughter would be away from the horses for a while.

"You go on inside with them and take a break," Sid said. "You've been working hard all day."

"Thanks, Sid. I'll be back out soon," Alexis said.

They made their way into the house, where Brenda served the girls cookies and glasses of milk. They sat at the table to eat them.

"These are delicious," Alexis said as she tried one.

"Would you like one, Ben?" Brenda asked.

"Oh, yes, I would love one. First, may I use your bathroom?"

"Of course, dear. It's just down the hall and to the left."

Ben went down the hall and splashed some water on his face not only to cool himself down but also to calm his nerves. The image of Estella falling down the mountain flashed through his mind, and suddenly an image of a horse kicking Nichole replaced it. He squeezed his eyes shut.

"I'm worrying too much," he told himself. "Right?"

A few minutes later, he came back down the hall to the kitchen, where Alexis was wiping up some milk off the floor with a towel.

"Sorry, I spilled it," Sophia said.

"Don't worry, dear," Brenda assured her. "Accidents happen. Nothing to worry about."

Ben looked around the room, but he didn't see Nichole anywhere. "Where's Nichole?"

Alexis stood up, holding the dripping towel. "She was just here a second ago."

Ben's heart pounded as he rushed out the door and ran outside toward the stables. What if she had gone through the fence into the pasture?

Sid was speaking with one of his employees outside the barn, and Ben hurried over to them. "Have you seen my daughter?"

"No," Sid said. "I'm sorry. I thought she was inside."

"I think she came out here," Ben said, scanning the pasture, but she wasn't inside the fence. "Maybe she went inside the barn."

"We'll help you look," Sid and his employee said, following him into the barn.

"Nichole!" Ben called, looking into each stall. With every passing second, his heart pounded in his ears even louder, the sound closing in around him until he could barely hear anything else.

Alexis ran into the barn. "Did you find her?"

"Over here!" Sid called.

Ben ran over to the other side of the barn where Sid had been searching. He looked over the stall door to see Nichole inside with one of the horses, standing beside the animal and petting it.

"Nichole!" Ben cried. "Come out here this instant."

Nichole looked up with wide eyes and stepped out of the stall as Sid opened it. Ben knelt down in front of her. "Why did you leave the house? When I came out of the bathroom, I didn't know where you were. I was so afraid something happened to you."

"I just wanted to pet one of the horses," she said meekly, frowning. "I'm sorry I scared you, Daddy."

At the sight of her big, brown eyes welling with tears, Ben put his arms around her. "It's okay, baby. Just promise me you won't run off like that again. And you definitely can't go inside the horses' stalls, okay? You could get hurt or let one of the horses out by accident."

"Your father is right," Sid agreed. "You shouldn't go in the stalls alone, even if the horses are gentle. It's one of the safety rules, remember?"

"Yes." Nichole sniffed, then he let her go. "I'm sorry."

"At least you didn't get hurt," Sid said.

"Maybe we should go," Ben said, standing up.

"No, please!" Nichole cried. "I won't do it again, I promise. I'll follow all the rules."

"Ben," Alexis said, briefly pulling him aside. "She didn't know. I think once she learns all the rules, she won't do it again."

"Her being around the horses makes me nervous," Ben admitted.

"I know you're protective of her, but being with horses can be very therapeutic. I know even in the short time I've worked here that it's helped me. I think it would help her too, if you let it. She doesn't even need to ride a horse for this place to help her," Alexis explained. "Won't you let her?"

Ben sighed, glancing back at Nichole, who was still giving him that puppy-eyed look that he couldn't say no to. "Okay, we won't leave yet, but you need to learn and follow all the safety rules."

"Okay," Nicole readily agreed.

"How about we go back inside? Sophia is still inside. We can sit down, and I will teach you all the safety rules," Sid offered.

"Sounds good," Ben agreed.

Inside, Sid taught them all of his safety rules, and the girls listened intently. Afterward, Sid showed the girls how to brush the horses under Ben's careful supervision. They watched as Sid exercised a few of the horses, and then they filled water buckets with the hose and put oats in the food containers. The girls worked enthusiastically, wanting to take care of the horses and prove that they could do the work, but soon enough, Ben could see they were feeling tired.

It's time to go back for dinner," Ben said. "Or Maria will be upset if we're late and the food is cold."

Alexis chuckled. "You're right. Thank you for bringing them, Ben." She smiled warmly at him, making his heart soar. Suddenly, he was very glad he had come today and stayed.

"The girls clearly loved it," Ben said as he took Sophia's booster seat out of his car. Nichole trudged wearily over to the car and climbed in.

"I'm tired," she muttered.

Ben chuckled. "You're going to bed early tonight."

"I'm glad you stayed. They had so much fun taking care of the horses, and I'm sure it was good for Nichole," Alexis said softly, stepping closer to him.

"You're right. I'm glad we stayed too. I'll bring her back soon," he found himself saying, unable to look away from her dark eyes that were drawing him in.

"Good," Alexis said, taking the booster seat from him. "I'll put this in my car. We're about to leave too."

"See you around," Ben said, getting into the driver's seat.

Sophia waved goodbye. "Bye!"

22

As Ben drove away, Alexis started her car to get the air conditioning going.

"Sophia, I need to talk to Sid for a moment. Do you want to go see the horses by the fence for a few minutes before we leave?"

"Yeah!" Sophia cried, running over to the fence as Alexis walked over to Sid.

"Thank you so much for teaching the girls today," she said. "They loved it."

"It was my pleasure." Sid grinned.

"It gave me an idea," Alexis began. "I know you don't offer riding lessons publicly, but would you ever consider it? I could help you. We could teach children and adults how to ride in small groups."

"We're quite busy already," Sid said, tapping his bearded chin. "However, I would consider it if you were willing to teach the classes. I can teach you all the basics, then you can teach the lessons. We could offer both group and private lessons."

"It would be a whole new stream of income for your business," Alexis agreed, then hesitated. "Me? I don't even know how to ride yet myself."

"Sam and Jacob have been riding since they could walk, but I don't think they would want to teach the lessons. If you lead the lessons, they will help you, and I'll continue on managing the stables," Sid said. "I'll talk to them about it. It's a great idea, Alexis."

"Really?" Her heart fluttered with the idea of teaching people how to ride. "Being here and working with the horses even for such a short amount of time has already helped me. It's very therapeutic. I just want to help other people in the same way. To be honest, it's my dream to open an equine therapy center." She chuckled. "I've always loved horses, but I just don't know much about them, and I would have to get certified. Maybe it's a pipe dream."

"Nonsense," Sid said. "You will learn about horses and how to ride, so that dream might not be as unrealistic as you think. You're doing a great job here, Alexis."

"Thanks." Her face heated at the compliment.

"Now go on home and get some rest," Sid said as Sam and Jacob also came out from the barn and started preparing to leave. "I'm going to talk to them, and I'll let you know what they think tomorrow."

"Okay." Alexis nodded. "Time to go, Sophia."

That evening after dinner, Alexis drove to the local coffee shop. Dorothy and Abner had offered to take care of Sophia, so she went alone.

When she walked through the door, she saw her two Amish friends sitting at a table already, happily chatting away. A fireplace beside them crackled, and soft music played as customers drank their tea, coffee, and hot chocolate. Industrial-style lightbulbs hung from the ceiling, giving the room a soft glow. A moment later, Freya walked in behind Alexis.

"Alexis!" Freya cried, pulling her into a hug. "It's so good to see you."

"It's good to see you too," Alexis said as they made their way to the table. They sat down with Maria and Liz and greeted each other.

"What's new? How are you, Alexis?" Freya asked.

"Alexis went on a date with Ben," Liz supplied with a playful smile.

"I'm not even sure I'd call it a date," Alexis said, her face reddening. "It was just a picnic."

"Oh, that's a date, sweetheart!" Freya smiled, patting her hand.

"But our daughters were there," Alexis argued.

"Doesn't matter. It was a date," Freya assured her.

"I tried to tell her," Maria added. "Ben told Derek all about it after. He definitely thought it was a date. He's clearly smitten with you."

Alexis' blush deepened even more. "I just feel so...unworthy of him. He's such a wonderful man, and I have so much baggage."

"But he is a widower," Liz reminded her. "He understands what it's like to lose a spouse too."

"That's true, but that's not the whole reason I didn't come back here for so long. It was also because I felt so guilty. I knew being here would remind me of Joshua, but it's not as painful as I thought it was going to be. We're making new memories. I'm so sorry I ignored your calls and stayed away from all of you for so long. I guess I thought if I shut everyone out, I could pretend like none of it had ever happened. But I was a fool to think that," Alexis apologized.

"We understand," Freya said. "When I first returned, being here reminded me of the accident when Robert died. It was hard at first, but now I've made so many new friends, and I have a wonderful husband from here. I believe God brought you back for a reason, Alexis. You already seem joyful. You have a glow about you."

"Really?" Alexis asked, subconsciously touching her face.

"It's true," Maria said. "You seem happier than when you first arrived. You're here now, so live in the moment and lift up your worries to the Lord. Just listen to what He's telling you and trust in His plan. Everything will fall into place as it should."

Alexis nodded in agreement, feeling as though a weight was beginning to lift off of her shoulders. "You're right, Maria. I need to lift up my concerns to the Lord and just be still and trust Him. I want to be present and stop worrying so much. I do feel like this place is already changing me. God is changing me. So many good things have happened since I arrived. I got a job, we've reunited with Joshua's parents, and now Sophia has her grandparents in her life. She's also made new friends."

"It is so cute how they play together," Maria added. "I love seeing them spend time together. You should bring your son Kyle by some time, Freya, so all the kids can play together."

"That would be great," Freya said. "He'd love that."

"And you have been reunited with Ben," Liz added with a wistful sigh. "You're both getting a second chance at love. How romantic."

Maria chuckled. "You're a hopeless romantic."

"What?" Liz asked, shrugging and lifting her hands. "It's true."

"And I think God has even more blessing in store for you," Freya said, and Maria nodded in agreement.

"I feel like Joshua was still alive just yesterday," Alexis said. "Part of me feels guilty for being interested in another man."

"Ben probably feels the same way, but I think Joshua would want you to be happy and fall in love again. I'm sure Ben's wife would want the same for him. You don't need to feel guilty," Maria said. "I felt the same way at first when I met Derek, then I realized Robert would have wanted me to be happy."

"Oh," Alexis said with realization. "Of course. You went through the same thing. So, does it get any easier?"

"With time," Maria said. "I will always love my late husband, and I will never forget him, but I've made room in my heart to love Derek too."

Alexis admired Maria's steadfast faith. "I'm so sorry. I didn't mean to make the mood so glum and talk about me. What's going on in all of your lives?"

"I'm pregnant with baby number two," Freya said with a wide grin. Liz squealed with delight and Maria threw her arms around Freya.

"Congratulations!" Alexis cried, joyful for her friend. One day, she hoped to have children of her own. She wanted four or five, maybe even more, with a house full of playful laughter.

After they each offered Freya their congratulations, Alexis asked, "So, Maria and Liz, what's new in your lives?"

"I've decided to start selling my pies and jams at the farmers' market," Liz said, and Maria clapped her hands.

"Finally! I've been telling you for so long that you should do that," Maria said.

"They're so delicious. I'm sure you'll have plenty of business," Freya added.

"That's wonderful, Liz," Alexis said.

"Maybe I should start selling my quilts at the farmers' market," Maria added.

"You're having a baby soon," Freya added with a chuckle. "Take it easy."

Maria laughed. "Maybe when the baby is older. I do like to keep busy though. I could start making them now and then I would have some to sell by next summer."

"That's a great idea," Liz said. "And I'll help you as much as I can. Maybe we can get our booths next to each other."

Alexis smiled as they continued to catch up with each other's lives and exchanged playful banter. The light-hearted conversation lifted her spirits, but deep down she knew she had some praying to do when she got home.

That night, when she arrived at the house, everyone was sleeping. Alexis checked on Sophia, who was sleeping. Alexis kissed her on the cheek, sweeping her daughter's blonde hair off her forehead.

"I love you," Alexis whispered. She pulled up the blanket to cover Sophia's shoulders, then crept up to her room and knelt at the bed. The moonlight streamed through the window, illuminating the colors on Dorothy's handmade quilt that covered the bed. Alexis folded her hands and rested them on the bed.

"Lord, I want to cast my cares upon You completely, but it's so hard. I keep worrying, and I keep hanging on to this guilt, letting it hold me back. Maybe it will take time, but please take it all away from me. Please help me trust in Your plan and be still. Thank You for bringing me back here and reuniting me with family and friends. Thank You so much for my friends. Just talking with them tonight helped me so much. Thank You for reuniting me with Ben. I don't know where things will lead with him, but I will trust You and listen to Your voice. Please show me what to do. Please help me to live in the moment and not worry about the past and future. In Jesus' name, amen," she prayed.

She climbed into bed and pulled the quilt over herself. Within moments, a peaceful stillness overcame her as she fell into a deep, restful sleep.

23

That evening at Derek's house, after charging his laptop at the nearby diner, Ben typed furiously. He marveled at the way Alexis was so brave and courageous even though she had probably endured more trauma and hardship than he had. He envied how fearless she was, living life to the fullest while he retreated to safety like a coward, trying to protect his daughter from everything that could possibly go wrong.

He loved Nichole so much and didn't want her to get hurt, but where was the line between being over-protective and just being cautious?

His mind replayed the events of the day, especially how Alexis had convinced him to stay at the stables, and he was so glad she had. The look on Nichole's face throughout the day warmed his heart. He hadn't seen his daughter that happy in so long.

Maybe Alexis was right about horses being therapeutic. Maybe it was just what his daughter needed.

As he continued to think about the times he had shared with Alexis so far, and how she made him feel, the words continued to quickly flow from his fingers to the keyboard.

His phone beeped, and he checked it to see it was a text from Margaret: *Any pages yet for book four? The book launch party is coming soon for book three.*

He replied: *Yes, but it's not for the book the publisher wants.*

She wrote back: *I was thinking about what you said before. What if we combine the two genres and you write an Amish crime story?*

He laughed. *Oh, so now she thinks it's her idea.*

His phone rang, and he answered it. "Hello, Margaret."

"So, what do you think?"

"I already asked you about combining the two genres into one story. I thought the publisher wanted this story to be about the secret agent going undercover as a house cleaner."

"I told them how popular Amish books are, and while they don't want you to branch off into the new genre entirely, they said you could combine the two. It's something new and different for you, but it still stays in line with the series. Can you come up with a storyline for an Amish crime story featuring Bobby Henderson, your secret agent character?" Margaret asked.

Ben hesitated. "Bobby could be undercover in an Amish community and fall in love with a woman who lives there. She is a survivor of sex trafficking, and he helped rescue her from the traffickers, then they get to know each other and fall in love."

"That's fantastic!" Margaret cried. "Brilliant, Ben. See? Now we all get what we want. The woman is Amish in the story, right?"

"That would work." Ben nodded slowly. "It's actually a good idea. I've been working on the story. I wasn't sure what to name the main male character, but he could be Bobby. I just need to make some changes. I like the idea of blending the two stories together, but it might take me a while to make it work."

"Just send me what you have now," Margaret said. "Then make the changes after. I'm curious to see what you have."

"Okay," Ben said hesitantly. "This is my first time writing a romance, so don't judge me. I'm emailing it to you now."

"Great. I'll read it and get back to you. Have a good night," Margaret said and hung up.

Ben sighed. Would she hate it? He shook his head as if trying to clear away his doubts and kept on writing.

The next morning, Alexis showed up for work even earlier than usual, eager to hear what Sam and Jacob thought about helping her teach riding lessons. She knew she needed all the help she could get, but with their help, hopefully, one day, she could even do it on her own.

"You're early," Sid said cheerfully as she got out of her car.

"I know. I hope that's okay. I was just really looking forward to hearing what Sam and Jacob think about the lessons. Did you get to talk to them?"

"I did," Sid said. "I was right in thinking they wouldn't want to actually teach the lessons, but they said they will help you organize them. I'll teach you to ride, but they will help you along the way as well. If we end up getting even busier, one day, I'd like to have you take over teaching the classes all by yourself, if you want to."

"Yes!" Alexis cried, clasping her hands together. "I just hope I'm a good enough rider to even teach the basics. I mostly want to teach kids how to ride, but I'd like to teach adults too."

"We'll start with the basics. That's what most people want to learn anyway. If they want to learn how to barrel race or do fancy tricks, this won't be the place for that." Sid chuckled, then a serious expression came over his face. "I was thinking about how you said working with horses is therapeutic for you and how you want to share that with others. I think that's a mighty fine mission, Alexis. I'm glad to be a part of it."

"Thank you," Alexis gushed. "I'm so glad you are on board."

"Of course," Sid said, walking toward the barn. "And if you'd like, you're welcome to put Sophia in our first children's class at no cost."

"Wow, thank you, Sid. I'm sure she would love that."

"Ben could put Nichole in the class too, if he wants," Sid offered.

"I'm not sure if he would let her, but I'll talk to him about it," Alexis said, hoping she could speak with him about it soon. Nichole would certainly love to learn to ride, and Alexis knew it would be great for her.

"Now, are you ready to learn the basics of riding?"

"I'm ready," Alexis said, anticipation and excitement surging within her as she followed him.

24

That evening, Alexis went home sore and tired, but she'd enjoyed every minute of her first lesson. Sid had started with the basics. He had shown her how to groom the horse, tack up, and mount, which she hadn't mastered yet. Then they'd gone on to do all their regular work of caring for the horses.

She hadn't even finished learning the basics, but she was still exhausted. She sat down at the table, rubbing her feet.

"Mommy!" Sophia cried, hurrying over from the living room where she'd been playing a game with Abner. "Did you learn how to ride today?"

"I did, sort of," Alexis said. "I just learned the basics."

"But you actually rode a horse?" Sophia asked with wide eyes.

"Yes, I did. Guess what? Sid is going to let me teach riding lessons at the stables. Isn't that great?" Alexis told her.

"Riding lessons? Can I do it? Please?" Sophia begged, clasping her hands together.

"Sid said you can join the class, so yes, you can." Alexis grinned.

"Yay!" Sophia threw her arms around Alexis' neck, almost making her fall off her chair. "Thank you, Mommy!"

"You can thank Sid later. Listen, it could be a while. I don't know how long it will take me to learn what I need to learn in order to teach classes."

"I'll wait. I'm so excited! Nichole wants to learn how to ride too. Do you think her daddy will let her learn how to ride too?" Sophia asked.

Alexis said, "It will be a long time before the lessons start, and Ben and Nichole are going back home soon. He will probably say no, baby. I don't want you to get your hopes up."

Sophia nodded. "I'll be sad if she can't do it, but I'm just glad I get to do it. Though, it wouldn't be the same without her."

"That's great news, Alexis," Dorothy said, wiping her hands on a towel. "Sid is such a kind, generous man."

"I'm surprised he hasn't offered lessons at the stables before to broaden the business," Abner said from the living room. "It's a great idea. Why didn't he think of it before?"

"I asked him about it yesterday. Before, he was always too busy, so that's why he's going to have me teach them. His employees, Sam and Jacob, are going to help me," Alexis explained.

"I'm really happy for you," Abner said, walking over and patting her shoulder. "I think you'll do a great job. You seem happy."

"I really am. Working with the horses has helped me in so many ways," Alexis said. "So, I'm just grateful I get to work there. Thank you."

Dorothy smiled at her thoughtfully. "Is it really just working with the horses that's making you so happy?"

Alexis blushed, her face heating with embarrassment. "That's not all of it, no."

Sophia scampered back to the living room to finish her game with Abner, and Alexis stood at the counter, chopping vegetables as Dorothy kneaded the dough for biscuits.

"I'm really glad to see you so happy with Ben," Dorothy said beside her, "but you were asking me before about joining the Amish. Have you given any more thought to it?"

"I've only been here a few days, but I have thought of it some. It's still all so new to me. I'll need to be here much longer before I can make a decision," Alexis said, peeling a carrot.

"No one will rush you into it. It's a big decision," Dorothy said. "I was just thinking that if you do decide to join, where does that leave you and Ben? He's not Amish, so you wouldn't be able to marry him if you joined the church."

"I don't think Ben has any intention of joining, so I see what you mean," Alexis said in a low voice as she brushed the carrot peelings off to the side. "That leaves me in a predicament. I want to ask him about it, but I don't want him to see me as desperate and already thinking about marriage when we've only seen each other a few times."

"Of course. That's understandable," Dorothy agreed. "So, you're a bit stuck, aren't you?"

"For now, yes, but I'm not in a hurry. Things are going well in my life for once, and I don't want to rush things and mess it up. I have you and Abner, my relationship with Ben is good right now as it is, and I love my job. Honestly, things haven't been this great for me since..." Alexis sighed. "Since before my sister died."

Dorothy stopped kneading the dough and turned to face Alexis. "I'm so sorry to hear that, Alexis. I didn't know you had a sister."

"She died when I was a teenager." Alexis squeezed her eyes shut. She could still hear the screams of her horrified friends when they'd discovered Jessie's body floating in the water, and a sick feeling washed over her. Alexis grabbed the countertop for support as her head spun.

"You don't have to tell me about it if you're not ready," Dorothy murmured.

No, she wasn't ready. As the images flashed through her mind, she pushed them away again, suppressing them as she had for years.

Maybe one day she would be able to talk to someone about what happened that day, but not today.

"I haven't spoken to anyone about it since I left home," Alexis said, opening her eyes. "After that, I ran away and got involved in drugs. My life spiraled out of control. I lived on the streets for a few years, then I got kidnapped and trafficked." Alexis sighed, breathing deeply to calm her racing heart. "Anyway, my life hasn't been this good since before she died. We used to be one happy family, just the four of us."

"What about your parents? Do you see them often?"

"I haven't spoken to them since I left home," Alexis admitted. "I know I should, but I can't bring myself to call them."

"Maybe they've forgiven you."

Alexis shrugged. "I guess because things are going so well right now, I'm afraid of facing their possible rejection now more than ever. That's silly, I know."

"No, it's not." Dorothy continued kneading the dough. "We all fear rejection, but is not ever taking that chance worth not knowing?"

Alexis chopped the carrots with more force than necessary. "I'll call them one day. I know I need to. Sophia has asked about them. She should have both sets of grandparents in her life."

"You know in your heart what to do," Dorothy said with a knowing smile. "Just pray for the Lord to give you the strength and courage to do it, and He will."

Alexis nodded slowly. "You're right. I need to pray about it more."

As they continued preparing dinner, Alexis vowed to herself to pray more about the decisions she had to make that loomed in her mind like a threatening storm.

Sid invited Ben and the girls back to the stables again, so the next afternoon, Ben drove the girls there to visit the horses.

"There's Zeke!" Nichole cried as she flung herself out of the car and ran toward the fence. "Hi, Comet." She stepped up onto the fence, waving to them. Sophia was right behind her and joined her at the fence. Ben chuckled at the tender sight.

"That is so sweet," Alexis said as she came up behind him. "They love it here so much."

"I can hardly keep her away. She's always asking when we'll come back," Ben said, smiling and shaking his head. "I just hope Sid doesn't mind."

"Of course not. He loves having them here. Actually, there's something I want to talk to you about."

Ben's heart leaped in his chest. Was she going to ask him on a date, perhaps? Or could it be more than that?

Alexis told Ben all about the riding lessons. "Sophia was wondering if you'd let Nichole join the class. I'm sure the girls would both love it, but I know you're going back home soon, and it would be too far to drive," Alexis said in a rush.

Ben sighed, ignoring the disappointment of her not asking him on a date. "You're right. We are going back home soon to Kennebunkport. That would be a long way to drive for riding lessons. Even if we lived closer, I don't think it would work out."

"Why not?" Alexis asked, crossing her arms.

"Nichole? Riding a horse? She's so young. She could get hurt." Ben's stomach churned at the thought. "I should have known that bringing her here would lead to other things beyond just visiting and taking care of the horses. It's one thing for her to stand near the fence and talk to them and change their water, but I can't let her ride a horse. They're so big, and she's so small. What if she falls and breaks a bone—or worse?"

"It would be a lie if I said there were no risks involved," Alexis said. "But look at how happy she is just talking to the horses. Imagine how excited she'd be to ride one. Maybe there is a place offering lessons closer to where you live."

"I don't want her on a horse." Ben shook his head adamantly. "I know you think this might help her work through her grief of losing her mother, but I can't let her get up on one of those massive animals. I'm sorry, Alexis. I just can't do it." His voice cracked, and he turned away, embarrassed at the sudden emotion that had overtaken him.

"Are you going to do this her entire life and never let her do anything? What about when she's ready to learn to drive? Are you not going to let her?" Alexis retorted. "You can't bubble wrap her, Ben. She'll only resent you for it."

"I thought you understood why I'm protective of her," Ben said in a low voice, turning to her. "I'm surprised you're not more protective of Sophia."

Alexis crossed her arms, offended. "It's better to live life and take risks than to not try anything out of fear."

"You're the one who won't even call your parents because you're too afraid. Sophia should have her grandparents in her life, but you're keeping them out of her life because of your own fear," Ben snapped, then his face paled. He felt the blood rush from his face as the weight of his words settled over him like a cold, wet blanket. How could he have said something so cruel? "I'm so sorry, Alexis. I shouldn't have said that."

Pain and shock flashed across Alexis' face, and she narrowed her eyes at him. "You don't know anything about what happened," Alexis said through clenched teeth. She turned and walked away toward the girls and joined them at the fence.

She was right—he had no idea what had happened between her and her parents.

Guilt settled like a rock in Ben's stomach. He wished he could take his words back, but it was too late. How could he have said that to her? He had no right to tell her how to raise her daughter or give her unwanted life advice.

Overcome with shame, he turned and walked down the long driveway to clear his head.

25

Sophia looked at Alexis, then Ben, who was now walking down the driveway. "Why is Ben leaving?"

"He's probably just taking a walk," Alexis said, anger roiling in her stomach as she remembered what he'd said. He had no idea what had happened between her and her parents, so how dare he say such a thing. If he only knew how Jessie had died, he never would have said such a thing.

"Did you and my daddy have a fight?" Nichole asked.

"No," Alexis said. "I mean, sort of. We both said some things to each other that weren't very nice. Adults do that sometimes."

"Kids do that too," Sophia added.

"You're right, but we shouldn't. We are supposed to be kind to each other." Alexis sighed. "When he comes back, I'll tell him I'm sorry."

"My daddy and mommy used to fight sometimes, but Daddy always said he was sorry after," Nichole said.

"Really?" Alexis asked thoughtfully. "It's good to apologize when you've done something wrong."

Nichole nodded and smiled. “Well, my mommy was always right.”

“Was she?” Alexis chuckled.

“Alexis, can you help me with something?” Sid asked from the barn door. “It’ll just take a minute.”

“Sure.” She turned to the girls. “Stay right here, okay? I’ll be right back.” Alexis turned and walked into the barn.

“My mom seems sad,” Sophia said.

“So does my daddy. I think they had a bad fight,” Nichole said, resting her chin on her arms, which rested on top of the fence.

“We should go pick them some flowers to make them feel better. I see some right over there.” Sophia pointed to a grassy area behind the barn.

“But your mommy said to stay right here,” Nichole argued.

“It’ll just take a minute. We can surprise them, and then they won’t be fighting anymore. I think they love each other, but they had a fight. Do you think they still love each other?” Sophia asked.

“I don’t know,” Nichole said, frowning.

“We could give your dad flowers and tell him they’re from my mom. Then we can give my mom flowers and tell her they’re from your dad,” Sophia said.

Nichole nodded. “Okay.”

“If they love each other again, maybe they could get married. Then you and I would be—”

“Sisters!” Nichole gasped, her hands flying up to her cheeks in shock.

"So, we have to go get those flowers," Sophia urged. "So they get married, and we can be sisters. Then we can play together all the time."

"Okay, let's go." Nichole hopped down from the fence, and they ran toward the patch of wildflowers behind the barn.

"Oh, I found daisies," Sophia said, picking several flowers. "And purple ones."

"I found pretty little white ones," Nichole said, then looked up to see a round stone structure, overgrown with weeds, that had been hidden behind some trees and tall grass. "What's that?"

"I don't know," Sophia said, walking over to it.

Nichole climbed on top of it. "I'm queen of the hill!" she cried as Sophia laughed.

"Come on up here. This is fun!" Nichole cried, jumping up and down on top of the wood that covered the top of the structure. It bent and creaked under her weight.

That didn't look very safe. "Nichole, maybe you should—" Sophia began to warn her.

Suddenly the rotted wood crumbled away, creating a gaping hole. Nichole fell through, tumbling into the well with a shriek.

"Nichole!" Sophia screamed. "Help! Help!"

"Go get my dad!" Nichole cried from the bottom. "Hurry!"

"Are you okay?" Sophia called.

"Just go get my daddy!" came the panicked cry from the bottom of the well.

"I will," Sophia promised and sprinted toward the barn. "Mommy! Mommy! Help!" She stumbled inside, and Alexis came out of one of the stalls with Sid.

"What's wrong?" she asked.

"Nichole fell in the big hole back there!" Sophia shouted in a shrill, terrified voice. Her heart pounded in her ears. Would Nichole be okay? Was she hurt? "It's all my fault. You told us to stay near the fence, but I wanted to go pick flowers."

"Oh no. It must be the old well. It was boarded up, but she must have fallen through." Sid grabbed some rope on the wall, then he and Alexis ran out of the barn with Sophia following close behind them.

26

"Help!"

Ben whirled around at the sound of a young girl's cry for help. Was that Sophia? He ran up the long driveway toward the stables to see Sid, Alexis, and Sophia hurtling out of the barn.

"Where's Nichole?" he demanded, panic rising in his chest. He'd been gone less than five minutes—he should have known better than to leave them, but he thought that Alexis and Sid would keep an eye on them. He'd let his emotions cloud his judgment—something that CPDU had trained him not to do since day one. How could he let this happen?

"She fell in the well," Alexis said, already hurrying toward an area behind the barn. "Let's go."

Not bothering to be polite and ask, Ben grabbed the rope from Sid and took off running toward the old well that had been partially hidden behind tall grass and some trees. Was there still water in it? The idea of Nichole sinking to the bottom, unable to swim to the surface, urged him forward as he ran as fast as he ever had in his life to the well. If there was no water, there would be nothing to cushion her fall, so either way, she was in danger. In a matter of seconds, he reached the well before the others looked over the edge. It was dark at the bottom, but he could barely make out the form of Nichole at the bottom, looking up at him, sitting in a shallow pool of water.

"Nichole? Are you hurt?" he called.

"My foot hurts," she shouted.

"Don't worry, baby. I'll get you out soon. I promise," Ben said, his heart racing. The memory of Estella plummeting down the mountain burned through his memory as he pulled up the rope. But he couldn't think about that now. This wasn't a mountain, and they'd get Nichole out somehow.

He wasn't sure if she could hold on to the rope long enough for them to lift her up. What if she lost her grip and fell again? He couldn't risk it.

Alexis and Sid ran up behind him, followed by Sophia, who now had tears streaming down her face.

"I'll go in after her. Can the two of you pull us up?" Ben asked.

"I have arthritis in my hands," Sid said. "I won't be able to grip the rope well, and Sam and Jacob aren't here today. We can saddle up my horse, Zeke, and tie the rope to the saddle horn. You can climb down and get her, and then he can pull you both up."

"Are you sure? We could just call the fire department," Alexis suggested.

"It could be a while until they get here. This is a small town, and we share a fire department with the neighboring town," Sid explained. Yes, Ben, I promise you that Zeke can do this. I've trained him well."

Ben took a deep breath and nodded. "She's scared, and she could have broken bones. Let's do this and not waste any time."

"I'll be right back," Sid said, hurrying toward the barn.

"While he's getting the horse, I'm going to tie the rope to this post and lower myself down," Ben said, pounding the post with his hand to test its strength. It didn't budge. "It seems strong. Besides, I could climb down if I need to." He secured the rope with a strong knot. "Just have him untie it and secure it to the horse when he gets back." He lowered the rope to the bottom. "I'm coming, Nichole," he called down to her.

"Okay," Alexis said. "As long as you're sure."

"I don't want her to spend another minute alone down there," Ben said, grabbing the tied rope and hoisting himself over the edge of the well. He carefully lowered himself down, and the feelings of the day Estella fell down the mountain came rushing back. The same panic and anguish filled him as if it were happening all over again.

He wasn't going to waste any time now.

"Daddy?" Nichole cried from the bottom, her sobs echoing off the walls. "I'm scared."

"I'm coming down to get you." Ben continued to carefully lower himself down, even though the walls felt as though they were closing in around him. He had been trained for situations like this, and at that moment, he was thankful he had. As images of his wife falling to her death continued to assault him, he pushed the memories away, focusing on the mission at hand—to rescue his daughter.

Finally, he reached the bottom. "Nichole, I know you're scared, but I'm here now. Tell me what hurts." He reached out and gently put his arm around her shoulder.

Nichole cried, "My ankle hurts."

Ben gently felt it, running his fingers gently over the bones in her ankle, which was already swelling. "Can you move your ankle?" It could be broken, but at best, it was sprained.

"No." Nichole's sobs came harder as her body shook with every breath. She shook her head. "It hurts too much."

Ben carefully wrapped his arms around her, careful not to disturb her injuries.

"You'll be okay, baby," he crooned. "We'll be out in a minute."

"Sid's here with Zeke!" Alexis hollered down the well. "He's tying the rope. Just a minute."

"See? We'll be out in a minute." Ben explained what they were going to do as he made a double lineman's knot to slip his legs through. "I want you to wrap your arms around me and hold on tight. Can you do that?"

"What if I fall?" Nichole asked, eyes wide with terror.

"I will never let you fall," Ben promised her. He pulled away from Nichole to look into her eyes as he gently placed his hands on the sides of her face. Tears stung his eyes as Estella's screams echoed in his mind. He was there on that mountain again, hearing her crash through the trees as she fell farther and farther from him.

No. I couldn't do anything to save her, but I'll save Nichole now. She'll be okay, he told himself.

"I'll never let you fall. I promise. I have to hold onto the rope, but I'll hold you too," Ben assured her, his voice cracking.

"Promise?" Nichole whispered.

"I promise," he murmured.

He finished the knot, then put his legs through the holes, sitting in it like a sling chair. "Here, you're going to sit on my lap." He tried as carefully as he could to lift her up, but she still cried out in pain. "I'm sorry. Hold on, okay? I've got you." He put Nichole in his lap between the line going up and his body and put one hand on the rope and one on her. "See? This isn't so bad."

"Okay, you can come up now. The rope is secured to Zeke," Sid called down. "We'll take it slow and steady."

"Let's go, baby," Ben said.

"Okay," Nichole squeaked.

"We're ready. Pull us up!" Ben shouted.

"Here we go," Sid called.

Ben gripped the rope tightly in one had and cradled his daughter in his other as the rope began to rise up. They slowly made their way up the well as Ben used his feet to walk up and keep them both from scraping against the sides. He still felt anxiety deeply in his gut, but was also appreciating the strength and steady pulling power the horse was giving the rope. Not having several stops and starts jerking their ascension was making it easier on Nichole's injured ankle.

"Don't let me go," Nichole whimpered.

"I'll never let you go," Ben promised. "I've got you. We're almost there. It's okay."

Finally, they approached the top, and Alexis and Sid helped pull them up over the edge of the well. Once they were on the ground, Ben breathed a sigh of relief as he held Nichole in his arms.

"I'm so glad you're okay, Nichole. I completely forgot this was here," Sid said in a pained voice. "The cover rotted through. I should have made a new cover and included talking about it when I taught you the safety rules. I'm so sorry."

"This isn't your fault, Sid. I need to take her to the hospital right now. I think she broke her ankle." Ben was already carrying Nichole over to his car.

"I'm sorry, Nichole! This is all my fault," Sophia cried as she followed them, her long brown hair streaming behind her as she ran. "I'm so sorry. It was my idea to go pick the flowers."

"This isn't your fault either, Sophia," Ben said as he gingerly set Nichole in the back seat of the car and buckled her. "It was an accident."

"You and Mommy had a fight. So I just thought if Nichole and I gave you each flowers, then it would fix everything so we could be sisters," Sophia cried, tears coursing down her cheeks. "Now she's hurt!"

Alexis ran over and put her arms around her daughter's shoulders comfortingly. "No, sweetie, it's not your fault. But what do you mean?"

Ben looked at Alexis, who seemed as puzzled as he was. What was Sophia talking about? He bent down to her eye level. "I'm not sure what you mean, Sophia, but we will talk about it when we get back. Right now, I need to take Nichole to the hospital so she gets better, okay?"

Sophia nodded, wiping her eyes.

"We'll be back," Ben said, then got in his car and drove to the hospital.

27

Later that day, after dinner, Alexis sat with Sophia on the couch in the living room. Sid had let her go home to take care of Sophia, who was overcome with guilt and was still crying by Alexis' side.

"It's all my fault!" she cried, wiping her red eyes.

"No, it's not," Alexis assured her for the tenth time, keeping her arm around her daughter's shoulders.

"We just wanted to pick flowers." Sophia sniffed.

"I know," Alexis said. "But that's why it's important to do as I say, right? I told you to stay near the fence so you would be safe."

"See? It is all my fault." Sophia shook her head.

"Poor dear," Dorothy said, bringing over a tray of tea and cookies. "Sophia, you should drink something."

Sophia sat up, probably due to the delicious smell of the warm chocolate chip cookies on the tray.

"My mother always said that cookies make everything better." Dorothy winked, and Alexis smiled.

At the sound of a car engine, Alexis looked up to see Ben's car pulling into the driveway.

"They're here!" Sophia cried, leaping off the couch and running to the door.

A few minutes later, Ben and Nichole came through the door. Nichole's foot was in a cast, and she was on crutches.

"What happened?" Sophia demanded. "Did you break your leg?"

"She has a broken ankle," Ben explained. "She'll be okay, Sophia."

"I'm fine," Nichole said. "Zeke rescued me. He's my hero."

"Hey. What about me?" Ben joked.

"You've always been my hero, Daddy," Nichole said, grinning up at him.

Ben smiled proudly, standing up a bit taller.

"Come on in and sit down," Dorothy called. "I just made some tea and cookies. Did you eat dinner? I can warm you up some beef stew if you'd like."

"Actually, that would be great, if you don't mind," Ben said. "We were at the ER for a while, so we'd appreciate it."

"Of course, dear." Dorothy bustled into the kitchen to heat the stew on the woodstove, and Ben carefully helped Nichole sit down on the couch before he sat down himself.

"Sophia, I was confused about what you were saying about the flowers earlier. You said you wanted to give us flowers so you and Nichole could be sisters. What did you mean by that?" Ben asked.

Sophia shrugged as a pink blush colored her cheeks. "Well..."

"She wanted to give you flowers and pretend they were from Alexis, and we were going to give Alexis flowers pretending they were from you, Daddy. We thought then you'd forgive each other and get married so we can be sisters," Nichole explained with an innocent look on her face.

Alexis hid a smile and blush while Ben shifted uncomfortably in his seat. He and Alexis weren't even officially dating yet. What did she think of all this? He glanced at her, and her eyes met his. She looked amused, but he wished he knew what she truly thought about it.

"That's very sweet, girls," Alexis said, patting Sophia's knee. "Now I see why you left the fence to get the flowers. But you didn't have to do that. Ben and I would have worked things out on our own."

"Adults can be stupid sometimes and say things they don't mean to each other," Ben said.

"Daddy, don't say that word!" Nichole chided him.

Ben raised his hands. "You're right, Nichole. But it's true. The important thing is that we apologize to each other after and forgive each other."

He still needed to work it out with Alexis. Did she forgive him for what he had said? He had felt terrible about it all day, replaying it over and over in his mind.

"Well, good. So, you love each other, and you'll get married then?" Nichole asked.

Alexis coughed. The awkwardness in the air was as thick as humidity on a summer day.

"Uh..." Ben stammered. "Let's talk about this later." He had no idea what else to say, and that was the best he could come up with.

"Stew's ready," Dorothy called out from the kitchen, and Ben breathed a sigh of relief, thankful for the interruption.

As Ben and Nichole sat at the table to eat Dorothy's delicious beef stew, Alexis and Sophia sat down to keep them company. Alexis couldn't help but want to laugh at what the girls had said—it was adorable how sweet and thoughtful they had been to want to pick them flowers, thinking that would fix everything.

If only it were that simple.

But what did Ben think of what they'd said? He'd looked extremely uncomfortable as he'd fidgeted in his seat. Did he think the idea of marrying Alexis was preposterous, or was he just being shy and awkward?

He was a hard one to read. She wanted to ask him, but how could she without being too bold?

Now that Sophia was clearly feeling better and smiling again, she ate cookies at the table with a glass of milk as Ben and Nichole ate their stew. Alexis also bit into a cookie, which was downright heavenly after just coming out of the oven. She'd always loved to bake cookies with her mother growing up. Oh, how she missed that.

I really should give her a call, she thought to herself for the hundredth time, then pushed that thought away.

"I want to go visit Zeke again tomorrow and the next day and the next day," Nichole said as she ate her stew and biscuits. "He saved my life. I want to see him all the time."

Ben drew his eyebrows together apprehensively. "You want to go back there after what happened?"

"Yes! I love the horses," Nichole cried.

"You better promise to stay away from that well, follow all the safety rules, and do what you're told," Ben warned.

"We will," Sophia and Nichole both said.

"I guess we could go back, if Sid is okay with it," Ben said. "I'll have to talk to him about it. I just don't think we can go every day. That's a bit much. Besides, we have to go home at the end of the week, so I can go back to work at CPDU."

Nichole looked up at him with wide eyes. "We have to leave soon?"

"Yes. Remember I told you we were only staying about a week?"

"Well, yeah, but I forgot." Nichole stared into her bowl.

"Me too. Mom and I are staying here forever, so I forgot you have to go back home soon," Sophia said glumly. "Can't you stay forever?"

"No, I'm sorry, Sophia. I have to get back to work," Ben explained.

"But if you leave, then you and Mom won't get married, right?" Sophia asked.

Once again, Alexis lifted her hand and covered her mouth to hide a small chuckle. "Sophia, let's talk about this later, okay?"

"Why?" she asked innocently.

"You shouldn't ask people things like that," Alexis whispered, leaning closer to her. "I'll talk to you about it later."

Sophia frowned.

Once again, Ben fidgeted uncomfortably. What did he think of the idea of getting married again at all? Was he open to the idea? What if he never wanted to get married again?

After Ben and Nichole finished eating, Ben stood up. "Thank you for the delicious stew, Dorothy."

"You're welcome," she said as she washed dishes in the sink.

"Nichole, we need to get you to bed. You've had a long day, and I'm sure you're tired. You need to rest," Ben said, and Nichole reluctantly let him help her to the door.

"Sophia, I'll be right back," Alexis said, following them outside. After Ben carefully placed Nichole in the back seat of the car and shut the door, he turned to her.

"I'm sorry about what Nichole said," he stammered, kicking a pebble with his toe.

"Sophia said it too. Kids say the funniest things," she said, trying to lighten the mood. She peered into his face, trying to read his expression, and he finally met her eyes.

"I mean, we aren't even officially dating, and they think we're going to get married," he stammered.

Alexis forced a laugh. "Right. It's silly."

"Not only that, but we have to leave soon." Ben continued kicking at pebbles in the driveway. "I think when we leave, it might break the girls' hearts."

"Do you really have to go back to work at CPDU? Didn't you say you were thinking of resigning?" Alexis asked.

"Well, yes, I was considering it."

"How about you consider staying?" she blurted, then said quickly, "I mean, for Nichole. It seems like she might want to stay here."

"You mean, sell my house and move here?" Ben asked, eyebrows raised.

Alexis shrugged, trying to act casual. "I don't know. It's none of my business, really. It just seems to me like Nichole really loves it here."

"She does." Ben sighed. "But we haven't even been here a full week. Estella's parents passed away, and mine are gone too. She has a brother, Jeff, but I haven't been good about staying in touch with him. I'm sure we would still visit him. Still, moving here would be a big decision."

"Of course." Alexis nodded. "Never mind. It was just a silly idea."

"It's not silly," Ben said, his voice softening. "Actually, Derek suggested the same thing. Being here has made me reevaluate my life. Nichole shouldn't have to be worried about me when I'm working at CPDU. I want her to know I'll always be here for her, and writing does keep me busy. Derek even offered me a job at his cabinetry shop."

Alexis looked up at him expectantly. Was he really thinking of quitting and moving here? Would he really do it? "Wow. That's great. You should pray about it," she said.

"I will. Listen, I wanted to apologize for what I said to you at the stables. That was completely out of line and none of my business. I don't know why I got so emotional. I'm really sorry."

"I'm sorry too. I shouldn't have said those things, either. I don't know what came over me. And I'm so sorry about Nichole getting hurt."

"Honestly, it's not anyone's fault. Kids will be kids, right?"

"Right," she said, sticking out her hand. "All is forgiven. Truce?"

"Truce." He smiled and shook her hand. "Yes, all is forgiven."

"Good." She took a step back and scratched behind her ear nervously. "Well, have a good night. I hope Nichole feels better soon."

"Thanks." Ben got in his car and rolled down the window. "Good night, Alexis."

She watched as he backed out of the driveway and drove away.

Will he really quit his job? she wondered. *If he does, then what's keeping him from moving here? Could it be possible?*

28

The next morning, Ben walked outside and sat on the porch.

"Should I really resign from CPDU, God?" he prayed, looking up at the sky. A sense of peace washed over him, followed by anxiety. "Should I take the job working at Derek's shop? What if I'm terrible at building cabinets? Will I still have time to write books?"

Or I could sell my house, he thought, knowing it was worth much more now than it used to be. *I could build a new house for us right here in Unity, big enough to fill with more children.*

His mind returned to last night when Alexis had brought up what the girls said about them getting married. He knew he'd want to get married again if he met the right person, and he could see himself marrying Alexis. Was that crazy after only getting to know her this past week? Ben had heard several people say they knew right away when they met the person they were going to marry—even his own parents had said that about each other.

But what if he moved here and it didn't work out between them? Wouldn't that just make things awkward?

Again, that feeling came over him. He knew he had to quit his job, even if it made him anxious about the future and how he would provide for his daughter.

"If God wants me to do this, He will provide a way," Ben told himself. Besides, he'd rather be broke than have his daughter continue to worry about his safety at work.

Ben dialed the number on his phone and waited until his boss, Branson, answered.

"Aren't you supposed to be on vacation?" Branson asked in his usual blunt way.

"I am," Ben said. "I'm calling because..." He sighed. "I'm resigning, Branson."

"Resigning?" Branson asked, sounding shocked for once. "Why?"

"My daughter needs me," Ben explained. "I don't want her to worry that she'll lose me too. Besides, I'm thinking about moving."

"Where?"

"Unity, Maine."

"Where Derek lives?"

"Yeah. I want to try to get a job here and write more. Actually, Derek offered me a job."

"What is it about that place? There must be something in the water there. It seems as though something interesting is always happening there. That place changes people, or so I've heard," Branson said.

"It's true. Being here really makes you think about your life and what matters most. That's why I'm resigning, so I can be here for my daughter and focus more on my writing. Listen... I am seeing a woman who was rescued from that sex trafficking ring that targeted the Amish. I know they're in prison, but if anything ever changes with those traffickers, especially Sebastian, will you have the DA let me know?"

"Of course, Ben. I'll ask them right after this."

"Thanks. I appreciate it."

"We will miss you. You've always been one of our best. It's been an honor serving with you," Branson said in a solemn tone.

"Thank you, sir," Ben replied.

After the call ended, Ben sat back on the porch swing, feeling more at peace than he had since...

Since before his wife had died.

Now that he wasn't working in Kennebunkport, what was keeping him there? His parents had passed away, and so had his wife along with her parents. Sure, he had some friends from work there, and Estella's brother, but Unity was only a few hours from Kennebunkport. They could still visit and stay in touch.

His house meant so much to him, but being there only made him think of Estella and how much he still missed her. If he was honest with himself, it only made him sad.

Ben picked up the phone and called his brother-in-law, Jeff, to let him know that he had resigned and was considering moving here. Jeff fully supported his decision, and they promised each other that they would get together soon either way.

How would Nichole feel about all of this? He had to talk to her about it and find out. He stepped into the house to see Nichole reading a book in the living room by the window. Derek was at work, the other children were playing in the backyard, and Maria was busy outside in the garden. Now was his opportunity to talk to her alone.

"Nichole, I have to talk to you about something." Ben sat on the couch beside her.

Nichole set down her book and looked up at him. "What is it?"

"I just quit my job at CPDU."

"Really?" Her eyes went wide. "So, you won't be in danger anymore?"

"No. And that's not all. I was thinking... How would you feel about leaving our house and moving?"

"Leaving our house? But we love our house."

"I know. That house is special."

"It reminds you of Mommy, doesn't it?"

Ben nodded. "It does."

"Me too." Nichole frowned.

"Well, what do you think about leaving that house behind and living here instead?" he asked.

"Here?" Nichole covered her mouth and gasped. "Like, in this house?"

"Well, not this house. We could buy land and build our own house or maybe buy a house here in town. Derek offered me a job, so I could work with him."

"Yes!" Nichole cried, throwing her arm around him. "Yes! I want to live here in Unity. Then Sophia and I will be sisters, right?"

"We talked about this, remember? I do like Alexis, and I think she likes me, but we haven't known each other very long. A couple needs to get to know each other for a long time before getting married."

"How long?"

Ben shrugged. "It depends. But we definitely need more time than a week to know if we'll get married or not."

"Do you want to marry Alexis?" Nichole asked.

Ben smiled. "Well... Maybe someday, but I'm not sure if she wants to marry me yet. That's why we can't talk about it in front of her. I don't want to make things awkward."

Nichole nodded, grinning. "Okay. But it could happen."

"It could, but don't get your hopes up, okay? We have no idea what the future holds." He would hate to see Nichole heartbroken if, for some reason, things didn't work out between him and Alexis.

"I'm just so happy we're moving here!" Nichole clapped her hands and bounced in her seat. "Can we go tell Sophia?"

"Well, I need to get our house on the market, so it's not quite official yet, but yes. First, I'll see if I can take Alexis out on a nice date and tell her our plans. I need to talk to her about it first, okay?" Ben said.

Nichole nodded, grinning widely again. "I'm so happy, Daddy. Thank you." She hugged him once again, filling Ben with warmth and gratitude. "Now call Alexis for your date."

"Okay, miss bossy," Ben laughed, then pulled out his phone and called her.

"Hello?" Alexis said when she answered.

"Hi, Alexis. I know you're at work, but I was just calling to see if I could take you out to dinner tonight. There's a nice Italian place downtown where we could go," Ben said, smiling as Nichole watched him expectantly. "I have something to talk to you about."

"That sounds great," Alexis said. "I'll have to go home and shower first so I don't smell like manure."

Ben laughed. "I'll pick you up around six."

"Sounds great."

After hanging up, Nichole was still grinning at him.

"What?" Ben asked.

"You look happy, Daddy," Nichole said.

"You're happy, too. We're both happier than we have been in a long time, aren't we?"

Nichole nodded.

There truly was something about this place.

***

Later that day, on his way to pick up Alexis at Abner and Dorothy's house, Ben gave Margaret a quick call.

"I hope you're calling to tell me you're about to send me more pages because the publisher is just eating this up," Margaret said on the phone.

"Well, yes, I do have more for you I could send. But I'm calling to let you know I resigned from my job today at CPDU," Ben said.

"Do you plan on getting another job?"

"My friend offered me a job at the cabinet shop, and I'm going to take it. Also, with the release of the third book coming up soon, if it goes well, maybe the publisher might have more work for me," Ben said. "Maybe that's wishful thinking."

"I'll see what I can do, Ben, but I'm glad to hear this news. I think book four might be your best yet."

"Really?"

"I really do. It's new and different. I'm excited to see what's next for you. I'll speak with the publisher about more books in the series."

"Thanks, Margaret. Well, I have to go. I have a date."

"A date?" Margaret crooned. "With an Amish woman?"

Ben laughed. "She's not Amish, no. She lives here in Unity."

"Is she the inspiration for your story? Are you going to bring her as your date to the book launch party? Don't forget, that's coming up soon in Portland."

"I didn't forget. I'll be there. I've got to go, Margaret. Talk to you later," he said, ignoring her nosey questions.

"Have fun!" Margaret called before hanging up.

A few minutes later, Ben pulled into Abner's driveway and walked up to the front door. After he knocked, the door opened to reveal Alexis, who was standing there in a knee-length black dress with her dark hair curled and cascading over her shoulder.

She smiled at him. "Hi."

"Hi. Wow, you look beautiful," he stammered.

"Thanks. It's different than my usual work clothes." She chuckled, then looked over her shoulder. "Sophia, go to bed when *Mammi* tells you, okay?"

"I will!" Sophia called, waving from the living room, where she was once again playing games with Abner.

"She'll be fine. Have fun," Dorothy called, waving. "Bye now!"

They went out to the car and drove downtown to a small Italian bistro. Online, Ben had read that this place had the best breadsticks and chicken alfredo around. He'd always loved Italian food.

"Wow, this is nice," Alexis said as they walked through the doors. Inside, small candles lit each table in the dim lighting. Soft Italian music played, and something smelled delicious.

After they were seated, Alexis hung her purse on the back of her chair. "So, what did you want to talk to me about?"

"Well, first of all, I resigned from CPDU today," Ben told her.

"Wow," she said, eyes wide. "You really did it. I'm happy for you. Do you feel like it was the right decision?"

"I really do," he said. "I've felt at peace about it. So, there's more. I've decided to put my house up for sale and move to Unity. I want to either build a house or buy one, and I'm going to work for Derek."

Her eyes went even wider. "Really? Wow, that was fast. I thought you'd need more time to think about it."

"I realized there's nothing tying me to Kennebunkport anymore." Ben picked up the menu and glanced at it. "That house just reminds me of Estella, which makes me sad. Nichole was ecstatic when I talked to her about moving here. She can't wait to tell Sophia."

"Oh, she'll be so happy." Alexis grinned. "Wow, this is all such a big surprise."

"A good surprise?" he asked, peering at her.

"Yes," she murmured. "Of course. So..." She looked down at the table and picked at the table cloth. "What does this mean for us?"

Ben reached across the table and took her hand, which sent a spark up his arm, sending his heart racing. "Now that I'm staying, I was wondering the same thing."

She looked up at him and smiled. "And?"

"Will you be my girlfriend, Alexis?" Ben blurted out, then gave a nervous laugh. "That was blunt, but that's what I wanted to ask you. We've both already been married before, so why keep dancing around it? I am falling in love with you, Alexis. I don't want to waste any time. I want you to know how I really feel."

Alexis blinked, just staring at him. Oh, no. Had he said too much too soon and scared her?

29

“I feel the exact same way,” Alexis said breathlessly. “I’m falling in love with you too. So, yes. I want to be your girlfriend.”

Ben grinned. “I’m so happy right now.”

Alexis laughed. “Me too. I never thought I’d feel this way again.”

“Me neither.”

The waitress came over. “Can I get you something to drink?”

Ben cleared his throat, wishing she had waited another minute or so. “I’ll have water, please.”

“Me, too,” Alexis said.

After the waitress left, Alexis looked down at the tablecloth again. “So, Ben, I have something to ask you, too. I know this might be sudden, but would you ever consider joining the Amish?”

“Joining the Amish?” Ben asked, leaning back in his chair. “Why, are you?”

“Well, I’ve been considering it. There’s nothing left tying me to my old life, which I’ve put behind me. I never cared much for technology, and I love the simple life that the Amish lead. I want to be closer to the

Lord, and I believe that lifestyle would help me do that." She looked up at him. "What do you think?"

"Me? Amish?" He laughed nervously. "I'm not sure. I hadn't thought about it much, to be honest."

"The reason why I ask is... Well, I don't want to sound presumptuous or desperate or too bold, but now that we are officially dating, I might as well say it. If I do join the Amish, I could only marry someone who is also Amish."

"Oh, I see," Ben said slowly with realization. So, was she thinking about marrying him? "I'd really have to give it some deep thought."

"Of course," she agreed. "It's a huge decision."

"Anyway, I just hope you'll think about it and let me know either way. Dorothy says that even if I live here, I don't have to join. They have plenty of non-Amish neighbors. You wouldn't have to join either if you moved here. And if I do decide to join, there's no hurry. I'd want to be completely sure before making a decision like that, and if I do decide to, it would be because I want to. I haven't even talked to Sophia about it yet, but I'm sure she would want to."

Ben nodded. "I'll pray about it, Alexis. I do see why you would want to join. The sense of community in the Amish church is incredible. A simple life would bring one closer to the Lord. I know that even just in this past week, I've already changed my way of thinking so much. As people say, there's something about Unity."

Alexis chuckled. "Yes, there sure is."

They ordered their meals, then a comfortable silence fell over the table.

"I said there's nothing left tying me to my old life, but that's actually not completely true," Alexis revealed. "I still haven't called my parents, and I know in my heart I need to do that before I can truly move on with my life."

"Not to sound blunt, but why are you so afraid? You said at the stables that I had no idea what happened, and that's true. I don't know what happened. You don't have to tell me if you don't want to, but I want to let you know I'm here for you if you want to talk about it," Ben offered.

"I had a younger sister. She died," Alexis explained, wrapping her arms around herself. "Her name was Jessie."

"I'm sorry," Ben said. "I didn't know you had a sister."

"I don't talk about her," Alexis said. "Because her death was my fault."

"Your fault? That can't be true, Alexis," Ben said, reaching for her hand again.

"No, it was my fault. Even my parents knew it. My father is a pastor, and they always expected a lot from me. They didn't ask me to be perfect, but I felt like I had to be or else I'd be an embarrassment to them. I was a teenager when it happened, and she was eight years old. I was going to my friend's house, and she wanted to come along and swim in the pool. My parents asked me to bring her along, so I did, reluctantly. They told me to keep a close eye on her. She could swim with a life jacket on, but not without it."

Alexis shivered at the memory that she had suppressed for so long. She hadn't spoken to anyone about it in years. "All of us were inside eating lunch. I started talking to this boy I had a crush on. Before I knew it, I realized I didn't know where Jessie was. I ran outside to see her body...floating in the pool. She'd gone in without her life jacket. Or maybe she'd fallen in. I'm not sure what happened because no one witnessed it, but she drowned in the deep end." Alexis' eyes burned with tears she had held back for years as she stared into her glass of water. Suddenly, the water became a pool in her mind's eye with Jessie's body floating lifelessly on the surface.

"Alexis, you were a kid." Ben squeezed her hand. "It was an accident."

"I was stupid and irresponsible," Alexis said. "The thing is that Sophia is close to the age she was, and I just wonder sometimes if I might turn away for one minute and something like that could happen again." A shiver snaked down her spine. "It makes me sick to even think about it. Yet, at the same time, I want her to experience life to the fullest because I had my teen years ripped away from me."

"You want her to have the experiences you missed out on," Ben said. "But what do you mean? What happened after that?"

Alexis sighed. "After that, I knew my parents agreed it was my fault, but they didn't want me to know that. One day we had a fight about it, and my mom admitted that she thought it was my fault. We all said things we didn't mean—horrible things. I ran away that day and lived on the streets. I didn't give my parents any way to contact me, so they couldn't reach me. I couldn't cope with the guilt, so I got in with the wrong crowd and started using drugs. Eventually, that's when Sebastian's groomers found me. One of them, a cute young guy, flattered me with empty words and promises. He told me I was pretty and started buying me expensive gifts. He made me feel special and took me to fancy restaurants and hotels. I trusted him. Then one day, he said that I owed him. He didn't just toss me into the back of a windowless van. No, it was much more calculated than that. He drove me from a restaurant to the warehouse where Sebastian was waiting for me. You know the rest." She looked out the window beside them, then squeezed her eyes shut to block out the memories.

By the time she had realized what was happening, it was too late. She'd been trapped like a caged bird, unable to break free.

"I feel terrible for what I said about you calling your parents," Ben said in a choked voice. "I had no idea. Now I understand."

"You didn't know. Besides, you were right. I should have called them by now. I'm just not sure if they still blame me for Jessie's death or not. That's why I haven't called them. I guess I'm too afraid they haven't changed their minds and haven't forgiven me."

"Here's your chicken alfredo," the waitress said, bringing two plates over to their table. She set the plate in front of Ben. "And here is your chicken parmesan, dear." She set the other plate in front of Alexis.

"Thank you," Alexis said, grateful for the interruption.

After the waitress left, Ben said, "Shall we pray?"

Alexis nodded, and they bowed their heads.

"Dear Lord, thank you for our evening together and thank you for this food. Please bless our time together. In Your name, amen." He looked up at her. "Are you okay?"

She gave a weak smile. "I'm fine. This looks delicious." She took a bite, and her eyes went wide. "This is the best Italian food I've ever had."

"This place has great reviews online," Ben said, digging into his chicken alfredo. "So, I have a book launch party coming up in Portland for my third book. It's not the one I'm writing now, but the one that comes before it. My agent said I could bring a date. It's a semi-formal event at a nice hotel. Would you like to come with me?"

Alexis raised her eyebrows. "I'd love to! Wow. You have book release parties?"

Ben shrugged. "It's not a big deal."

"Yes, it is," Alexis said. "You're like a celebrity, and I had no idea. I can't wait to go. When is it?"

"The weekend after next," Ben said, his cheeks turning an endearing shade of pink. "I'm no celebrity. Not that many people came to my last ones, but they did say they think there will be more people at this one. My agent is really harping on me to get more chapters of my fourth book written before then for some reason. I think they want to announce the title or say what it's about or something. I'm not sure."

"Well, I think it's exciting. I'll be looking forward to it." Alexis smiled.

After their meal, Ben drove Alexis home since she had to be up early the next day. He walked her to the front door, not sure if Abner and Dorothy were in bed yet or not. He didn't want to risk it, so even though he wanted to kiss Alexis, he held back.

“Nichole wants to visit Zeke again, so we might be back at the stables tomorrow if Sid doesn’t mind,” Ben said.

“He said to come by any time,” Alexis said.

“Well, then, I might just have to take him up on his offer so I can see you more.” Ben grinned at her in the twilight.

“I’ll see you tomorrow then,” Alexis said, reaching for his hand and briefly squeezing it. His heart soared, and he reluctantly let her hand go as she quietly went inside and shut the door.

Alexis watched from the window as Ben drove away. She had hoped he might kiss her, but he seemed as though he didn’t want to, and maybe it was because they were at Dorothy and Abner’s house, which she understood. Maybe after the book launch party, he might kiss her then. Her heart raced at the mere thought of it.

Alexis glanced at the clock. It was almost nine o’clock. The house was dark and quiet, so Abner and Dorothy were definitely in bed. She walked over to the couch and pulled her phone from her purse. Was it too late at night to call her mother and father? She knew she had to wake up early for work tomorrow, but she had the feeling that it was important that she called them tonight. If she got to bed late tonight and was tired tomorrow, it would be worth it.

Her heart pounded in her ears. What if they just hung up on her?

Now was the time. She dialed the phone number before she could stop herself. Hopefully, they still had the same number. Her heart raced as the phone rang.

30

"Hello?"

"Mom?" Alexis asked.

"Alexis? Baby?" Lisa Fernandez asked.

At the sound of her mother's voice, tears welled in Alexis' eyes. "It's good to hear your voice, Mom."

"Oh, you too, sweetie. Martin! Martin!" Alexis held the phone away from her ear as her mother loudly called her father.

"Alexis?" she heard her father ask, his voice cracking with emotion.

"It's me, Daddy." She wiped a tear from her eye, overcome with guilt for how she'd treated them. They were wonderful parents. They didn't deserve what her terrible choices had put them through.

"We're so glad you called. Are you okay? How are you?" Lisa asked. "Where have you been?"

"I'm okay. Actually, I moved to Unity, an Amish community. I have friends here. Actually, three of the women here were kidnapped, then they were rescued on the same day I was. It's a long story, but we're friends now."

"If you ever want to talk about what happened, we are here for you, Alexis," said her father.

"I know the police explained to you what happened, but I never got to tell you in my own words."

"Oh, you don't have to if you don't want to, Alexis. It must be hard for you to talk about," her mother said. "But yes, they did tell us what happened to you. I'm so sorry, Alexis. My poor baby." Her mother began to sob, and Alexis heard her father trying to comfort her.

Alexis' heart wrenched. "It's all over now, Mom. I think I should finally tell you my side of the story. But first, this place has shown me what's important in life. It's teaching me life is short and things shouldn't remain unsaid. My friends have been teaching me about God, and it's changed me. So, I called to say I'm sorry. I'm so sorry, Mom and Dad, for those things I said before I left." A sob shook Alexis, and she wiped her eyes. "I didn't mean it. I was just upset. I don't think you're bad parents. I know you did your best with me, especially after Jessie died. Most of all, I'm so sorry about letting Jessie die."

Now Alexis heard her father crying too. "We're sorry too, baby. We know. We forgive you. But we realize now that Jessie's death was not your fault. It was wrong of us to ask you to take her with you that day and to be in charge of her when she couldn't swim. We're so sorry about what we said the day you left. There's not a day or hour that goes by when we haven't regretted it."

Alexis smiled, feeling even more weight lifted off her. "I forgive you too. Actually, I've wanted to call you for a long time, but I've been a coward."

"We're so sorry we didn't know you were missing when you were taken. If we had known, we would have reported you missing right away," Lisa said.

Alexis said, "You had no way to reach me. It's not your fault.

"I can't even imagine what you went through." Lisa's voice shuddered. "If we would have reported you missing right away, maybe—"

"Mom, Dad, please don't blame yourself. We have no idea what would have happened if things had been different. None of this is your fault," Alexis assured them. "I'm doing okay now. I've moved in with my late husband's parents."

"You were married?" her father asked, dumbfounded.

"Yes, but he died of cancer three years ago. I have a daughter. Her name is Sophia," Alexis explained, her heart constricting as a sob escaped her chest. "I'm so sorry I didn't call you sooner. I convinced myself that you still blamed me for Jessie. I have caused you to miss out on so much time with Sophia."

"All that matters is we love you, and all is forgiven," Martin said. "We would love to meet her."

"She'd love to meet you, too. She's been asking about you, actually."

"We want to know all about your life," Lisa gushed.

"I've made really good friends here, and it's a nice area. I have a full-time job at a horse stable, and I've met a really nice guy who also has a daughter."

"Oh, sweetie," her father cried. "That's great news. It's about time we spend more time together like we used to. We've missed you so much."

"I've missed you too."

"Can we come see you? We want to meet your daughter. We can't wait to meet her! Can we come by tomorrow? It's not that long of a drive, is it?"

"It's only about forty minutes to drive to Augusta from here," Alexis said. "Let me check with Dorothy and Abner in the morning, then I'll call you back and let you know when to come. It's their house, so I want to ask them first. Maybe Saturday would work."

Alexis and her parents talked for over an hour, catching up and reminiscing, and Alexis moved to her bedroom. After Alexis hung up, she fell back on the bed and smiled, letting out a long, cleansing breath. It felt so good to finally have made peace with her parents. She just wished she'd done it sooner. She'd be tired tomorrow, but it would be worth it.

"Thank you, God, for giving me a second chance. Please help me make the most of it," she whispered. "Thank you for showing me how important it is to forgive and make things right. And most of all, please help me forgive myself and move on from my past."

Peace washed over her as she fell asleep.

The next morning after breakfast, Alexis helped Dorothy wash dishes as the morning sun illuminated the farm fields out the window.

"I called my parents last night," Alexis told her.

"You did? How did it go?" Dorothy asked.

"Great, actually. They want to visit. They've never met Sophia before, and I told them I moved here. They were wondering if they could come by and meet you and Sophia and visit for the day," Alexis said. "Would that be okay?"

"Of course," Dorothy said. "They can come any time. How about Saturday?"

"That's what we were thinking," she said. "Thank you so much. I'll call them and let them know." Alexis glanced at Sophia, who was playing with Abner in the living room. "Sophia will be so excited to meet them. She's been asking why she doesn't have two sets of grandparents like the other kids at school. Now she'll finally have both sets of grandparents in her life."

"That's wonderful!" Dorothy cried. "I'm so glad you called them. You must be relieved."

"I really am. We forgave each other, and now I know our relationship is on the mend. I haven't seen them in so long." She sighed. "Everything in my life is coming together for once."

Dorothy smiled. "I have a feeling many more good things are coming your way, dear. How was your date last night?"

"Well, Ben and I are officially dating," Alexis said.

"That's very good news!"

"He quit his job at CPDU so he can write more, and he's selling his house and moving here. He's going to try to get a job here."

Dorothy turned to Alexis as her eyes widened. "Wow. That happened fast. He must really love you." She gave her a knowing smile.

"I think this place made him realize what's important in life, just like it did for me. I have to admit, it was a surprise, but I do think he's doing it mostly for Nichole. I asked him if he'd ever consider joining the Amish, and he said he'd think about it," Alexis said. "The thing is, I'm not even sure if I will yet. We both will pray and think about it."

"Good. Remember, don't feel obligated just because you live here. The Amish way of life is not for everyone and shouldn't be taken lightly," Dorothy explained. "I'm sure you will make the right choice, though."

Alexis nodded, then glanced at the battery-operated clock on the wall. "Oh! I have to go. Ben will pick up Sophia this afternoon."

Alexis gave her daughter a kiss, said goodbye, and hurried out the door to work.

"I resigned from CPDU," Ben told Derek the next morning at breakfast.

"You did?" Derek asked. "I'm happy for you. I mean, I know it's bittersweet. You worked there a long time. But I honestly think that you'll be happier, and this is for the best." He patted Ben on the back. "You'll see."

"I hope so," Ben said as they sat down to eat. Maria was cooking eggs and sausage, and the savory smells were tantalizing.

"One of my employees just gave his notice," Derek said. "My offer still stands. Will you come work with me at the cabinet shop?"

"I was going to ask you about that. Yes, I would love to." Ben smiled with gratitude. "Thank you."

"I really do need the help," Derek said. "We're busier than ever, and I was going to have to find someone to replace him anyway. You'd be doing me a favor."

"Thank you so much," Ben said. "I used to do construction when I was younger, but it's been years. I enjoyed it."

"It's good, honest work. When you see your cabinets in someone's home, it's very satisfying. I'm so glad to have you come work with us, Ben," Derek said, smiling at him from across the table.

"That's great news," Maria said, setting down a large platter of eggs, sausage, bacon, and toast on the table. She called the kids to come sit down, and they shared a silent prayer together.

Thank you, Lord, for my new job, Ben said. *I didn't even have to go looking.*

31

Later that afternoon, Ben arrived with the girls so Nichole could visit Zeke. Ben helped her to the fence, where she stroked Zeke's nose.

"You're my horse hero," Nichole told him. "You saved my life, buddy. I want to come see you every day."

"That is so sweet," Alexis gushed, a hand over her heart.

Ben chuckled as Sid walked over.

"If she didn't love the horses before, now she's really enamored," Sid remarked.

"Thanks for letting us come by again," Ben said. "She thinks we're going to come here every day, but I let her know that after today, we can't. I don't want them to be in the way."

"In the way? Pish posh. I'd love to have those sweet kids come by every day," Sid said. "I know my wife loves having children around." A serious expression shadowed his face. "Our children are all grown up and have moved away. That's why we love to have the girls over so much. Brenda loves spoiling those girls. Bring them by every day, if you'd like. We love it."

"You sure it's not a bother?" Ben asked.

"A bother? Not at all!" Sid laughed. "They're a blessing, not a bother."

"Thank you," Ben said.

"They both sure love to be here," Alexis added.

"But you're going back home soon, aren't you?" Sid asked Ben.

"Well, actually, I'm selling my house and moving here," Ben explained. "We love it here, and we love the people here." Ben winked at Alexis, who felt her cheeks burn. "Actually," he said. "Derek just gave me a job at his cabinet shop."

"Wow, that's great news!" Alexis said.

"Are you two officially dating yet or what?" Sid asked out right.

Alexis laughed. "Yes, Sid, we are."

"Don't forget to invite me to the wedding," Sid said with a mischievous grin.

Alexis just smiled. "Oh, Sid."

"You know, I have to admit I was wrong about the horses," Ben said as he watched Nichole and Sophia talk to Zeke. "I only saw them as dangerous creatures. I was scared to bring Nichole here, but Zeke did rescue her. Now I see why Nichole loves horses so much. They're truly incredible."

"They truly are one of God's most magnificent creations," Sid agreed. "Zeke knew Nichole was in trouble. He could sense it."

"Well, he truly is a hero. You know, I've thought about it, and I've decided that once she's healed, I will sign her up for the riding class after all," Ben told them. As he watched his daughter's face light up with pure joy, he made his mind up right there on the spot.

"Really?" Alexis asked, eyes wide with excitement. "Sophia! Did you hear that?"

"I haven't told Nichole yet. I just decided," Ben added. "But I'll tell her now."

Sophia turned around at the fence. "Hear what?"

Now, Nichole was looking at her Dad and seemed to be all ears.

"Once your ankle is all better, you can take the riding class, Nichole," Ben said. "If you want."

"Yes, I want to! Thank you, Daddy!" Nichole cried, using her crutches to make her way over to him and hug him. "Thank you so much! It's my dream come true. I get to learn how to ride a horse. Mr. Hoffman, can I ride Zeke?"

"He is one of the gentler ones," Sid said. "Sure. Once you're better, we'll teach you how to ride Zeke." He turned to Ben. "They're going to love it."

"Yay!" Nichole cried, then went back to the fence to tell Zeke all about it.

Sid went into the barn, and Alexis turned to Ben with a smile. "You just keep on surprising me."

"What can I say? I'm full of surprises." He shrugged.

"Well, I'm glad you changed your mind. They really will love it. It'll be great."

"You helped me see that," Ben said. "So, thank you. You're making me see a lot of things differently."

"You've done the same for me. I called my parents last night," Alexis said with a smile.

"You did? It went well, I hope?"

"It did," Alexis said. "They forgave me, and we got to talk for a while and catch up. They're coming to visit soon, and I want you to meet them."

"I'd love to." Ben grinned. "I'm so glad you got to talk to them."

"Me too. I just wish I did it sooner." Alexis sighed. "I have to get back to work." She briefly touched his hand, then looked up at him before she walked toward the barn. "God is working on both of us, isn't He?"

Ben nodded in agreement. "That could take a while."

But he could be a patient man when he wanted to be.

32

That following Saturday morning, Alexis paced in the living room while Sophia kneeled on the couch, staring out the window, waiting for her grandparents to arrive. "When will they be here, Mommy?"

"Soon, baby," Alexis said. "They sent me a text saying they were on their way."

"Don't fret," Dorothy said, bustling around the kitchen. "They'll get here when they get here."

"Let me help you with something," Alexis insisted, going to the sink to wash the dishes from breakfast. "Sorry. I was distracted."

"Are you nervous? You seem nervous," Dorothy observed.

"I guess I am," Alexis admitted, dunking a pot into the sudsy water. "I haven't seen them since I was a teenager. It's been so long… Will it be awkward? Will they even recognize me? What if we have nothing to talk about?"

Dorothy patted her arm. "Don't you worry about that. I'm sure they're excited to see you and meet Sophia. You'll have plenty to catch up on. You know, we could invite Ben over to meet them if you want."

"Why didn't I think of that? I've been so frazzled that the thought never occurred to me. I guess let's see how it goes, and then I can give him a call later."

"Sure. I always like having Nichole and him over."

Abner came inside and kicked off his boots. "I thought I heard a car."

"A car?" Sophia said, jumping up to look out the window. "Is that them? I see a car!"

Alexis looked out the window over the sink to see a red car driving slowly down the lane toward them. "That must be them." Her heart pounded as she removed the gloves and ran a hand over her hair.

"They're here!" Sophia cried, leaping off the couch and running toward the door. She opened it as the car pulled into the driveway and parked. A man and woman in their sixties stepped out of the car, looking up at them.

"Hi," Alexis' father, Martin, called out cheerfully. "You must be Sophia!"

Sophia ran out the door and down the steps to them. She threw her arms around Martin, then Lisa.

"Look at you," Alexis' mother gushed. "You're so beautiful. You look just like your mother when she was your age."

Sophia grinned shyly. "Thank you."

Lisa looked up to see Alexis standing in the doorway.

"Hi, Mom. Hi, Dad," she squeaked out.

"Oh, my baby!" Lisa cried, already sobbing as she met Alexis on the porch and threw her arms around her. "I'm so sorry for everything. We've missed you so much!"

"I'm sorry for everything, too," Alexis cried, her eyes filling with tears. "I missed you too. I'm so glad you're here." She thought one of her ribs might crack as her mother squeezed her tightly.

Finally, Lisa let go and held her at arm's length. "Let me look at you. Oh, you're even more beautiful than I remember."

Alexis smiled, noticing more lines around her mother's eyes that hadn't been there the last time she'd seen her. "Thanks, Mom."

"So, can I call you Grandpa?" Sophia was asking Martin.

"You can call me whatever you want, cupcake!" Martin laughed.

"Grandpa it is." Sophia laughed, then turned to Lisa. "And can I call you Grandma?"

"Of course, sweetie." Lisa nodded. "Oh, how sweet." She turned to Alexis. "She's adorable."

"Thanks," Alexis said. "Want to come inside?" She finally noticed Dorothy and Abner standing in the doorway, giving them space and observing quietly.

"Come on in!" Abner called, waving them inside. Alexis introduced the two sets of grandparents to each other, and they made their way into the living room where they sat down on the couches and chairs.

"I'll get some tea," Dorothy said, bustling off. When Alexis got up to help, Dorothy waved her away. "You sit. I'll be right back."

Alexis sat back down next to her mother, who kept looking at her and smiling. Sophia peppered Lisa and Martin with questions, and they chatted pleasantly throughout the morning. When there was a lull in the conversation, Sophia pulled out a board game and got Abner to play with her. Dorothy made an excuse and whisked away to the kitchen again, giving Alexis and her parents some privacy.

"So, your late husband grew up here?" Lisa asked.

Alexis nodded. "They invited me to come stay here with them. I love it here."

"You know, you could have come to stay with us if you had only contacted us," Lisa said in a constricted voice. "You could have moved in with us."

"I'm sorry I didn't even call," Alexis said. "For some reason, it seemed easier to come here, where I was part of the reason why Joshua was shunned."

"Shunned? What does that mean?" Martin asked.

"Joshua left the Amish to go to college, become a veterinarian, and marry me," Alexis whispered, glancing at Sophia and Abner, who were playing the game on the other side of the room. "His family wasn't allowed to speak to him, and I was part of the reason why that happened."

"So even with all of that, it was easier for you to come here than to come home to your own parents?" Lisa snapped, then sighed and shook her head.

"Lisa," Martin whispered, putting an arm around her shoulder. "That's in the past."

"I'm sorry. I just wish you would have called. We would have told you a long time ago that we forgave you. We just wanted to see you," Lisa cried. "I have to admit that I'm jealous of Dorothy and Abner that they got to spend time with you first."

"I know," Alexis said, reaching for her mother's hand. "I am glad I came here, though. I plan on staying here forever. I think it was meant to be." She explained how she had been forced to spy on Maria and Liz during her captivity. "We're good friends now, and I've never had close friends before. This is where I met Ben again, and now we're dating. He helped rescued me when he was working at CPDU."

"Really?" Lisa put a hand over her heart, tears filling her eyes. "We have to thank him."

"Wow," Martin said. "He sounds like a good man."

"He really is. Actually, if you want to meet him, I can invite him over. He has a daughter who is Sophia's age."

"We'd love to meet him," Lisa agreed. "And thank him for rescuing our daughter. Wait, what did you say his name was?"

"Ben Banks," Alexis said.

"And he works for CPDU?" Lisa asked.

"Well, he just resigned, but yes, he did. Why?" Alexis looked at her mother quizzically.

"Oh, nothing." Lisa smiled. "But yes, have him come over." She glanced at her husband.

What is going on? Alexis wondered, picking up her phone and calling Ben.

33

About a half hour later, Ben arrived with Nichole. Alexis introduced Ben to her parents, and she couldn't help but notice how strange her mother was acting.

"It's so nice to meet you," Lisa stammered, shaking his hand.

"I hope you're being good to our daughter," Martin said, trying to sound serious though he was smiling.

"He is, Dad," Alexis said with a laugh. They returned to the living room, where Nichole and Sophia began playing a new board game. Alexis went into the kitchen where Dorothy was making lunch for everyone.

"I'm so sorry about this," Alexis said. "I invited all these people over, and I'm not helping you cook!"

"It's important for you to spend time with your parents. And now Ben is out there with them, so you should go back out there, so he doesn't feel awkward without you. I love cooking for a crowd," Dorothy assured her. "Besides, this recipe isn't any trouble to make for several people. Don't worry about me. Just go spend time with them and enjoy yourself." Dorothy grinned and waved her away.

"Thank you," Alexis said, then turned and walked back toward the living room. Before she came around the corner, she heard whispering.

"Did you tell her?" Lisa was whispering to Ben.

"No," Ben said in a low voice. "I should have by now, but it's been going so well..."

"Tell me what?" Alexis demanded, stepping into the living room.

Lisa looked up at her and blinked, and Ben just looked down at his hands folded in his lap. Martin fidgeted nervously.

"Alexis, you know that CPDU called us to tell us what happened after you were rescued, right?" Lisa asked her softly.

"Yes, I know that," Alexis snapped. "What do you need to tell me?"

"I was the one who was assigned with calling your parents," Ben admitted to her. "I let them know that you'd been rescued, but I'd been informed that you didn't want personal contact with them, so I wasn't supposed to tell them much more than that. Your mother begged me to tell her more, saying she had no way to reach you, and she wanted to know more."

"Ben was kind enough to give us updates on you," her father filled in. "And we appreciated it so much."

"What do you mean by give you updates?" she asked, breathing rapidly as her heart pounded in her ears. Had Ben been spying on her all these years for her parents?

"He let us know that he spoke to you the day you were rescued and how you had those scars on your arms," Martin said with tears in his eyes. Subconsciously, Alexis crossed her arms around herself, hiding the scars as her father continued. "He told us how afraid you were and how he saw the pain in your eyes. We just wanted to know if you were okay. It didn't go beyond that. We didn't even know you got married."

"That's because I was getting married around the same time. I got so busy, and I stopped giving them the updates," Ben told her. "We lost touch. I'm sorry, Alexis. Your parents were so worried about you, and you wouldn't talk to them, and I felt like I had to help."

"Help? You spied on me, and you call that helping? Why didn't you tell me until now?" Alexis cried, her hands balled into fists.

"Because he knew you'd be upset," Lisa said in a calming voice which only irritated Alexis. Then Lisa's voice rose in pitch with each word as she lost control of her emotions. "You had just been rescued from traffickers, and you still wouldn't call us to let us know how you were doing! So, what else were we supposed to do?" She slammed her hand down on the couch, making Sophia jump.

"What are...traffickers, Mommy?" Sophia asked.

Suddenly, she was back in that warehouse with Sebastian standing over her. The scars on her arms felt as though they were burning, as if he was hurting her again.

But he's in prison, she told herself. *He can't hurt me anymore.*

She could hear the screams of the woman she had spied on, the one they had killed for trying to escape when Alexis had been forced to report her.

A sudden force of anguish and horrible memories bubbled up within Alexis, spilling over in the form of tears streaming down her cheeks as she found herself running out the door, toward the barn, straight to Daisy's stall. Once again, she found comfort in being near a horse.

"Horses are easier to talk to than people, sometimes," she whispered, patting Daisy's nose. "Why are relationships so complicated, Daisy?"

Alexis sniffed, and the horse whinnied and nudged her with her nose. When Alexis heard footsteps approaching, she sighed. Expecting to see Ben or one of her parents, she slowly turned to see Sebastian standing in the doorway of the barn.

Bile rose in her throat as her stomach lurched at the sight of the man who had caused her so much misery and pain for so many months, who had stolen so much from her. He was heavier, but it was him. His dark, hate-filled eyes stared her down, causing a sickening shiver to snake down her spine.

Didn't Sebastian have a tattoo of a tear on his face? It was gone now. Her brain barely registered the fact as she stood there trembling, frozen, and unable to run or even move as her heart slammed against her ribcage.

A strangled scream finally escaped her throat once she caught her breath, and Daisy stomped and whinnied as Alexis heard the sound of the front door to the house open. Sebastian looked toward the sound, then took off running toward the woods.

34

Alexis collapsed against the stall door, feeling as though her feet might give out from under her. Daisy prodded her gently as if to comfort her.

Ben ran into the barn, eyes wild. "What happened? Why did you scream?" He was followed by Martin and Lisa.

"Are you okay, dear?" Lisa asked.

"I saw... I saw..." Alexis choked out, her hand on her chest.

Ben gave her parents a knowing look. "I'll stay with her." He walked over to them and whispered something she couldn't hear well followed by something like, "She just needs a minute."

Lisa gave her a worried look. "We'll be right inside if you need us." Her parents went inside, then she and Ben were alone.

In a moment, he had already crossed the barn. As she began to collapse, his arms slid under hers and he held her to his chest, wrapping her in a close embrace.

For a moment, the image of Sebastian left her as she focused on Ben's woodsy scent, the way she could feel his muscles under his shirt as she rested her head against his chest and his arms surrounded her. His scratchy chin brushed against her forehead, and she found it comforting—until she remembered what he'd done and what he'd hidden from her.

Yet, right now, that didn't seem to matter.

"Alexis, what happened?" he asked softly.

"I saw... I saw... Sebastian," she stammered. "He was here. I know you said he's in prison, but he was here, I swear. He was standing right there in the doorway."

She felt Ben's chest rise and fall in a sigh. "I'm so sorry about what happened back there with your parents and me and how I hid that from you, but I thought I was truly doing the right thing by letting them know how you were doing. I think it triggered your PTSD."

Alexis scowled and pulled away, then instantly regretted it.

"Trust me, Alexis. I also struggle with it, from my days in the military and Estella's death. Certain things will trigger it. I could see it in your face when the panic set in. It can cause you to...see things," Ben explained.

"I wasn't seeing things," Alexis insisted. "He was here. He was real. He was staring right at me! You don't believe me?"

"It's not that I don't believe you," he said. "But Sebastian is in prison. I was just talking to Branson. He said he would have the DA let me know right away if there were any changes."

"Does he have a twin?" Alexis asked breathlessly.

"No, Alexis. I worked on that case, and I know he doesn't have a twin. He's behind bars for the rest of his life. You're safe." Ben pulled her into his arms again, and she closed her eyes and let herself melt into his embrace. Slowly, her anger toward him faded away.

"So, how many times did you update my parents?" she asked curiously.

"I called them only once or twice after you were rescued," Ben said. "Then we each got married and you moved. As I said before, I meant to track you down and check in on you, but life got in the way. So, it didn't last long. They were desperate to know how you were doing, Alexis, and I wanted to ease their minds. Cut them some slack."

"Maybe I overreacted in there," she murmured into his arm. She let out a long breath. "I felt betrayed when you were all talking about it behind my back, keeping it from me."

"I should have told you. I admit that. I'm sorry," he said. "I just knew it would upset you."

"Well, I shouldn't have gotten so mad about it. What you did for them was actually kind of...sweet. Thank you," she found herself saying.

He pulled away and looked into her eyes, stunned. "Thank you?"

"Thank you for staying in contact with them when I couldn't even muster the courage to call them."

Ben smiled. "I wasn't expecting that reaction, but you're welcome, I guess. Do you want to go back inside?"

"In a minute." She nestled closer to him. "Let me enjoy this."

"I won't object to that." He chuckled and held her even closer.

A few minutes later, she reluctantly pulled away. "I should go back in. They're probably worried about me."

They went back into the house, where Lisa was talking to Dorothy in the kitchen as she helped her finish making lunch.

"Are you feeling better, sweetheart?" Martin asked as her mother came over to give her a hug.

"I thought I saw..." She shook her head, trying to erase the image of Sebastian in the doorway, glaring at her. "I thought I saw...some-one...but I was wrong. It was my mind playing tricks on me."

Wasn't it? Was her mind really just playing tricks on her?

It hadn't been real, had it?

It was just in my mind, she told herself.

35

"I'm so sorry I got so upset," Alexis told her parents. "Ben explained everything. I completely overreacted. It just brought up some bad memories for me."

"It's okay, baby," Lisa said, running a hand over her hair. "We can't even imagine what you went through."

"Maybe some food will help you feel better, dear," Dorothy said, setting a basket of rolls on the table. "Lunch is ready."

They spent the rest of the afternoon talking and reminiscing, and Martin and Lisa told funny stories about Alexis as a child, which Ben and Sophia loved to hear. Later, they played some games together, filling the entire house with laughter.

At the end of the day, when it was time for Martin and Lisa to leave, Alexis' mother held her at arm's length.

"Promise you'll call us whenever you need anything or just want to talk," Lisa said, tears glistening in her eyes. "We want to hear from you and see you as much as we can."

"And we want to get to know our granddaughter better," Martin said, hugging Sophia.

"Yeah! Come over again soon," Sophia said.

"If you want, you can come to our house, too," Lisa offered. "We live near an ice cream place and a playground."

"Ooh!" Sophia cried in delight. "I want to go."

"We will definitely do that soon," Alexis agreed. "Thank you. And again, I'm sorry I got so mad earlier."

"Please don't worry about it a moment longer," Lisa said, pulling Alexis into a hug.

"We're just so glad we're all reunited, and we got to meet our granddaughter," Martin said, hugging her next. He pulled away and lowered his voice. "And we really like Ben. He's a good one. You better keep him."

Alexis chuckled. "I'm glad to hear that."

After they drove away, Ben and Nichole walked out with Alexis and Sophia onto the porch as the sun set behind the farm fields, casting a pink and orange glow over the tall grass. The girls talked amongst themselves, giggling.

"Don't forget my book launch party is coming up next Saturday," Ben said. "You still want to go?"

"Of course, I do!" Alexis cried. "I'm looking forward to it."

"Do you have a nice dress?" Nichole asked curiously.

Alexis blinked. "Actually, no. Now I have an excuse to go shopping."

He chuckled. "I'll see you later." He helped Nichole down the steps and carefully set her in the car before driving away.

"Today was the best day ever," Sophia said. "I got to meet my grandma and grandpa, and Nichole came over. That was so fun!"

Alexis wrapped her arm around Sophia's shoulder. "I'm so glad you had a good time."

"Can I help you pick out a nice dress at the store?"

"Sure. You probably have a better sense of fashion than I do," Alexis joked as they went inside.

Thank you, God, Alexis prayed, *for bringing Mom and Dad back into my life. Please help me have better control of my emotions, and please help me stop seeing Sebastian.*

The week passed quickly as Alexis was busy at work, and before she knew it, the night of the book launch party had arrived. Alexis had gone shopping with Sophia earlier that week, and they had picked out a knee-length, shimmering emerald green dress. Alexis put it on with some black heels and stood in front of the mirror, running her hands over the sequined fabric. Was it too much? She felt awkward wearing such a fancy dress, and would she even be able to walk in these shoes?

Sophia came bursting through the door.

"Do you knock?" Alexis laughed.

Sophia looked at her and gasped. "Mommy, you look so pretty!"

"Really? Thank you," Alexis said hesitantly. "You like it?"

"Yes!" Sophia cried. "It's perfect."

A few minutes later, when Ben arrived to pick her up, she opened the door.

"Wow. You look beautiful," he stammered.

"Thanks." She smiled and kissed Sophia goodbye. "Have fun with Nichole, Carter, and Rachel."

"I will," Sophia said with a grin. Maria would be picking up Sophia soon so she could sleep over at their house.

"Have fun!" Dorothy called.

They drove to downtown Portland, a historic city in Maine known for its many restaurants, and parked in a parking garage for a hotel. Inside, the lobby was flooded with people.

"Are they all here for the party?" Alexis asked.

Ben shrugged. "I don't know."

"There he is!" a young woman cried, and a group of several middle-aged women cried out and flocked around Ben.

"Mr. Banks, will you sign my book?" one woman asked.

"Where do you get your story ideas?" another asked.

"Is this your girlfriend?"

At this question, all of the women suddenly stared at her.

"I'll be signing books later," Ben stammered, then pulled on Alexis' hand as they hurried out of the lobby to a large auditorium where many of the seats had already been filled.

"Wow," Alexis murmured, stunned. "You're really popular. You seem to have quite the fan club. I had no idea you were so famous."

"I am not." Ben shook his head. "I'm just a normal guy who happens to write."

"All the ladies love you." Alexis chuckled, remembering the way they had looked at her as if they hated her.

"I only care about you, Alexis," Ben assured her, looking into her eyes.

"There you are!" A woman in her fifties wearing cat-eye glasses with her hair in a French twist approached them.

"Ben, there you are. Come on, let's get you backstage," the woman said.

"Margaret, this is my girlfriend, Alexis," Ben said with a wide grin.

Girlfriend. It was the first time she heard him say it out loud to someone else, and she had to admit, it sounded nice.

"So nice to meet you." The woman smiled at Alexis. "I'm Margaret, Ben's agent and the one who discovered his incredible talent. You're a lucky woman, Alexis. Watch out. Some of Ben's female admirers might get overly jealous of you." Margaret winked.

Alexis let out a nervous laugh. "Should I be worried?"

"No. Just ignore them," Ben said, squeezing her hand.

"Come on, let's go. You can come backstage too, Alexis," Margaret said, waving them onward. They walked behind the stage, behind a large red curtain where sound equipment was kept. Out on the stage was a podium with a microphone.

"Now, I'm going to announce you, then you're going to read from your new release," Margaret explained to Ben. "Then I'm going to open it up for questions and answers. Okay?"

"Fine." Ben fidgeted. "I really don't like being in the spotlight."

Margaret flicked her wrist. "They all love you. Don't worry about it. You could make a blubbering fool of yourself and still win them over."

Eventually, the rest of the seats in the auditorium were filled.

"We're about to start," Margaret said. "I'll go make you sound good." She walked up on the stage and addressed the audience, speaking about Ben's former books and then his newest release, the third book.

"Are you nervous?" Alexis asked, noticing how much Ben was tugging at his tie and his sleeves. "You look handsome." She smiled up at him.

"Thank you," he said, giving her a crooked grin. "But yes, I am nervous. I don't like public speaking."

"You'll do great," Alexis assured him. "Just pretend like you're talking to Nichole or me and no one else is here."

Ben tugged on his tie. "Okay, I'll try that."

"Please welcome Ben Banks," Margaret said into the microphone, and Ben gave Alexis a smile before walking out onto the stage. For the next several minutes, Alexis listened closely, enraptured as he read a chapter from his third book in the series. She had no idea he was such an incredible writer. She'd been busy, but she should have made the time to read his work. She now realized just how much she'd been missing out on and why his fans adored him so much.

After a question-and-answer session, Ben returned backstage.

"That was incredible!" Alexis gushed.

"Thanks," Ben said. "I just can't wait to get out of here."

"Mr. Banks, we need you to come this way for the book signing," someone said, taking Ben away and asking him several questions.

Alexis was about to follow them, then stopped when she heard what Margaret said next.

"Now I'm going to read an excerpt from Ben's new fourth book, which is still being written. I knew he'd get mad at me for reading this because it's not done yet, but I think it's brilliant, and I think you will too," Margaret said.

Alexis decided to stay and listen, curious to know what his new book was about.

The more Margaret read, the more horrified Alexis became. The story was about a secret agent, Bobby Henderson, who rescued a young woman from sex trafficking and how he fell in love with her. The woman's description sounded exactly like Alexis, even though her name had been changed to Alice. From her long, dark hair to the scars on her arms, Alexis realized Ben had been writing about her since the moment he'd arrived in Unity, maybe even before then.

Was that why he was dating her? To see where their relationship would go and get ideas for his story? He had said he had writer's block that day at the pond.

Had their entire relationship been a lie? Did he love her at all? She should have seen the red flags when he'd given her parents updates on her and kept it a secret from her. How had she been so blind?

Had he really just been using her this entire time for his book? Now all of his fans knew about their relationship, and worst of all, about her past traumas.

36

The familiar feeling came over Alexis—ears ringing, vision tunneling, and rapid breathing as she grabbed onto a nearby chair for support. Instead of sitting down, her feet carried her out the backdoor into the hallway. She broke into a run, her heart pounding in her ears as she headed for the door, as a cold sweat broke out over her skin.

Ben was at a table, surrounded by both fans and staff alike, who were talking to him. They blocked his view of her running out the door. As she left the building, she almost bumped into a young hotel employee carrying luggage for guests.

"Are you okay, miss?" he asked her.

"I'm fine." She gave him a fake smile and walked toward the street.

She didn't know where she was going but had to get out of there. Maybe a walk would calm her down. As she made her way down the sidewalk, she wished she had worn better shoes.

How do people wear these on a regular basis? she wondered. She could already feel the blisters starting to form on her feet. Maybe there was a bench nearby where she could just rest her feet for a minute.

Finally, she found a bench near an old brick building and sat down. The sun was beginning to set, and several people milled about on the sidewalks, browsing the local shops and going in and out of the local restaurants. Alexis slipped off one shoe and massaged her foot, and the ache finally began to lessen.

Suddenly, a rough hand grabbed her around her neck, and another hand pressed fabric against her face, cutting off her air supply. In a wild panic, she tried to scream, but no air could get in or out of her lungs. She tried to twist around and hit her attacker, but he had her arms pinned down. Because she was pressed into the bench, kicking him was futile.

The images of Sebastian standing in the barn doorway and watching her from the woods flashed in her mind. It was him. It had to be. Why had CPDU said he was still in prison? Had he escaped?

Her thoughts raced as quickly as her heart, and her head began to spin from lack of oxygen. Finally, she was able to get a small amount of air into her lungs—along with the chloroform that was on the handkerchief held against her nose and mouth.

Her vision began to blur and darken until blackness swallowed her.

"I'll be right back," Ben said, pushing his way past the crowd of people that had somehow grown larger around the book signing table.

He hadn't meant to leave Alexis behind like that, but they had taken him away suddenly and were asking him so many questions that he'd been unable to let her know she could follow him. Although, she probably would have if she wanted to. But why had she stayed backstage?

Ben returned to the backstage area and realized Margaret was still at the podium. As he listened, Ben's heart sank to his feet as he realized she was reading from the book he was still writing—the one that Alexis had inspired.

Ben's eyes went wide. She hadn't told him she was going to do this. Had Alexis heard any of it? He looked around. Where was she?

Ben waved his hands, trying to get Margaret's attention and make her stop, but she was already finished. How much had she read? Had it really been the entire first chapter?

She thanked the audience and walked off the stage as thunderous applause filled the auditorium.

"They love it!" Margaret cried. "Do you hear that applause?"

"How much did you read?" Ben demanded.

"The first chapter."

"Where is Alexis?"

"I have no idea. She was here when I started reading."

"Where did she go?" A sick feeling filled his stomach. Had she left when she realized she'd been the inspiration for his new story? He hadn't intended to write about her, but she was on his mind and heart so much that it had just...happened. She was so inspiring; he couldn't help but write about their story.

And he had certainly never intended for Margaret to read it tonight before he could change more than just her name. He had been planning on going back through and changing most of the details, making it into a new story.

I am such a fool, he realized. *What was I thinking?*

People would have read it eventually. She would have found out one way or another, even though he hadn't intended to keep it a secret from her.

She must have realized the book was about them. Had it caused her to panic like she had when she'd found out he'd given her parents information on her but hadn't told her?

Have I completely lost her trust? he wondered. *How can I ever gain it back?*

Ben's head swam with questions.

"We need to get you out there to sign books," Margaret said. "People are going out into the lobby."

Ben barely heard her. "I have to find Alexis. I think she's having a sort of panic attack if I know her as well as I think I do. She might have gone outside to get some air."

"You can't leave now!" Margaret cried.

He waved his hand, already walking toward the back door into the hallway. He kept his head down, moving quickly toward the exit, trying to keep a low profile so no one might recognize him. He heard someone call out his name, but he ignored them, just focused on getting out that door.

Once he was outside, he saw a young man carrying luggage. "Excuse me, did you see a woman in a sparkly green dress?"

"She walked that way just a few minutes ago," the young man said. "She looked upset."

Alexis had mentioned how much she hated wearing heels, so maybe she had been walking slowly, or maybe she had even stopped.

"Thanks." Ben turned and walked down the sidewalk at a fast pace, hoping he could catch up to her.

37

Ben continued straight and came upon a quaint, shop-lined street where people were browsing and shopping. Maybe he could ask some of them if they'd seen her. A bench came into view, and as he approached it, he saw something on the ground that made him sprint forward.

A black, high-heeled shoe was on the ground beneath the bench as if it had been kicked off and forgotten. This was Alexis' shoe; he was sure of it. Why would she just leave one shoe here behind like this?

A sick, cold feeling seeped into his veins. She wouldn't do that by choice. Something must have happened to her.

In a panic, he pulled out his cell phone and dialed Alexis's number. He heard a phone ring about ten feet away on the ground. It was Alexis' phone. His heart nearly stopped. He then dialed Branson's number.

"You don't work here anymore, remember?" his former boss joked.

"I know, but I'm calling for your help. I think something terrible happened to Alexis. She ran off in downtown Portland, and I just found one of her shoes. Are you sure nothing has changed with Sebastian's prison sentence? He didn't get out somehow?"

"What are you talking about? Sebastian is in for life without parole. There's no way it's him."

"Alexis said she saw him watching her twice, and I brushed it off as her mind playing tricks on her. I know he doesn't have a twin, so I can't think of any other explanation," Ben said, holding the shoe in his hand.

"Hold on," Branson said, and Ben heard him typing and clicking in the background. "At Sebastian's sentencing, there was a man there who made a huge disturbance and started yelling during one of the times when Alexis was giving her testimony. The person who caused the disturbance was Sebastian's cousin. Back then, he was much heavier, but I just found him on social media, and he has lost a lot of weight since then. Now, he looks a lot like Sebastian. I'm so sorry I didn't know until now."

"His cousin? Maybe they look enough alike that Alexis thought it was Sebastian who was watching her," Ben said. He slammed his forehead with his palm. "I should have listened to her. I'm such an idiot!"

"You weren't at the trial, Ben, so how would you know? You had a lot going on in your life at that time."

"I think he took her, Branson. The local police won't look for her until twenty-four hours have gone by, and you know it could be too late by then. Can't you send me some people to help me find her?" Ben pleaded.

“Anything for you, Banks,” Branson said. “Where are you?”

“My car is at the hotel, but it’s packed there.” Ben gave him another nearby location where they could meet.

“We’ll see you soon,” Branson said.

Ben ran all the way back to the hotel and fumbled with his keys as he approached his car. He had to get out of here.

“Where are you going?” Margaret shrieked. “Everyone is wondering where you’ve been. You can’t leave now. Your fans are waiting.”

“My girlfriend has most likely been kidnapped, so I have to go find her,” Ben said, not bothering to explain any more than that as he got inside his car and started the engine.

Shock registered on his agent’s face, then understanding. “I’ll let everyone know. Good luck.”

Ben tore out of the parking lot.

Something bumped against Alexis’ head, waking her up. She was leaning against a window inside a truck, which smelled like cigarette smoke, body odor, and marijuana. She slowly opened her eyes, realizing they were now on a dirt road. How long had she been unconscious? Her hands were tied together.

Groggily, she turned her head to see her assailant.

Sebastian.

She felt for a moment like she might retch, but now that she was closer, she could see this was not Sebastian. That was why the tear tattoo on his face was missing, and now she could see the snake tattoo on his forearm was gone. Instead, this man had other tattoos, including a skull on his upper arm. Though the shape of his nose and face were different, she could see now that even though this man looked like Sebastian at a distance and had the same dark hair and piercing black eyes, he was not the person she'd thought he was.

"Who are you?" she asked in a raspy voice.

"You don't remember me?" the man growled. "I was at the trial when you testified."

"At the trial?" Alexis' mind went back to one of the days she'd sat in a courtroom and had given her testimony which had helped significantly with putting the traffickers—especially Sebastian—behind bars. She'd had to testify for every trafficker, which had only brought up horrible memories.

"Your testimony put my cousin in prison for life!" the man shouted.

Alexis looked even closer at him, and a memory formed in her mind. She remembered a heavy-set man shaking his fists at her after she'd finished testifying. He'd shouted threats at her from the back of the courtroom, but he'd been escorted out by security so fast that she hadn't been able to hear much of what he'd said. He'd also been outraged at Sebastian's sentencing.

"You're...Sebastian's cousin?"

"Yes," he sneered. "My name is Marcos. I've lost a lot of weight since then, so I look different, but now do you recognize me?"

"Now I remember," she murmured.

38

"So, it was you watching me," Alexis concluded.

"You thought I was Sebastian." Marcos let out a sickening cackle. "I figured if I lost the weight, I'd look more like him. We were inseparable growing up, and everyone said we looked alike until I gained weight. I always wanted to be just like him."

"Why?" she spat out. "He sold women to the highest bidder. He's a monster."

"He's not a monster!" Marcos yelled, slamming the steering wheel. "Sebastian always knew how to get what he wanted. I was always letting people push me around, but no more. I want to be like him. He's all the family I have left. That's why I'm going to get him out of prison."

"How are you planning on doing that?"

"By holding you for ransom so your rich boyfriend can give me the money I need to hire a better lawyer. Then I'll get him out," Marcos said.

He's delusional, Alexis thought.

Maybe she could sympathize with him and get him to see how terrible of an idea this was. "What do you mean he's all the family you have left?"

"My dad left when I was a kid, and my mom died a few weeks ago," Marcos explained. "Sebastian is the only one left in this world who cares about me."

"I'm sorry about your mom," Alexis said. "That must have been hard."

Marcos shrugged. "Sebastian and I are more than cousins. We're like brothers. It's not fair that he's in prison, and I'm all alone without him."

One small part of her heart went out to him, then turned stone cold. He had kidnapped her, and who knew what he planned to do to her? Still, she had to pretend like she was on his side. "There must be someone besides Sebastian who cares about you."

Marcos shook his head as he drove. "I don't have anyone else."

"Where are we going?"

"My trailer in the woods," he replied. "I'll call your boyfriend and have him meet us alone, then he can give me the money, and you can go free. But if he brings anyone with him or doesn't have the money, I'll kill you." As he drove, he gave her an icy, sidelong glance.

Alexis gulped. "There must be another way to get a better lawyer for your cousin."

"I've checked. There is one who says he can get him out if I pay him enough, so I need fifty thousand dollars."

Alexis bit her lip. Ben didn't have that kind of money, did he? She wasn't sure, but she said, "Ben isn't wealthy, Marcos. What if he doesn't have the money?"

"He'll have twenty-four hours to get it," Marcos said.

"That's not enough time!"

"Not my problem," Marcos huffed.

"You know that Sebastian would still have gone to prison for life even without my testimony, right, Marcos? I wasn't the only one who testified, and there was plenty of evidence against him. It wasn't my fault that he went to prison. He's the one who committed the crimes. Why are you blaming me?" Alexis pleaded with him.

"You don't know that! Your testimony was the most detailed of all. You were with him the longest. He might have gotten a shorter sentence if you hadn't testified," Marcos roared. "Now shut up. We're here."

The truck rumbled down a dirt path in the woods to a small campsite, where Marcos' trailer was parked, probably illegally. He got out of the driver's side and opened her door, yanking her out. She almost stumbled as she scrambled to keep up with him. When they reached the trailer, he opened the door, shoved her inside, then secured her hands to a table leg, which was attached to the floor.

Trapped again. Memories of being tied up in the warehouse after she'd refused to spy on one of the women flashed through her mind. They'd locked her in a room for two days. It had been so dark, and just like this, she'd been unable to move...

"We're far enough from the city now, so I'm going to make the call," Marcos said. "And if you try anything..." He moved his jacket aside to reveal a knife tucked into the waistband of his jeans. "I'll kill you."

Alexis' mouth went dry as his cold black eyes bore into hers, but as soon as he turned around to dial the number on his phone, her fingers quickly began working on untying the knots.

Ben pulled into the parking lot of the abandoned building where he had instructed CPDU to meet him.

"Thanks so much for coming," Ben said to Agent Holmes, whom he'd worked with previously.

"Glad to help," said Agent Holmes.

Ben's phone rang, and he glanced at the screen to see an unknown number. Who on earth was calling him? A sick feeling filled the pit of his stomach. Ben held up a finger. "Sorry, I'm going to take this. I'll be right back." He turned and walked away, out of anyone's earshot.

"Hello?"

"Ben Banks?"

"Yes. Who is this?"

"All you need to know is that I have your girlfriend. You can get her back unharmed if you do exactly as I say," said the gravelly voice.

"What do you want?" Ben demanded through clenched teeth.

"I want you to come here alone with fifty thousand dollars," the voice ordered. "Alone. If I see anyone else with you or even get a feeling someone else is with you, I'll shoot your girlfriend. Got it?"

Ben's veins filled with fiery indignation toward this man who had taken the woman he loved, but he took a deep breath to steady his emotions. He had the money that his parents had left him, but he had been planning on using it for Nichole's college education and in case of an emergency. "I need time to get the cash."

"Fine."

"Where do I meet you?"

The man gave Ben directions on how to get to him.

"Remember, you have twenty-four hours. If you're not here alone with the money by this time tomorrow, you can say goodbye to your woman."

The call ended, and Ben stared at the phone, stunned.

"Is there a problem, Banks?" Agent Holmes asked, walking up behind him.

"No," Ben stammered, feeling a cold sweat break out over his body. Should he risk taking a team with him and attempting to take the kidnapper out? The man had said that if he saw anyone with Ben, he'd kill Alexis. CPDU agents and officers were stealthy, but he couldn't risk it. He didn't know if the person who took Alexis had any type of military or police training and might spot the team.

But Ben had the training he needed to take out this criminal alone if things went south.

"I was wrong," Ben said. "I'm so sorry. Alexis went home. That was her calling. She's safe. I'm so sorry I wasted your time."

"Oh, she's safe? Well, that's good news then," Holmes said. "It was just a misunderstanding. It happens. We'll pack it up and go."

"Thank you anyway," Ben said, turning toward his car. He drove away, a knot forming in his stomach. Was he making a mistake? Would it be riskier to go alone than to secretly bring the team?

No, he had to do this alone. He'd get the money, go back to Derek's house, grab his weapons and gear he brought on their vacation, then go get Alexis. Hopefully, the kidnapper would take the money and let them go. And if not, Ben would be prepared with his pistol, assault rifle, and stun grenades.

39

After getting the cash, Ben drove back to Derek's house. He could have gone back home to get the equipment, but the meet-up location was much closer to Derek's house than his own, and he didn't want to waste any time.

Ben had brought his case filled with weapons to Unity, which had a safety lock on it so none of the children could open it. Old habits die hard, and he had almost laughed at himself for bringing it to the Amish community, but he felt vulnerable without it. Besides, years ago, he had helped Derek protect Maria from a stalker here, and with all of the other crimes that had taken place, he wanted to be cautious.

Now he was glad he'd brought it, though he wished he had kept it in his car instead of having to waste time driving to pick it up.

He pulled up to Derek's driveway, where the children were playing in the yard. He hurried inside, waving to them casually.

"You're back already?" Maria asked as she chopped vegetables at the kitchen counter. "Where's Alexis?"

"She's still there, at the conference," Ben said. "I just forgot something. I'm going right back." Before she could pry any further, he ran up to his room, grabbed the case, covered it with a suit jacket, then ran back downstairs.

On his way out the door, he bumped into Derek.

Oh, no. Derek could read him better than anyone. He wished more than anything that he could ask Derek for help, but he couldn't risk it. Besides, Derek had left that way of life behind when he'd joined the Amish, and Ben couldn't ask him to break the rules.

"What are you doing here?" Derek asked quizzically.

"Nothing," Ben said, trying to sound as cool as possible. "I just forgot some stuff my agent wanted me to bring. I have to get back. Alexis is there waiting."

"She didn't want to come with you?"

"Uh, no. She was talking to some of the other people there and wanted to stay behind. I'm going back right now." He turned and walked out the door.

"What do you have there?"

Ben kept on walking. Was part of his case showing underneath the jacket? "Just some books and stuff for a presentation I forgot." He should have grabbed an armful of books or some papers to make it seem more convincing, but it was too late now. "See you later."

As he was walking toward the car, Nichole called out to him in the yard as she played with the other children. "Daddy!"

He wanted to get going, but what if things went sideways and something happened to him? The mere thought made his stomach churn. Just in case, he should say goodbye to Nichole.

No, this is not goodbye, he told himself. He walked around the side of the house to where the kids were playing. Sophia was there as well because she was spending the night there.

"Are you leaving again?" Nichole asked, sitting on the grass beside her crutches. Paper and crayons were scattered on the grass, and Carter, Sophia, and Rachel played tag.

"Yes, but I'll be back soon," he assured her, kneeling.

"Where's my mom?" Sophia asked, running over to them. "I thought you both went to the party."

"We did. I'm going to get her right now," he assured them.

"Sophia and I drew a picture of our family," Nichole said, handing him a paper.

Ben took it to study the image of a man, a woman, and two girls. Above each person was their name: Daddy, Alexis, Sophia, and Nichole. Up in the clouds was another woman with the name Mommy above her, and there was a man with the name Daddy above it.

"That's my daddy," Sophia said, pointing. "He's in heaven."

"And that's Mommy," Nichole said, pointing to the woman in the clouds.

Tears stung Ben's eyes as he swallowed a lump in his throat.

"It's our new family, Daddy. Even though Mommy is in heaven, she's still in our family, but we can have new people join our family, right?" Nichole asked.

Ben could only nod.

"And my daddy is in heaven. Mommy says he will always be a part of our family, but I could have a new daddy someday, like my friend at school," Sophia said.

"Alexis and Sophia can join our family if you marry Alexis. Then Sophia and I would be sisters," Nichole said.

"You would be my new daddy, and my mommy would be Nichole's new mommy." Sophia grinned enthusiastically.

Ben only nodded. "I don't know what's going to happen, girls."

"You'll ask Alexis to marry you, right?" Nichole asked with big, hopeful eyes.

"My mommy loves you," Sophia told him.

In his heart, Ben knew Alexis was the one. Even though they hadn't known each other very long, Ben knew he wanted to ask Alexis to marry him.

"Yes, girls. I'm going to ask her to marry me. It's up to her if she wants to say yes or no, though."

"She'll say yes, Daddy. Don't worry. She loves you. I can tell." Nichole grinned.

Ben smiled through his tears and touched his daughter's face. "I love you."

"I love you, too, Daddy."

"And I love you, Sophia, and so does your mom," Ben said, hugging both of them.

"I love you, too, Daddy. I mean, Ben," Sophia whispered in his ear, melting his heart.

What if something happened and he couldn't fulfill his promises to them? What if they only ended up with their hearts broken?

"I have to go now. I'll be back soon with Alexis." He forced himself to turn and walk away to his car. Ben threw the case in the back of his car, waved to Nichole, and drove down the lane.

40

"He should be here soon," Marcos said as he paced the trailer, which seemed to be getting smaller with every passing minute. Alexis felt as if the walls were closing in around her. Whenever Marcos had his back turned, she worked on loosening the knot on the rope that was tied around her wrists, but she didn't want him to notice, so she couldn't make it too loose.

"And he has the money?" she asked.

"He just called and said he does," Marcos said.

Did he really have the money? Alexis didn't want him to waste his money on this goon. Maybe it was fake, or maybe he was lying.

A few minutes later, she heard the rumbling of an engine.

"He's here," Marcos said, looking out the window. "I'll make sure it's him."

Alexis could just barely see Ben's car park outside the trailer. "It's him," she said.

"Get out of the car with your hands up," Marcos yelled from the trailer window. Ben opened the car door and did as he said, standing outside the car with his hands up and the door left open.

"Now, give me the cash," Marcos ordered.

Ben reached across the driver's seat and grabbed a bag of cash, then held it up to show Marcos.

"I'm not giving this to you until you show me Alexis," Ben ordered.

"Fine." Marcos stomped over to Alexis, untied the rope that anchored her to the table leg, and then yanked her toward the door. He opened it and showed her to Ben while holding the cold, steel blade of a knife to her throat, which sent an icy shiver down her spine.

"See? Here she is," Marcos said. "Give me the cash."

Ben slowly backed up near his car. "First, send her toward me. Then you get the money."

"Walk toward him slowly," Marcos seethed into her ear, causing her to flinch away from him. "And if you try anything, I'll kill you. Got it?"

She nodded slightly. "Yes."

"She'll walk toward you slowly, and at the same time, you come toward me with the money," Marcos said.

"Okay. Nice and easy," Ben said, coming toward them.

Marcos pushed her forward, and she began walking slowly toward Ben. The entire time she made her way toward him, she focused on his face, which helped calm her racing heart.

"It'll be okay," he whispered.

They crossed, and she continued toward the passenger side of the car. Suddenly, she heard a shout.

Ben was just about to set the bag down on the ground when Marcos suddenly lunged at him with the knife, screaming, his eyes blazing with rage. The bag of money fell to the ground, cash spilling out onto the dirt.

"You arrested my cousin!" Marcos roared. "Now you'll both pay! First, I'll kill you, then the woman, and I'll keep the money."

Ben kicked the knife out of the man's hand, taking him by surprise as they both fell to the ground, grappling. "Stay back, Alexis!" Ben called. He tried to reach for the gun tucked into the back of his jeans, but Marcos was stronger and faster than he'd anticipated. The knife was just out of Ben's reach as he stretched his arm out toward it, but Marcos grabbed it and held it to Ben's throat.

"Say goodbye," Marcos seethed, spit flying from his rancid mouth.

Suddenly, the knife at his throat dropped away and it felt like the hand of God jerked Marcos off of Ben, but then someone cried out in pain. Ben scrambled to his feet while turning to see Derek standing there, holding a thick tree branch in one hand which now had one end resting on the ground and sporting a red slash on the right side of his chest blooming through his now torn shirt as his other hand began pressing on his injury. What was *he* doing here?

Apparently, Derek had hit Marcos in the head, then grabbed him and pulled him backward. Marcos had managed to keep hold of the knife and twisted around and cut him. Marcos was now rubbing the back of his head, swearing profusely, while he kept just out of range of Derek and the branch.

Ben pulled the pistol from his waistband and aimed it at Marcos. "Drop the knife! Kick it toward me."

Marcos froze with his hands up. "Don't shoot!" he cried, dropping and kicking the knife toward Ben. It landed near his feet. Ben slowly bent down and picked it up while keeping his eyes on Marcos. "Back up! Toward the rear of the trailer."

"Please, don't kill me, man," Marcos cried, backing up until he was only a few feet from the trailer. "I don't want to die! I just wanted the money to get my cousin out of prison."

Ben didn't want to shoot Marcos, but he wouldn't let him know that. "Your cousin hurt the woman I love and trafficked so many other innocent young women," Ben shouted. "He deserves to rot in prison."

Suddenly, Marcos reached behind him, pulling out a pistol that had been hidden under his shirt, and aiming it straight at Ben's heart.

Alexis finally loosened the rope around her wrists and slipped her hands out of the restraint. As she looked in the front passenger seat of the car, she noticed an open bag with weapons in it—including a grenade. She opened the door and grabbed it. In the movies, she'd seen soldiers pull the pin and throw it; a few seconds later, the fragmentation grenade would explode.

She hoped this would work. Ben and Derek seemed far enough from the trailer not to be injured. *How far will the shrapnel travel?* she wondered.

Marcos was standing about ten feet away from the trailer and she would be protected by the car.

Heart pounding in her ears, Alexis pulled the pin and threw the grenade as hard as she could toward Marcos and the trailer.

"Get back!" she screamed at Derek and Ben as she ducked down inside the car.

The grenade sailed through the air toward the trailer, and Ben and Derek ran toward the car, getting behind the open driver's side door just in time before a deafening boom sounded.

41

Instead of the explosion she expected, a bright white flash burned Alexis' eyes like a massive camera flash. Even though she'd covered her ears, the sound was so loud that her ears rang. She could barely hear Marcos screaming as he fell, the gun forgotten on the ground as he covered his ears, screaming, with his eyes squeezed shut in agony.

Derek and Ben recovered quickly because they were not so close to where the flash-bang grenade went off and didn't waste any time. While Marcos was disoriented, Ben grabbed the same rope that had been around Alexis' wrists and picked up Marcos' gun and knife from the ground. Derek held Marcos down as Ben tied Marcos up, and they secured him to a tree.

Meanwhile, Alexis grabbed Ben's phone from the center console cup holder and dialed 911.

"Were you hiding in my trunk?" Ben asked Derek.

"I knew something was wrong back at the house," Derek said. "I figured you were carrying weapons the way you were trying to hide them with your suit jacket. So, while you were talking to Nichole in the yard, I got in the trunk. It was hot in there, I'll tell you. It's a good thing that newer cars have a phosphorescent trunk release mechanism. I could see it in the dark."

Ben chuckled and shook his head. "I thought you left all this behind you when you joined the Amish."

"I had to help you," Derek said. "I had no intention of killing anyone, but I was going to knock someone out if I had to."

"I'm sorry you got hurt," Ben said, gesturing toward the cut on Derek's chest.

Derek dismissed it with a wave of his hand. "You know I've had worse."

"The police are on their way," Alexis said as she walked toward them. Ben nodded to Derek, signaling for him to keep an eye on the criminal as he wrapped his arms around Alexis.

"I'm so sorry this happened to you," Ben said, pulling her close to him. "And I'm sorry I didn't believe you. I should have known something was wrong, but I knew Sebastian was in prison, and I just didn't know he had a cousin who looked more like his twin."

"He used to not look like his twin," Alexis said. "Now I remember seeing him in the courtroom when he yelled threats at me."

"My boss, Branson, told me about how they look alike now. I should have realized it wasn't just your mind playing tricks on you." Ben sighed. "I'm so sorry, Alexis. I'm so sorry."

"It's over now," Alexis said, squeezing him tightly. "Did you really almost just lose fifty-thousand dollars all because of me?"

"Oh, that? Most of it is fake." Ben laughed. "That bag was mostly stuffed with paper bags, and I put some fake cash on the top that I got at the local department store in the toy department. Up close, it's obvious that it's fake. I thought it might fool him long enough for us to get away. The bank was closed, and I didn't want to waste time getting here, so I could only withdraw a few thousand dollars at the ATM."

Alexis laughed out loud. "Oh, good. I thought I almost cost you fifty-thousand dollars."

"Even if you did, I wouldn't care. You're priceless, Alexis, and I thank God you're safe now." He looked down at her, smiling at her so warmly that her heart stuttered in her chest. "I'm sorry about what happened at the book launch party. I had no idea Margaret was going to read that."

"Why did you write about me?" Alexis asked, looking up at him with tearful eyes.

Ben sighed. "I couldn't help it. I was uninspired for so long, and then I met you. All I could think about was you, so all I could write about was you. I didn't mean for it to happen. It just...did. I tried to write the book I was supposed to write for the publisher, but my heart wouldn't let me. So, yes, I wrote about you. I wrote about us. I changed our names and personal details, but it's still us. I'm sorry, Alexis. I understand if you're angry with me."

Alexis bit her lip, deep in thought as she looked past his shoulder, staring off into the distance. "I was angry at first. That's why I left the party. But after what just happened, I've realized life is too short to shut people out, which is what I always do. Hearing Margaret read our story in front of all those people was a shock to me, I have to admit. You didn't tell me that you were writing about us, and it made me feel like you were using me for your story."

"I promise, I never intended to do that. I didn't tell you because I was embarrassed, to be honest. I thought you might think I was a weirdo or something." Ben chuckled.

Alexis smiled. "Well, you can be a weirdo sometimes, but that's beside the point. Now that I think about it, it's kind of...sweet that you wrote about us."

"Really?" he asked, blinking in surprise.

"Now we will have something to look back on when we're old and gray. The story of us."

"I love you, Alexis," he whispered, his heart so full of love for her he feared it might burst. Every nerve ending was lit with the electrifying need to be close to her, to hold her and love her for the rest of his life.

"I love you, too, Ben," she whispered.

Police sirens and lights approached, and soon officers swarmed the area, taking evidence, asking questions, and taking their statements. The EMTs looked them over and patched up Derek's injury. It was all a blur for Alexis, but once Marcos was arrested and taken away and they could go home, she breathed a sigh of relief as the three of them drove back to Unity.

Thank you, Lord, that we're all safe now, Alexis prayed. *I just hope nothing life-threatening happens to us again.*

42

They drove to Derek's house, and Alexis noticed another buggy in the driveway—most likely Abner and Dorothy's. After the police had arrested Marcos, they had notified Dorothy, Abner, and Maria of what had happened at Derek, Ben, and Alexis' request.

"Derek!" Maria cried, running out of the house, wagging a finger at him. "Don't you ever scare me like that again. I didn't know where you went."

"I'm sorry, Maria. There wasn't any time to explain, and I had to get in the trunk quickly when Ben wasn't looking."

"You were in the trunk?" Maria's face turned a shade redder.

"He saved my life," Ben told Maria. "Marcos, the man who kidnapped Alexis, was about to kill me. Derek pulled him off me just in time."

Maria smiled proudly at her husband and sighed. Her face was starting to slowly return to its normal color. "Well, I can't stay mad at you then. That was so brave, Derek."

"Mommy!" Sophia cried, running out of the house. It was past her bed time, but Alexis was glad she was still up. Carter and Rachel followed her along with Nichole, who was sprinting toward Ben. Dorothy and Abner also ambled out of the house.

Alexis wrapped her arms around her daughter, her heart filled with joy just at the sight of her. She held her close, savoring each moment. "Hey, baby. I'm back."

"We're so glad you're safe," Dorothy said.

"Thank you for coming to stay with Maria and the kids," Alexis said.

"Of course," Abner said with a nod.

"Did Ben rescue you?" Sophia asked, pulling away and looking up at them.

"Your mother doesn't need rescuing," Ben told her with a chuckle. "But yes, I tried."

Sophia grinned up at him. "How romantic."

Alexis laughed out loud, and Ben gave her a sheepish look.

"So, are you going to ask Alexis to marry you now, Daddy? Like in the picture Sophia and I drew?" Nichole asked, tugging on his arm.

Redness crept into Ben's face, coloring his ears and neck. "Nichole, we can talk about that later."

"What picture?"

"Here. We made it for both of you," Sophia said, handing it to Alexis. "You told me Daddy would always be a part of our family. Remember?"

Alexis studied the picture, tears welling in her eyes. "Yes, I do. He will always be a part of our family."

"And so will my mom," Nichole added.

"You both drew this?" Alexis asked.

The two girls nodded proudly.

"It's beautiful," Alexis murmured, noticing how she and Ben were together in the picture. She glanced up at Ben, who managed to smile back at her.

Could this picture come true? What if they all became one new family?

"Let's get you kids to bed, Rachel and Carter," Maria said. "That's enough excitement for one night, and it's way past your bedtimes." She turned to Alexis and Ben. "I still have Nichole and Sophia's beds set up. Do you still want them to spend the night here as we planned?"

"Please, Daddy?" Nichole asked.

"Can I stay, Mom?" Sophia pleaded with Alexis.

"Sure, if that's okay with you," Ben agreed.

"I'm fine with it too," Alexis agreed.

"We'd love to have them. Come on let's go, children," Maria called.

"Bye, Mommy," Alexis said, hugging her before running to join the other kids. She seemed to not realize how close her mother had come to death.

"They don't know the details of what happened," Abner supplied. "We didn't want to frighten them. We left that up to you."

"Thank you," Alexis said, relieved.

"I'll go help Maria," Derek said.

Ben clapped him on the back. "Thank you, Derek. I know you could have gotten in trouble for helping me back there, and riding in the trunk must have been hot in this weather. I appreciate it."

Derek shrugged. "What are friends for?" He smiled and went into the house with his family.

"We better get home to bed," Dorothy said. "Are you coming with us, Alexis?"

Ben gave her a soulful look, his gaze searching hers. "I was hoping to talk with you, Alexis. Can I drive you home after? It won't take long."

She nodded, her mouth suddenly going dry. What did he want to talk to her about?

"Goodnight, then," Abner said, before helping his wife into the buggy and driving away.

Once again, Alexis and Ben were alone in the driveway.

"Let's walk," Ben said, and they began to make their way down the lane. By now, the moon had risen, full and glowing among a sea of glittering diamonds. Ben reached for Alexis' hand and intertwined his fingers through hers. Warmth filled her entire body along with a feeling of safety and comfort.

And love. Oh, how she loved him. She looked over at him as he watched her intently in the moonlight as if he were studying every one of her features.

"I was so scared, Alexis," he began. "I don't know what I would have done if something had happened to you. I don't think I could bear to lose someone I love again." He stopped and turned to her, taking both of her hands in his. "It made me realize how much I love you. I know we haven't been together long, and I don't want to rush things, but I want you to know I fully intend to ask you to marry me one day. I love you."

"I love you, too," she murmured, "But I'm so broken. I have so many scars, physical and emotional. Today I realized I still have so much recovering and healing left to do."

"So do I," Ben said. "I will be there with you every step of the way. I love all of you, Alexis, even with the dark parts of your past that you have never told anyone before. Even with all of your fears and scars." He glanced down at their hands, and she instinctively let go of his hand to pull her sleeves down and cover the scars on her arms.

He rested his hand on hers, gently stopping her. "You don't have to hide your scars from me, Alexis. Every part of you is beautiful to me. I love all of you. Every bit."

She stood in disbelief at how such a wonderful man was in love with her.

Her eyes stung with tears as one slipped down her cheek, and Ben gently wiped it away. Her heart pounded against her ribs as he leaned closer, wrapping his arms around her waist. She reached up and pulled him closer, feeling his muscular back beneath her hands. Could he hear how loud her heart was beating?

Ben slowly lowered his face, and she stood up on her tip toes. He swept his lips over hers.

Thank you, God, for bringing Ben to me, she prayed as they kissed beneath the stars.

43

A year later...

Alexis could see why Maine was known for its fall foliage and why people traveled from far away to come to see it. The trees were ablaze with vibrant leaves colored gold, crimson, and fiery orange all around Unity, especially surrounding Sid's stables.

"You're doing a great job," Alexis said as she led Nichole on Zeke during an after-school children's riding lesson. Ben watched from the fence, but it was clear that he wasn't as tense as he would have been a year ago seeing his daughter on a horse, and Alexis was proud of him for coming so far.

Sam and Jacob helped with the other children until each one had a turn riding around in a circle, including Liz, Maria, and Freya's children: Hope, Peter, Carter, Anna, and Freya's son, Kyle.

Alexis smiled up at Sophia, who was smiling with delight as she rode. "You love riding, don't you, Sophia?"

"Yes!" Sophia said. "Riding Comet is my favorite."

Alexis chuckled. Soon the lesson came to a close, and the children took off their helmets.

Freya said, "Kyle is loving the lessons, Alexis. They are having so much fun."

"It seems like the word is spreading all over town," Liz added.

"Thank you. We have more people interested than we anticipated, so Sid is already making plans to offer more classes so we can break the lessons up into smaller groups," Alexis explained.

"You're doing a great job," Maria said with a smile. "It's obvious how much you love it. You're just overflowing with joy."

"Thanks," Alexis said, beaming. "I really am loving it. Right now, I'm not sure how life could be any better." Alexis was only helping teach the classes for now until she had more training and practice, which could take a while, but she was willing to wait.

"Oh, I think I know how it could get better," Freya said with a wink, glancing over at Ben, who was talking to another one of the dads.

Her friends said goodbye and took their children home.

"I have something to talk to you about after everyone leaves," Sid said to Alexis as she led the other children to their parents. By the twinkle in his eye, she had a feeling it was something good, but what could it be?

Once every child had gone home except for Nichole and Sophia, the two girls began playing tic tac toe in the yard, drawing with sticks in the dirt.

"Alexis," Sid said, walking up to her. "I have to say I am very surprised how full the class turned out to be. You and Sam and Jacob are doing an excellent job."

"I couldn't do it without them," Alexis said. "I just follow their lead."

"Even though they're teenagers," Sid said, "they are very good at what they do. You've come so far, Alexis. You have a knack for running a place like this."

"Thank you, sir." She beamed with pride.

Sid's long, white beard bobbed as he spoke. "I've been talking to my wife about retiring, and before now, we didn't see it as a possibility, but now we do. So, if you want it, I want to hand down my entire business to you, Alexis. Sam and Jacob are too young, but you're just the right person for the job."

Alexis blinked, barely comprehending what he was saying.

"You can continue to board horses," Sid continued, "but if you want your main focus to be teaching lessons, that's fine with me. And I will continue to train you and help you until you get going, of course, and you'll have Sam and Jacob's help. I already talked to them about it. So, what do you say, Alexis? Do you want to take over the stables?"

Alexis stood still, unable to move. She opened her mouth and then closed it, stunned. "You...want me to run this place? I've only been here a just over a year."

"Yes," Sid assured her. "Brenda and I are very sure. You clearly have a passion for horses and for teaching the lessons."

"Yes, I want to do it! Thank you!" She took his hand, shaking it enthusiastically.

"Not that I think you can't do it on your own, but it would help if you had a partner to help you run this place." Sid smiled and looked at Ben, who was laughing with the girls as they played. "He's a good man."

Alexis nodded. "He really is."

"Well, I'll go tell Brenda the news," Sid said with a smile before walking up to his house.

"What was that about?" Ben asked, walking up to her.

"Sid asked me to take over the stables and run it. He's retiring," Alexis told him.

"And?"

"I said yes!" Alexis grinned. "It's a dream come true."

"That's incredible!" Ben said. "Congratulations. I know how important this is to you."

"Thank you," she said, wishing she could ask him to run the stables with her, but she would only do that if...

"As you know, I sold my house in Kennebunkport," Ben told her, "and I have been leasing a place here in town for the last year, but now that lease is expiring. I know it is right for Nichole and I to continue living here and...I already have a house picked out here to buy."

"Where? What house is it?" Alexis asked, eyes wide.

"I've been talking to Sid, and I want to buy Sid's home and the stables. They're moving up to Smyrna to live with their son. I was waiting to see what you said first about taking over his business. We were both sure you'd say yes, but I just wanted to wait for that to happen first," Ben explained.

Sophia and Nichole looked over at them curiously.

Alexis eyed him, puzzled. Why would he do that? He could buy any house he wanted. Why would he want her opinion? Unless...

Ben pulled a small box from his pocket, causing Alexis' heart to pound. Was that what she thought it was? Was this really happening?

Ben knelt down on one knee in front of the barn, in the dusty yard, as the horses looked on. Sophia and Nichole gasped, then giggled.

"Alexis, I want to make a new life here with you and grow our family here. You make me want to be a better man, and you've already taught me so much. You're the most incredible person I've ever met, and I love you with my whole heart. Will you marry me?" Ben asked, tears glistening in his eyes as he opened the box, revealing a sparkling diamond ring.

Alexis could barely breathe as she took in everything around her, everything about this moment, especially the way Ben was looking at her—with so much love. She could see them raising their family here and having more children, and growing the business so that she could teach more and more people about therapeutic riding. But, most of all, she could see herself sharing a life full of love with Ben, her soul mate.

"Yes!" she cried. He put the ring on her finger, and she threw her arms around his neck as he stood up.

Nichole and Sophia cheered, dancing and clapping for their parents as they cried, "We're going to be sisters!"

Alexis and Ben laughed, staring into each other's eyes.

"It's just like in the pictures we drew," Sophia said with a grin, looking up at her mother.

"Exactly." Alexis hugged her daughter.

Now she felt that everything in her life was complete and resolved. With Ben's help, she had contacted all the women and girls who had been rescued by CPDU and the FBI and had apologized to them for her part in their suffering.

There was confidentiality to protect the victims, but as more trafficking survivors were recovered, Alexis went to court whenever Sebastian or his goons had any hearings or further trials on additional charges, and then the sentencing hearings.

The survivors testified in court against the traffickers, so Alexis was able to go and apologize to many of them in person, letting them know how sorry she was that she had spied on them and had not been able to help them before their lives were shattered. She told them about how the traffickers had murdered a woman named Caroline when Alexis hadn't done what they'd wanted, so she'd had no choice.

The court hearings and what they are for were public record, so Alexis and Ben followed all the traffickers' cases online.

Alexis remembered the names of many of the victims while she was held captive, before they were sold. She scoured social media and private messaged several of them.

Because they knew Alexis had spied on them against her will, to her amazement, all of them had forgiven her.

Finally, she felt complete peace in her soul. Complete closure. She had done everything she could, and she had forgiven herself completely. The rest was out of her control.

Thank you, God, for giving me this peace and forgiveness, she prayed for the thousandth time. *And for Ben. Thank you for my wonderful new family.*

Alexis turned to her fiancé. "And what about joining the Amish? We never officially decided."

"Let's pray about it some more. If you want to join, I will join. If you don't want to join and just live a simple life here among our Amish friends and neighbors, I'm fine with that too. Let's see where God leads us," Ben said. "I'm sure He will show us the way."

Alexis stood up on her tiptoes and kissed him. "That sounds like a plan."

GET 4 OF ASHLEY EMMA'S AMISH EBOOKS FOR FREE

www.AshleyEmmaAuthor.com

Your free ebook novellas and printable coloring pages

—•—

Visit www.AshleyEmmaAuthor.com to download free eBooks by Ashley Emma!

Ashley Emma wrote her first novel at age 12 and published it at 16. She was home schooled and knew since she was a child that she wanted to be a novelist. She's written over 20 books and is now an award-winning USA Today bestselling author of over 15 books, mostly Amish fiction. (Many more titles coming soon!)

Ashley has a deep respect and love for the Amish and wanted to make sure her Amish books were genuine. When she was 20, she stayed with three Amish families in a community in Maine where she made many friends and did her research for her Amish books. To read about what it was like to live among the Amish, check out her book Amish for a Week (a true story).

Ashley's novel Amish Alias was a Gold Medal Winner in the NYC Book Awards 2021. Her bestselling book Undercover Amish received 26 out of 27 points as a finalist in the Maine Romance Writers Strut Your Stuff novel writing competition in 2015. Its sequel Amish Under Fire was a semi-finalist in Harlequin's So You Think You Can Write novel writing competition also in 2015. Two of her short stories have been published online in writing contests and she co-wrote an article for ProofreadAnywhere.com in 2016. She judged the Fifth Anniversary Writing Contest for Becoming Writer in the summer of 2016.

Ashley owns Fearless Publishing House in Maine where she lives with her husband and four children. She is passionate about helping her clients self-publish their own books so they can build their businesses or achieve their dream of becoming an author.

Download some of Ashley's free Amish books at www.AshleyEmmaAuthor.com.

ashley@ashleyemmaauthor.com

>>>>Check out Ashley's TV interview with News Center 6 Maine! https://www.newscentermaine.com/article/news/local/207/207-interview/what-led-a-writer-to-the-amish/97-5d22729f-9cd0-4358-809d-305e7324f8f1

—•—

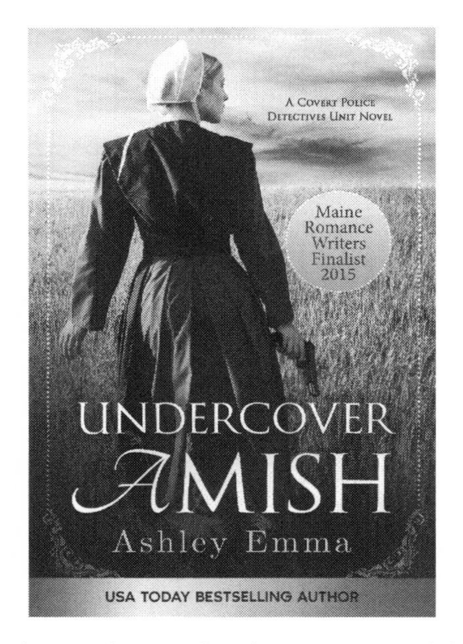

(This series can be read out of order or as standalone novels.)

Detective Olivia Mast would rather run through gunfire than return to her former Amish community in Unity, Maine, where she killed her abusive husband in self-defense.

Olivia covertly investigates a murder there while protecting the man she dated as a teen: Isaac Troyer, a potential target.

When Olivia tells Isaac she is a detective, will he be willing to break Amish rules to help her arrest the killer?

Undercover Amish was a finalist in Maine Romance Writers Strut Your Stuff Competition 2015 where it received 26 out of 27 points and has 455+ Amazon reviews!

Buy here: https://www.amazon.com/Ashley-Emma/e/B00IYTZ TQE/

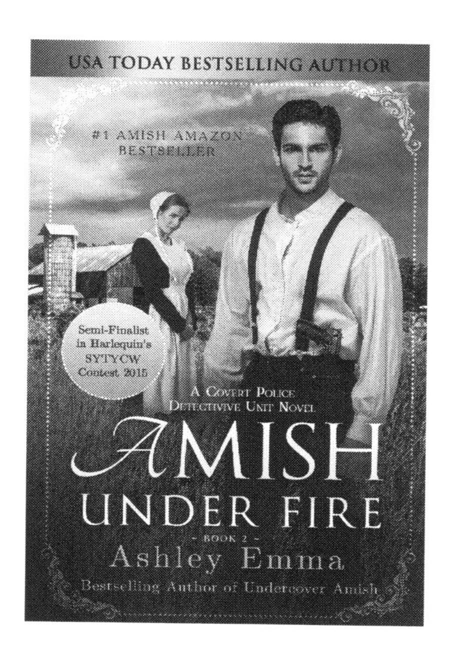

After Maria Mast's abusive ex-boyfriend is arrested for being involved in sex trafficking and modern-day slavery, she thinks that she and her son Carter can safely return to her Amish community.

But the danger has only just begun.

Someone begins stalking her, and they want blood and revenge.

Agent Derek Turner of Covert Police Detectives Unit is assigned as her bodyguard and goes with her to her Amish community in Unity, Maine.

Maria's secretive eyes, painful past, and cautious demeanor intrigue him.

As the human trafficking ring begins to target the Amish community, Derek wonders if the distraction of her will cost him his career...and Maria's life.

Buy on Amazon: https://www.amazon.com/Ashley-Emma/e/B00IYTZTQE/

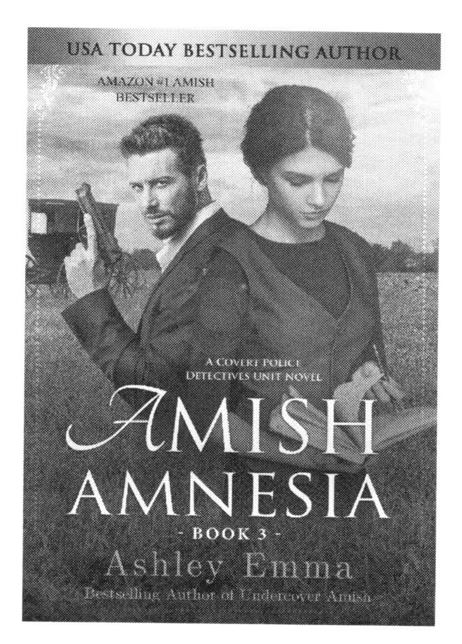

When Officer Jefferson Martin witnesses a young woman being hit by a car near his campsite, all thoughts of vacation vanish as the car speeds off.

When the malnourished, battered woman wakes up, she can't remember anything before the accident. They don't know her name, so they call her Jane.

When someone breaks into her hospital room and tries to kill her before getting away, Jefferson volunteers to protect Jane around the clock. He takes her back to their Kennebunkport beach house along with his upbeat sister Estella and his friend who served with him overseas in the Marine Corps, Ben Banks.

At first, Jane's stalker leaves strange notes, but then his attacks become bolder and more dangerous.

Buy on Amazon: https://www.amazon.com/Ashley-Emma/e/B00IYTZTQE/

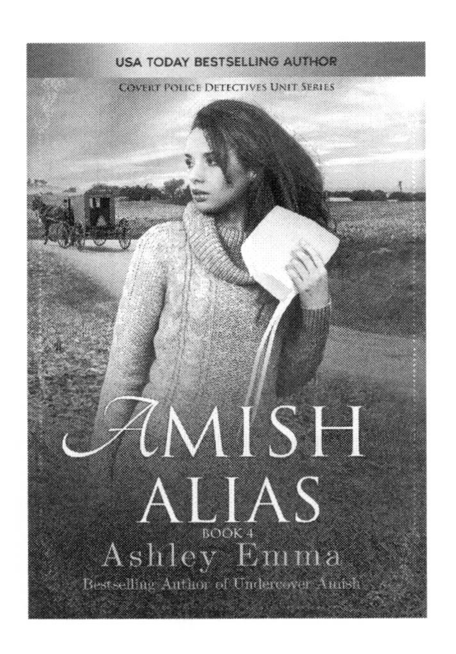

Threatened. Orphaned. On the run.

With no one else to turn to, these two terrified sisters can only hope their Amish aunt will take them in. But the quaint Amish community of Unity, Maine, is not as safe as it seems.

After Charlotte Cooper's parents die and her abusive ex-fiancé threatens her, the only way to protect her younger sister Zoe is by faking their deaths and leaving town.

The sisters' only hope of a safe haven lies with their estranged Amish aunt in Unity, Maine, where their mother grew up before she left the Amish.

Elijah Hochstettler, the family's handsome farmhand, grows closer to Charlotte as she digs up dark family secrets that her mother kept from her.

Buy on Amazon here: https://www.amazon.com/Ashley-Emma/e/B00IYTZTQE/

When nurse Anna Hershberger finds a man with a bullet wound who begs her to help him without taking him to the hospital, she has a choice to make.

Going against his wishes, she takes him to the hospital to help him after he passes out. She thinks she made the right decision...until an assassin storms in with a gun. Anna has no choice but to go on the run with her patient.

This handsome stranger, who says his name is Connor, insists that they can't contact the police for help because there are moles leaking information. His mission is to shut down a local sex trafficking ring targeting Anna's former Amish community in Unity, Maine, and he needs her help most of all.

Since Anna was kidnapped by sex traffickers in her Amish community, she would love nothing more than to get justice and help put the criminals behind bars.

But can she trust Connor to not get her killed? And is he really who he says he is?

Buy on Amazon: https://www.amazon.com/Ashley-Emma/e/B00IYTZTQE/

Ever wondered what it would be like to live in an Amish community? Now you can find out in this true story with photos.

Buy on Amazon: https://www.amazon.com/Ashley-Emma/e/B00IYTZTQE/

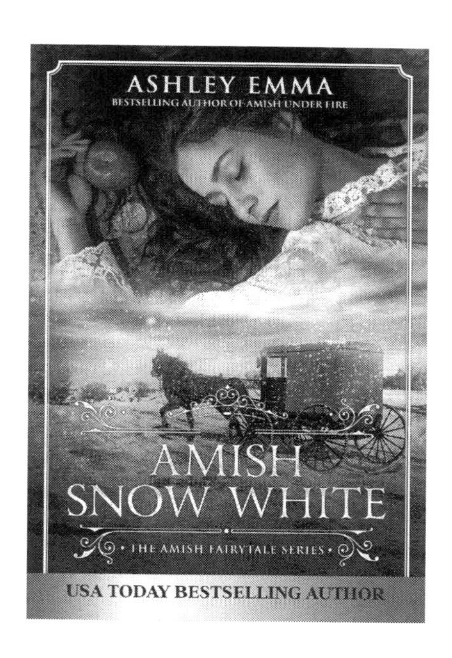

An heiress on the run.

A heartbroken Amish man, sleep-walking through life.

Can true love's kiss break the spell?

After his wife dies and he returns to his Amish community, Dominic feels numb and frozen, like he's under a spell.

When he rescues a woman from a car wreck in a snowstorm, he brings her home to his mother and six younger siblings. They care for her while she sleeps for several days, and when she wakes up in a panic, she pretends to have amnesia.

But waking up is only the beginning of Snow's story.

Buy on Amazon: https://www.amazon.com/Ashley-Emma/e/B00IYTZTQE/

She's an Amish beauty with a love of reading, hiding a painful secret. He's a reclusive, scarred military hero who won't let anyone in. Can true love really be enough?

On her way home from the bookstore, Belle's buggy crashes in front of the old mansion that everyone else avoids, of all places.

What she finds inside the mansion is not a monster, but a man. Scarred both physiologically and physically by the horrors of military combat, Cole's burned and disfigured face tells the story of all he lost to the war in a devastating explosion.

He's been hiding from the world ever since.

After Cole ends up hiring her as his housekeeper and caretaker for his firecracker of a grandmother, Belle can't help her curiosity as she wonders what exactly Cole does in his office all day.

Why is Cole's office so off-limits to Belle? What is he hiding in there?

https://www.amazon.com/Ashley-Emma/e/B00IYTZTQE/

Abraham and Sarah know in their hearts that they are meant to have children, but what if they are wrong? And if they are meant to have children, how will God make it possible?

Just when all seems lost, God once again answers their prayers in a miraculous and unexpected way that begins a new chapter in their lives.

In this emotional family saga, experience hope and inspiration through this beloved Bible story retold.

https://www.amazon.com/Abraham-Sarahs-Amish-Baby-family-ebook/dp/B09DWCBD7M

Gomer is not your typical Amish woman.

On the outside, Gomer seems like a lovely, sweet, young Amish woman, but she's hiding a scandalous secret.

Gomer was created to sing. Most of all, she loves to sing on stage for the audience--she loves the applause, the lights, and the performance--**but her Amish community forbids it.**

How can Hosea find his wife, bring her home, and piece their family back together again when it seems impossible?

https://www.amazon.com/Hosea-Gomers-Amish-Secret-family-ebook/dp/B09GQVCBM9

When Ruth's husband Mahlon dies one morning on his way out the door, she thinks she will never find love again--but little does she know that God has a miraculous plan for her future.

In Unity, Ruth catches the eye of successful farmer Boaz Petersheim. He's drawn to her not only because of her beauty, but because of her loyalty and devotion to her mother-in-law,

Naomi. When Ruth asks for a job harvesting wheat in his fields, he immediately hires her because he can see how much she wants to take care of her mother-in-law, even though she is the only female worker among his male employees.

When rumors sweep through the community after a near-death experience, who will Boaz believe?

https://www.amazon.com/gp/product/B09M7XV76C

—•—

Chapter One

Aladdin Samuels' eyes shot open at the sound of a loud truck on the bridge overhead, and when he realized it wasn't a threat, he took in a deep breath and slowly sat up on his sleeping bag.

Aladdin Samuels' eyes shot open at the sound of a loud truck on the bridge overhead, and when he realized it wasn't a threat, he took in a deep breath and slowly sat up on his sleeping bag.

His German shepherd, Abe, yawned and stretched beside him, his long pink tongue extending past his sharp teeth. Though the mild-mannered dog seemed sweet, he was well-trained. On Aladdin's command, he would attack anyone who threatened them. Ever since Aladdin's time overseas in the military had ended, Abe had been his lifeline, not only for protection on the streets but as a friend. In fact, Abe was more of a friend to Aladdin than any human had ever been.

"Good morning, Abe," Aladdin said to his companion, scratching him behind the ears. Aladdin looked around at where they had spent the night, a grassy spot under a bridge in Unity, Maine. At least it was summer now and not winter, which is when they would have to face possible frostbite.

"Let's go," Aladdin said, rising to his feet. He let out a low whistle, and the dog followed.

He'd never been to Unity, Maine, before, although he was originally from Maine. For now, he was just passing through the town. Aladdin didn't exactly know where he was going, but he liked it here in Unity so far. It was a quaint town with classic diners and old bookstores, and people actually greeted each other on the street.

At twenty-four years old, this was not what Aladdin had envisioned his life would look like. After growing up with an abusive stepfather and a mother who clearly hadn't cared enough about him to keep him safe, he'd left as soon as he was old enough to join the

Army. After three tours in Afghanistan, his time in the military was over.

His friends hadn't been so lucky.

Lucky? He scoffed, glancing down at his tattered clothes and running a hand over his long, scruffy black beard that desperately needed shaving. His fingers subconsciously traced the scar that ran down his arm, hidden by his tattered sleeve. It wasn't from combat but had been done by his stepfather—another part of the past he'd rather forget.

His stomach rumbled, reminding him that he hadn't eaten in two days. As he walked down the street with Abe, he received a few wary glances from shoppers on the sidewalk, but he ignored them. He was used to it by now—everyone avoiding the young homeless man and his dog. For all they knew, he was on drugs.

But he wasn't. No, he'd given that up quickly. After getting out of the military, it had been his only way to cope at first, but then he'd overdosed. Coming that close to death once again finally convinced him to give it up. There was still a gaping hole in his heart, and he longed for something—or someone—to fill it, but he knew that might never happen. At least now he knew that drugs would never fill the void.

"Street rat," an older man mumbled, glaring at Aladdin as he walked by. Aladdin ignored him, continuing on down the street. What if that person knew Aladdin had fought and risked his life for his country? Would he still treat him the same way?

"There's so much more to me, Abe," Aladdin murmured as they walked. "If people took a moment to talk to me, I think they'd realize that."

As Aladdin approached the farmers' market, the smell of baked goods and other homemade foods made his stomach growl again. He reached into the pocket of his worn camo jacket, feeling a few coins and one dollar bill between his fingers. Not nearly enough to buy enough food for the day for him and Abe.

He let out a long breath, glancing at his dog. He was going to have to steal their breakfast...again. It wasn't his first choice, but after searching in dumpsters for two days, he was desperate.

As he looked around, he noticed several Amish people since there was an Amish community just down the road, and many of them sold their goods here at the market. People bustled about, filling their shopping bags as vendors called out their goods to get the buyers' attention.

"Sugared dates and pistachios!" one vendor called, turning Aladdin's head.

Aladdin wandered over to a booth displaying Amish homemade cheeses, and his mouth watered just at the thought. He stepped up to the booth, and the elderly Amish couple gave him polite smiles and nods.

"Good morning. What a sweet dog you have there," the woman said.

"Thank you. This is Abe." Aladdin turned to the dog. "Abe, turn."

The dog quickly walked in a circle, spinning.

The couple laughed. "Oh, how charming," the woman added.

As the couple watched Abe do more tricks and draw the attention of everyone nearby, Aladdin swiped a block of cheese off the table and stuffed it into his sleeve.

"That's an impressive dog," the man said.

"Thank you." Aladdin nodded and turned. "Abe, come."

He knew Abe could smell the cheese in his sleeve, but the dog followed him obediently as they moved on to the next booth, not noticing the curious young woman who watched him.

Chapter Two

Jasmine Byler watched the strange young man with the performing dog from several booths away. As the dog covered his eyes with his paw and spun in circles, she watched as the man deftly pulled a block of cheese from Mr. and Mrs. Schuler's table and hid it in his sleeve.

So, he was a thief, and he used his dog as a distraction. She crossed her arms, eyebrows raised. Clever. Well, if he tried that at her booth, she'd be ready. She wouldn't let him steal baked goods from the Miller's Bakery.

"Cute dog, isn't he?" Laura Miller, Mae's younger daughter, asked enthusiastically.

"Yes, he is," Jasmine agreed.

"Seems to me like you're more interested in his owner." Laura wiggled her eyebrows.

"I am not." Jasmine turned and busied herself with straightening the tablecloth.

"He looks like he's homeless," Lydia, Laura's older sister, added. "Probably a common thief and pickpocket."

"Maybe," Jasmine said, studying the man as he moved from one booth to the next. His dark eyes darted back and forth as he moved through the crowd cautiously. His dog stayed right by his side, obeying his every command, whether verbal or through gestures. "He seems...lonely."

"Really?" Laura put her hands on her hips. "I knew it. You think he's handsome."

"Have you seen him?" Lydia asked. "His clothes are ragged, and he probably hasn't bathed in weeks."

"You're right, but underneath all that..." Jasmine stared at him again from across the market. If his beard was gone, what would he look like? His eyes were so mysterious that they drew her in, even from a distance. She found his deeply tanned skin handsome, and something about the way he moved intrigued her. "I think he really is good-looking."

"Me too." Laura nodded and smiled.

"You two are hopeless." Lydia threw her hands up and turned to help a customer.

"Don't listen to her. She doesn't have a romantic bone in her body," Laura whispered. "Do you think he will come to our booth?"

"How can he not? You can smell your cinnamon buns a mile away." Jasmine laughed.

Laura smiled and nodded. "True. I bet that dog can, at least."

As more customers arrived, Jasmine focused on boxing up donuts, pastries, pies, and cinnamon rolls and taking their payments. The line of customers finally ended, and Jasmine let out a breath of relief and leaned forward, resting her hands on the edge of the table.

Suddenly, the mysterious man and his dog stood before her. At the sight of his tan face and dark eyes so close to her, she drew in a sharp breath, her heart racing as adrenaline spiked through her veins.

"Good morning," she said breathlessly.

"Good morning," he said in a low voice.

Laura looked at the man, then at Jasmine. She turned to her sister. "Lydia, those vegetables over there look so good. Let's go buy some. Come with me." Laura grabbed Lydia's hand and pulled.

"We have vegetables at home, Laura," Lydia said dryly.

"Come on." Laura continued to drag her sister away, who rolled her eyes. Why was Laura leaving her alone with this man?

"I saw the tricks your dog can do," Jasmine said, turning to him. "He's very well-trained. Did you train him yourself?"

"Yes, I did," the stranger said. "I found him abandoned as a puppy. He truly is my best friend."

"He's blessed to have you. You probably saved his life."

"More like the other way around." The man looked down at his dog as though he meant the world to him, scratching behind the dog's ear. The sight was so tender that her heart flooded with warmth.

Jasmine smiled and met the man's eyes as he looked back up at her, and her stomach flip-flopped. Why was she feeling this way? She didn't even know this man.

The man turned to the dog. "Up."

The dog sat back on his hind legs and lifted his two front paws in a begging pose.

"Aw." Jasmine couldn't help but smile at the sight. She handed the dog a homemade bagel. "Here you go, buddy."

The dog devoured the bagel in two bites, then looked up at her with his tongue lolling out, the corners of his mouth turned up as if smiling.

"What kind of dog is he?" she asked.

"I'm not sure. He's a mutt, I guess." The man shrugged.

"A very cute mutt."

"Turn," the man said to the dog, and he did his spinning trick again. As the dog spun in circles, Jasmine watched the man instead of the dog, who discretely stole two bagels off the edge of the table and tucked them into his jacket. Jasmine raised one eyebrow. That trick might work on other people, but not her.

As the dog's trick ended, the man met her eyes again. "Thank you for his bagel. I'm sure he enjoyed it."

"You're welcome...for both his and yours." She crossed her arms.

His eyes widened, but only for a split second.

"I saw those bagels you stole while the dog was doing his trick. That's very clever."

"I...I'm sorry. I don't have any money. I'll go now." The man quickly turned away, and his dog followed.

"Wait." Jasmine quickly packed more bagels, cinnamon rolls, and donuts into a box and came around the table, handing the box to him. When their fingers touched, electricity shot up her arm, straight to her heart. "Please, take these."

"I couldn't. I've already taken too much from you." His warm eyes searched hers. "I don't deserve this."

"I want you to take this. Please, don't worry about it. We might not sell it all anyway."

"Really?"

She nodded.

"Thank you, miss..." he said, fishing for her name.

"Jasmine. My name is Jasmine."

"I'm Aladdin."

"Hmm. I've never heard that name before."

"I'm pretty sure my mother was high when she chose that name." Aladdin chuckled, then stopped himself. "Sorry. I shouldn't have said that in front of you."

"I don't live in a bubble, contrary to what you might think." She took a step back and crossed her arms again. "I hope you two have a nice day."

"Thank you, Jasmine." Aladdin smiled at her, causing heat to creep into her cheeks.

"You're welcome," she said softly, watching as he and his dog walked away.

"What just happened?" Laura's voice suddenly sounded behind Jasmine, causing her to jump.

"Were you standing over there the whole time?"

"Ja," Laura said, nodding rapidly.

"She was eavesdropping." Lydia rolled her eyes.

"Maybe I was. So, what happened?" Laura asked.

"Not that much. He tried to steal some bagels, so I gave him a box of baked goods," Jasmine explaned.

"You what?" Lydia's eyes went wide.

"Aw, that's so sweet." Laura clasped her hands together in front of her heart.

"You can take it out of my pay," Jasmine said. "I felt bad for him and his dog, even though he tried to steal."

"Hmmm, I think it's more than that." Laura elbowed her playfully.

"I don't even know him." Jasmine turned to hide the blush heating her cheeks. "He must have been really hungry, and he said he didn't have any money."

"Right. You don't even know him. He could be a serial killer," Lydia snapped.

"Oh, you're no fun." Laura waved her hand.

"Someone has to be logical here." Lydia shrugged.

"No, I think he has a good heart." Jasmine stared as the man disappeared into the crowd.

"How can you know that from only meeting him for a few minutes?" Laura asked.

"I just have a feeling," Jasmine said, her eyes still searching for him, but he was gone.

***

If you liked this excerpt, check out Amish Aladdin here on Amazon:

https://www.amazon.com/dp/B09RF7Y3NX

Made in the USA
Columbia, SC
01 July 2025

60190722R00217